Falling Into Rhythm

Falling Into Rhythm

A Crawford's Landing Love Story

Alexandra Christian

Mocha Memoirs Press
Rock Hill, South Carolina

ISBN: 978-1-7352195-2-3
Copyright© 2020 Alexandra Christian

Cover Art by Rocking Book Covers
Editor: Jessica Glanville
Proofreader: Susan Roddey
Publisher: Mocha Memoirs Press

For teachers everywhere.

Chapter One

Harper Winslow inhaled deeply and thought to herself that there couldn't be a more comforting scent in the entire world than a fresh box of crayons. Something about the combination of wax, the newsprint paper wrapping, and the cardboard box always managed to calm her nerves. There was probably a long, complicated name for what it was, but Harper was just thankful for it as she prepared to open the door for the year's first open house.

"Get a hold of yourself, Winslow," she said, checking her quirky blonde hair with its pastel pink peek-a-boo streaks once more in the mirror. It wasn't as if this was her first year teaching kindergarten. She'd done parent orientations five times before this one, so why was she literally shaking in her shoes? "You know exactly why."

Her principal had given her a heads up this morning when she walked in that a new student had been registered for her class at the last possible moment. Harper hated that. She'd had her class list for weeks and already she felt like she knew them. She'd read all of their files, looked at their preschool drawings, analyzed their previous teacher's notes so that she knew where they were. Janie likes to talk but can already read simple books. Charles has a lisp.

1

Mya and Mia are identical twins. *"Luther hasn't learned his alphabet yet, but he'll win you over with his smile."* With a glass of wine in one hand, she'd sat on her sofa carefully printing their names on cubby labels, folders, and pencil boxes. In Harper's mind, she'd already planned for stories she wanted to read them and games she wanted to play. She even had an idea about how to finally teach Luther his alphabet.

Then, Mrs. Nettles had sprung a new kid on her. It was okay. Harper was flexible and she would adjust accordingly. But she hated not being prepared. Once the principal had given Harper the news, she'd bypassed the coffeepot in the office and rushed down to her classroom to rearrange things. In the space of an hour Harper had managed to get an extra chair, cubby hole, and carpet square labelled for the late arrival. The pencil box, complete with three fat pencils, a pink eraser, a pair of safety scissors, and a fresh box of crayons was the finishing touch.

"Christopher Renfro," Harper said, printing the name across the box lid.

"Ready for the onslaught?"

Harper turned to see her friend Nicole leaning in the doorway, looking cool and collected as usual. "Oh hi. Well… as ready as I'll ever be I suppose."

"Ain't that the truth. I've been teaching twenty years now, and I've never been ready for a new class."

"Oh please. You've always got it together." Harper gestured toward Nicole's classroom across the hall. Through the doorway she could see the perfectly matched, themed décor that looked so inviting to the five-year-olds that would soon be swarming the halls.

"Only on the outside. And your room looks fantastic!" Nicole gestured to the room where Harper had diligently worked to make her classroom look like the bottom of the ocean.

"Thanks. I've been working on it for weeks. I wanted to do something different this year. I got tired of the same old stuff, ya know?"

"I don't know about that. There's something to be said for using the same watermelon slices bulletin board set for the last ten years." The two of them cracked and soon they were laughing until tears had collected in the corners of their eyes. Harper and Nicole always teased the teacher down the hall about using the same, decrepit bulletin board set of withered looking watermelons year after year.

"Oh well, it's easier for her I guess."

"And easy is probably for the best this year," Nicole said. Suddenly her forehead wasn't creased with laughter but worry. The last couple of years had been tough on their tiny, island elementary school. Ever since the swanky and very private Highgate School had moved into Crawford's Landing, Sojourner Truth Elementary had been struggling. Funding had been cut across the board, resulting in fewer teachers, fewer supplies, and one shared assistant for three kindergarten classes. "I think we're going to have our hands full."

Harper sighed, nodding sadly. "I'm not sure how they can justify doing this to us."

"That's what happens when the people in charge are in it for the money and not the children. Private schools come in touting better teachers and shiny new technology and with the voucher system, it's easy for our kids to get left behind. But we've still got a good group."

"It's going to be a great year," Harper said, more to reassure herself.

Before Nicole could agree, they could hear the throngs of parents and their students heading down the hall. "12 pm, on the dot," she said with a wink, heading back to her classroom to greet the squealing new arrivals standing at her door.

Harper grinned and pulled off her apron, folding it neatly and putting it away in the closet. Despite everything, she was excited. The beginning of the school year was always such a fun time. It was like a blank slate just waiting to be filled, and that gave her such a sense of hope, even when things seemed so uncertain.

"Hello?"

Harper wasn't prepared for what she saw when she turned around. Years from now she'd look back on this moment as the first and only time she'd ever been shocked beyond speech. After all, she was a kindergarten teacher. She'd seen a five-year-old flip up her dress, squat down and pee on the playground in front of God and everybody. She didn't scare easily, but when she turned around and saw Jude Renfro standing in her doorway, it was the closest she'd ever come to fainting dead away. It wasn't his muscular frame or his warm brown eyes, though that would have been enough. Jude Renfro was the frontman and lead guitarist for the band Affluenza, or had been. They had kind of disappeared three years ago, just as their stardom was at its peak. Even Rolling Stone had done a cover story entitled, "What Happened to the Saviors of Rock?" that chronicled Affluenza's rise to fame and their subsequent disappearing act. They also just happened to be Harper's favorite band.

"Hi!" she said, her voice climbing into the rafters against her will. "I'm Harper Winslow!"

"Yeah," he said. "It says so on your nametag."

Harper looked down at the large nametag plastered across her chest. The administration insisted that they wear these monstrosities instead of the regular ones for orientation citing that they were more easily identifiable for the children. "Oh... yeah."

Jude smiled and strolled into the classroom, leading a small, wide-eyed boy behind him that was desperately trying to hide behind his hip. "Are we too early to meet the teacher?" he asked.

"Oh. No," Harper stammered. "You're right on time. I just wasn't...I mean..." She mentally kicked herself for blathering like an idiot. For God's sake, she was supposed to be the teacher. "You startled me."

"I'm sorry," he said. Damn, he was beautiful. Much more so than she remembered. She'd seen Affluenza in concert the summer before she started teaching and immediately, like everyone else, Harper had fallen in love with his lazy baritone voice and deep, dark lyrics. Seeing him now, he looked almost exactly the same except that his long, wavy hair had been tamed into a shorter mane of misbehaving curls. "I'll try to be less scary the next time."

Harper chuckled and knelt down to the little boy's level. "And who are you, little one?"

The boy stared up at his father, looking for reassurance that this person was acceptable. Jude nodded. "It's all right, kid."

Harper offered her hand. "I'm Harper. Would you like to see the classroom? I've only been waiting all day for you."

"For me?" he asked, looking skeptical. "You didn't know I was coming."

"Of course I did!" Harper said. "Christopher Renfro, right?"

The little boy nodded. "You know my name already?"

"I know everything," she teased with a wink.

Christopher smiled and took Harper's hand. "They call me Kit for short." She threw a smile over her shoulder at his father and led him into the back of the classroom. "Okay, Kit. Here's your cubby. It has the seahorse on it."

"I like seahorses!" Kit exclaimed.

"Me too," Harper agreed. "They're my favorite sea creature." She gestured to the classroom around them. The whole thing was decorated in shades of blue. There were even swathes of blue gauze and strips of shiny bubble wrap hanging from the ceiling to make

5

it look like they were standing on the ocean floor. "You might have noticed that I like the water."

"Me too!" Kit turned to his father. "Dad! She likes the ocean too!"

"All the best people do."

Harper's heart gave a small flutter at his compliment. "Anyway, Kit, whenever you see the seahorse you'll know it's for you. Think you can find your table?" She pointed to the small tables in the back of the room with their tiny chairs. More sea animal decals had been placed at each chair. Kit immediately ran over to find his seat and pencil box. They watched as he fluttered from place to place, looking for his seahorse on everything.

"That's very clever, you know," Jude said.

"Well, I know some of my students won't quite be able to find their name written out. It relieves some of the confusion on the first day," Harper replied. "What about Kit? Does he read at all yet?"

"Almost as good as you or I," Jude said.

"That's great!"

"Yeah, he took to it pretty fast. He must have gotten that from his mother. I had a really hard time reading when I was in school. Music was more my speed."

Harper smiled. "Well, everyone is good at something. Every child can't be an A student, but every child has their own special talent."

"Boy, I wish I'd had you as my kindergarten teacher." He flashed one of those paparazzi smiles, and Harper nearly melted into her sensible flats. She could feel the flush rising up from under her collar. Any second her chest, neck and finally her cheeks would be lit up bright red. *Get a hold of yourself, Winslow!*

Harper guided them around the classroom, pointing out classroom policies and procedures. She was trying desperately to keep up her super teacher persona, but every time she caught a whiff of Jude's cologne, her heart skipped a beat. It was absurd.

She was no longer a college girl, fantasizing about wild nights of groupie decadence with the rock band. Pamela DesBarres hadn't been on her reading list for quite some time. Yet here she was, practically drooling over this man she barely knew.

"…so we're trying to keep a low profile. You know how people are."

Suddenly, Harper realized that Jude was speaking to her. And had been for a while. How long had she been standing there gaping at him, lost in her own ridiculous thoughts? "I'm sorry?"

"I was just saying that Kit and I are new in town and trying to keep a low profile. You probably don't remember, but I used to be in a band."

"Oh right," Harper said. Her feeble attempt to look unimpressed was ruined by the completely inappropriate laughter that bubbled up and out of her mouth before she could stop it. "Affluenza."

"You heard of us?"

She rolled her eyes. "Uhm, of course I have. Hasn't everyone?"

"Well, it has been a while." He rubbed his fingers through his hair absently, not really an itch, but more of a nervous tic.

"Music is immortal, I'm afraid." *What the hell did that even mean?* "They were one of my favorites in college."

He smiled, clearly pleased that Harper was a fan. "So yeah, I thought it was important for Kit to go to school in a nice, quiet community where there wouldn't be photographers documenting his every step. Boston had started to get a little claustrophobic for my taste."

"Well, you don't have to worry about that here. Crawford's Landing is about as low-profile as you can get without being off the grid. But still close enough to civilization that your wife doesn't have to drive for miles to the market." She watched him closely, trying to read his body language for signs of a wife or girlfriend. Or boyfriend. Maybe both.

Jude chuckled. "Good to know. But I don't think it will be much of a concern."

"My mommy is dead," Kit blurted from where he stood examining the blocks station.

Harper's throat closed up and an embarrassed flush rushed into her cheeks. "Oh my... I'm... I'm so sorry. I didn't think... Sometimes my mouth runs away with me."

"It's really okay. It isn't something that most people know. I kept it pretty hush hush at the time. Shelby died two years ago."

There were a million questions that Harper wanted to ask, but that would be rude and inappropriate. She gave his arm an awkward pat and cleared her throat. "So why don't I tell you a little about the curriculum?"

Chapter Two

Harper was a million miles away as people started to file into the auditorium for the beginning of the school year "rah rah" session. She had a notebook poised in front of her, ready to take down notes about new school policies and motivational quotes, but all she'd managed so far was a pencil sketch of Jude Renfro's eyes. Just a little too far apart and the color of melted chocolate, with long, sooty eyelashes—they were eyes to remember.

"God, I thought that woman was never going to leave." Nicole flopped down in the seat next to her, looking exhausted. "First she had to tell me about all her kid's allergies. Undocumented allergies, mind you. Then, she proceeded to critique all the art on the walls, the books on the shelf, and my schedule. And just when I thought I couldn't take it anymore, she finished up by telling me about how she really wanted her kid to be in Miss Allen's class, but that she supposed I'd have to do."

"Watch out. She'll be the bane of your existence all year."

"No kidding. I only managed to get away because they announced that the meeting would be starting in ten minutes."

Harper chuckled and shook her head. While teachers understood that parents were often apprehensive about sending their babies off to kindergarten for the first time, they couldn't help but be slightly annoyed by the overzealous parent. "Well you haven't missed anything. I have to admit that I'm not looking forward to this meeting."

"Oh, I know. More bad news about budgets and state regulations I'm sure."

"As usual."

But it wasn't usual. Harper and Nicole had been at Sojourner Truth Elementary for several years and this was the first time in their memories that the administration had seemed so agitated.

"Changing the subject entirely, tell me about your first visitor of the day," Nicole said with a mischievous arch of the eyebrow. "He was a tall glass of water."

Harper immediately flushed straight down to her toes. "Was he? I hadn't noticed."

"Oh right, Harper. I might be old, but I haven't been stricken blind just yet. The man is fine. And it's pretty obvious you think so too."

Harper giggled and made a concentrated effort to keep her eyes on the paper in front of her. "Well, he was very handsome. But he's the parent of a student."

"A single parent of a student?"

Harper hesitated and then nodded with a sheepish grin. "A widower no less."

"Ooooh... a tortured soul, even. How long has his wife been gone?"

"Two years. He seemed okay. I mean, he wasn't choking up talking about her or anything." Harper went back to scribbling in her notebook. "Must be a bit lonely, raising a child on your own like that. And not to mention..." Harper paused, not sure if she should say anything about Jude's musical career. It seemed as if he'd moved to Crawford's Landing specifically to get away from the prying eyes of fans and paparazzi. Not that she thought Nicole would blab about it all over town, but it almost felt like a betrayal. Luckily, she was saved by their principal taking the stage.

"Good afternoon, everyone and welcome to another new school year."

As suspected, their principal, Mrs. Nettles, began droning endlessly about how every new school year was a gift, the pride in carrying on the American tradition of public education, et cetera, et cetera…, but it didn't look like Mrs. Nettles' heart was in it this time.

"As many of you are aware, Sojourner Truth is in crisis this year. Our enrollment is way down and the state has cut our funding in half. In half. That means that many of our programs are going to be cut as well. After-school think tank for our gifted students, remediation for our at-risk students, and arts programs are all on the chopping block. I hate to be so blunt, but there's really no sense in sugar coating the truth. We're going to have to pull together and work hard to meet our achievement goals, but I'm confident we can do it. Our students are among the best in the nation and they deserve our best."

"What happens if we can't?" Jackie Inman, the resident cynic, asked. Jackie was one of those old-school battleaxes that had been teaching fifth grade since the dawn of time. "I think it's unfair to ask us to work harder with less materials."

Some of the other teachers rumbled in agreement.

"If they cut all our programs to reach out to these kids, how are we supposed to help them?"

"We can't just 'make it happen!' We're teachers, not miracle workers!"

Mrs. Nettles raised her hands in a calm down gesture. "Ladies and gentlemen, please. I can assure you that we are doing everything we can, but you can't get water from a stone."

Nicole raised her hand and stood up. "Mrs. Nettles, I think I speak for all of us when I say that we aren't willing to let our kids fall through the cracks. The truth is, the island kids — the ones we serve — are not the affluent population. But they are just as worthy of a good education as the kids over at Highgate."

Harper smiled at her friend's no-nonsense approach. Nicole had been teaching for years and was one of the most well-respected women in the school and on the island. Whatever she said, the community would listen. "We all agree they need experience and patience, but they are more than capable. We can rise to this challenge." This time the rumbling from the audience was positive and met with spotty applause.

Harper stood up and put an arm around Nicole's shoulder. "We just need a plan, Mrs. Nettles. We're going to have to get creative, and we might have to sacrifice some of our own time, but we can do this."

Nicole nodded in agreement. "I'd be glad to head up a committee to work on periodic fundraisers."

"This is going to take more than bake sales," Jackie said with a chuckle. "School level fundraisers won't make a dent."

Harper narrowed her eyes, staring pointedly at Jackie. If there was one thing she never could stand, it was negative naysayers who loved nothing more than standing in the way of those who wanted to try. "But it's a start. We can't just sit here and do nothing."

The music teacher, Mr. Butler, cleared his throat and stood up. "The arts are always under fire. I know a little about grant writing. I'd be happy to help find us some money. Maybe get the community organizations involved."

The grumbling waves of defeat were soon being drowned out by excited chatter, much to the chagrin of Jackie Inman who did very little to hide her displeasure. "Excuse me," she started, standing up again and clearing her throat.

"Yes, Jackie?" Mrs. Nettles said. "You had something to add?"

"I think you all need to be a bit more practical. The people on this island, most of them are unemployed or underemployed. Many work in the tourist industry, and in case you hadn't noticed, tourism dries up in October. What makes you think that they'll be able to cough up any extra money?"

"What makes you think they won't?" Harper snapped.

"Historical precedent," Jackie retorted. "Remember last year's gift wrap sale? I was on the organizing committee for that, and it tanked. Yearbooks? We ended up giving away most of them because parents never paid their balance off. Then of course there was..."

"Those things are too expensive," Harper said. Her voice was raised, but she was damned if she was going to let Jackie talk over her. "The reason why those things always fail is because we aren't meeting these people where they are. Our kids' parents are working class folks, for the most part. They don't care about foil wrapping paper and hand-sewn ribbon."

"So what do you suggest?"

Jackie was challenging her. She wanted Harper to look like a fool in front of everyone so her voice would be silenced, but it wasn't going to happen. Not today, Satan! "A carnival. A big, fall carnival where parents can take their kids and spend time with them while raising money for the school."

Jackie laughed, nudging some of her compadres to do the same. "Where are we going to get the money for it? Someone will have to pay for the food and the games... renting the rides. Have you thought about this at all?"

"Well..."

"I think it's a wonderful idea!" Nicole chimed in. "And we could get the community involved. The parents would jump at the chance to help us."

"And we could get people from the mainland to come and spend their money too!" Mr. Butler shouted.

"This is a great start," Mrs. Nettles said, before Jackie could offer more negative comments. "I can't wait to see your ideas. So I'm thinking we can count on you, Harper?"

"Pardon?"

"We can count on you to chair the carnival committee?"

"Oh... uh..." Harper saw her relaxing evenings spiraling down the drain. In a couple of days, she'd be neck deep in five-year-olds and assessment. There was no way she was going to have enough time to add carnival planning to the mix. "Well... I suppose. Yeah. Sure!" Harper heard herself answering in the affirmative though her brain was screaming for her to stop.

"Excellent!" Mrs. Nettles exclaimed. "And don't worry. We'll find you a flunkie on the PTA to help out."

Harper smiled nervously as she slid back down into her seat. Once again, her mouth had gotten her into a whole heap of trouble.

Chapter Three

"But what if they don't like me?"

Jude knelt in front of his son, trying to keep a smile on his face as he snapped the front of Kit's jeans. They'd been having this conversation ad nauseum since Kit opened his eyes, bright and early at 5:45 this morning. The poor kid had been fluctuating between giddy excitement and a full-on panic attack. It had been no small feat convincing him to eat some breakfast and then into the shower. It was barely eight, and Jude was already exhausted. "Why wouldn't they like you?"

Kit shrugged. "I don't know anybody here. And they all talk funny."

"What do you mean they talk funny?"

"You know. Like that lady at the vegetable stand."

Jude laughed. He knew exactly what Kit meant. There was an old lady who ran a vegetable stand near the house with an accent straight out of *Gone with the Wind*. It sounded so lazy and strange to their New England ears that both of them giggled every time they went to buy some of her luscious heirloom tomatoes.

"Well think of it this way, kid. If they sound funny to you, you probably sound funny to them. So, I wouldn't worry too much about it." He grabbed a black teeshirt with a skull emblazoned on the front and began tugging it down over Kit's head. "Sheesh, kid. You must have some big brains in there."

Kit giggled, peeking out from under the shirt. "Why, Daddy?"

"Cuz you got a *huge* melon," he said in his New York cabbie voice that never failed to make Kit laugh. He was struggling to get the shirt down over the kid's nose when there was a knock on the door downstairs. "Who can that be at this hour?" Jude grumbled.

"Maybe it's the ice cream man," Kit said. They played this game a lot whenever the phone rang, or someone came to the door.

"Maybe it's the dog catcher."

"Maybe it's the..." Kit paused, struggling to get his head out of the neck hole of his teeshirt. "My new teacher, Miss Winslow!"

Jude smiled. He kind of wished it was Miss Winslow. She was quite a refreshing bit of Southern charm, that girl. Those blue eyes that sparkled with mischief, a killer smile, and a wicked sense of humor. He liked that in a woman. His late wife, Shelby, had been that kind of woman. And he missed it.

"Somehow I don't think so, kid." He helped Kit get his arms through the holes and straightened out his shirt. "Go brush your teeth while I get the door."

"What if it's Godzilla?"

"Then I'll just have to invite him in for some coffee and your leftover waffle." He winked at Kit and gave him a gentle push toward the bathroom as the knocking at the door became more insistent.

"I'm coming," he called as he galloped down the stairs, two at a time. Who could it be knocking on his door so early? He didn't know any of his neighbors yet. Not to mention, the house didn't really look like receiving guests yet.

When he opened the door, a tall woman with a silver streaked, straight bob and tiny glasses stood on the porch. She greeted him with a smile that wasn't exactly warm, but friendly. "Hello there!" she said. "My name is Mia Goddard. I live in the house across the way."

"Oh, hi," Jude said, extending his hand. "So nice to meet you. I'm Jude Renfro. Sorry I haven't been over to say hello yet. It's been a busy couple of weeks."

"Oh no, no, no," she said, waving off his apologies. "I'm the one who should be apologizing. I should have been over here the second I saw the moving truck. Not living up to my duties as a hospitable Southern lady. I should have brought a casserole or something."

"If it makes you feel any better, I'm not exactly educated on etiquette in the south," Harper said. He was trying not to be annoyed, but he could see the clock out of the corner of his eye. He didn't want Kit to be late to his first day of school.

"I'm sure you're doing fine," Ms. Goddard said, practically shoving her way into the foyer. She looked around the room over the tops of her glasses, and Jude could feel her forming judgments already. The truth was, he'd bought this house on the internet, having never seen it in person, out here on the edge of the marsh, assuming it would be private and give him and Kit lots of room. It wasn't until they got here that he realized that the area was rapidly growing into an affluent neighborhood. "I see you're not quite settled in yet."

"Well, no. A mix-up with the moving company, so we're still waiting on some of our things." That was a bit of an understatement. Moving from Boston had been a nightmare in logistics. Most of their furniture was lost on the interstate somewhere between New York and South Carolina.

"Well, I didn't want to take up too much of your time, but I was heading out and saw your light on, so I thought I'd stop in and say hello." She wandered through the foyer and into the living room, her eyes everywhere. "This is such a beautiful place."

"It is," Jude said. "I think that old fireplace was what sold me." He gestured to an enormous stone fireplace against the far wall. Already he was having visions of a great, roaring fire in the hearth while he sipped a local brew and strummed his guitar.

"It's original to the house. Most of which was lost to Hazel in '54."

"Hazel?"

"The hurricane. It was rebuilt in the sixties, bigger and better, but the original house is much older. Probably dates back to Reconstruction."

"Oh yeah. The Reconstruction after the Civil War."

Ms. Goddard gave a thin-lipped smile that reminded Jude of one of those lizards that kept trying to get in through the French doors in the back. "Yes, this house has history. Around here people call it The Willows because of your lovely trees out back. I've always wanted to see the inside."

"Well, I have lots of plans for it. I'd be more than happy to give you the grand tour when everything gets settled."

Before she could reply, Kit came bounding down the stairs, shoes untied, with his bookbag thrown over his shoulders. "C'mon, Daddy! We're gonna be late."

"And who is this?" Ms. Goddard turned and knelt down on the little boy's level.

"I'm Christopher Owen Renfro, but everybody calls me Kit. I'm five years old, and today is my first day of school."

"Oh, how exciting," Ms. Goddard said. "You must be going to Sojourner Truth."

"Yep. I'm in kindergarten, and my teacher is Miss Winslow."

Jude could have sworn her eyelid twitched just a little at the mention of Harper Winslow. He wondered if there was some kind of history there that he should be aware of. There usually was in small towns.

"Well, you certainly look very handsome," Miss Goddard said, ruffling Kit's hair. She stood and began to stroll back toward the door. "Well, I won't keep you, but I just wanted to say hello. If you need anything, I'm just across the road there."

"Thanks, Miss Goddard," Jude said, offering his hand.

"Oh please, call me Mia." She smiled and shook his hand stiffly before turning to leave. Before she reached the door, she paused. "And just an aside. I give piano lessons, if you think Christopher might be interested in learning."

"Yes!" Kit shouted, nearly bowling them over in his excitement. "I always wanted to learn to play. Please, Daddy! Please, please!"

Jude sighed. This woman had unintentionally put him on the spot. He'd planned on teaching Kit himself when he got the house situated. His smallish grand piano was one of the things still missing in action. But he didn't want to offend his new neighbor by refusing her offer. Especially when Kit was now gazing up at him adoringly and bouncing. "That's so kind of you, Mia. Uh… when can he start?"

"Why, this afternoon if you'd like. You probably don't know, but I'm also the headmistress over at Highgate Academy. Our students don't come back for another couple of weeks, so my afternoons are still wide open."

"That sounds perfect," Jude said.

"Excellent. I'll expect you today around three." She handed Jude a card with the Highgate crest and contact information for herself.

"We'll be there." By this time, Kit was tugging on his arm and pulling insistently toward the door. "Sorry, but we have to go," Jude said, offering his son an ominous eyebrow arch.

"Of course," Miss Goddard said. She stepped out on to the porch with them and started back down the steps and across the road. "Give Miss Winslow my kindest regards," she called over her shoulder.

Jude shoved the card down into his pocket and guided Kit toward the car. The child had grown quiet and submitted without a sound as he was strapped into his booster seat in the back of the car. His excitement at going to school seemed to diminish as the reality that he was actually going set in. He was still smiling, but Jude doubted if that would last much longer.

Poor kid, he thought. The last couple of years had been rough on him. Kit didn't really remember Shelby that much. He had been barely three when she died, but he'd been left with a clueless father who had spent much of the last two years in a fog of depression. They'd moved out here because Jude's therapist thought it might be a good idea for both of them to have a change in scenery. It might clear out some of the darkness that Jude had kept close for so long, and also inspire him to write music again. He wasn't sure if it would work, but it couldn't hurt. And there was nothing to keep them in Boston.

As they drove toward the school, Kit had gone completely quiet. Jude looked up into the rearview mirror and could see the kid staring out the window with his worried face on. He used to make the same face when he was a toddler and had to go to the bathroom before he was fully trained.

"What's up, kid?" Jude asked.

"Nothing," Kit replied. He paused and then, "Are you sure I have to go to school today? That Miss Goody lady said she was a teacher and didn't have to go today. Maybe you got mixed up."

Jude grinned. "I don't think so. Miss *Goddard* is at the Highgate school on the other side of the island. It's a private school, so they don't have to go back yet."

"Oh." Kit thought for a minute. "Maybe I should go there instead."

"But what about Miss Winslow? I thought you liked her."

"I do," Kit said. "But maybe she was just being nice because you were there."

"I don't think so. She seemed pretty nice to me." *Looked pretty nice, too.* "I think once you get there and meet all the kids, you'll have a blast."

"You promise?"

Jude thought for a moment. He didn't want to make the kid a promise that he couldn't keep. There was a possibility that Kit would hate school. The truth was, Jude had not been a stellar student himself. Kids could be cruel, especially to outsiders. And weren't they outsiders in Crawford's Landing? But in all likelihood, Kit would love school and have a thousand friends by the end of the day. Maybe he was just projecting his own hang-ups on his five-year-old. God, how he wished Shelby were here. She had always known just what to do.

"I can't promise that everything will be perfect, Kit. But I think if you go in there and give it a chance, you're going to have a great time. Miss Winslow seems like a fun teacher, and remember how awesome it was to play in the park in Boston? You'll get to play like that all day at school."

He leaned forward and flipped on the radio. Even after all these years, it always surprised him when he flipped past a radio station and heard his own voice. The refrain of "Evil Angel" blared through the speakers. It had been one of Affluenza's biggest hits, even though Jude hated it. He'd written it after a particularly brutal college heartbreak. To him, the lyrics were whiny and bitter, but they'd needed a filler song on the album, so he pulled it out and the band recorded it. Jude always figured that was that chick's final act of revenge—he'd have to sing that song at every concert for the rest of his life.

"Daddy, look! It's my teacher."

Jude turned to glance inside the other car and sure enough, it was Harper Winslow in the car beside them. She held a pink travel mug, presumably full of high-test coffee, and using it like a microphone as she danced and flipped her hair to the music. He could faintly hear the music coming through her cracked car window. She was listening to the same station they were and matching the song note for note.

He secretly hoped the light wouldn't change so he could sit there watching her for a few minutes. The way she danced to the music was wild and free. She had a dark, smoldering look in her eyes that made him wonder what she did in the dark. The thought gave him a shiver even as they sat in the warm, early morning sun. Suddenly, she turned and sang his own words right to him.

Chapter Four

The first day of school dawned brightly. In years past, Harper had slept poorly the night before and had to drag herself out of the bed with the taste of bitter resentment in her mouth that summer vacation was over. Today was different. By the time the first rays of the morning sun peeked through her blinds, Harper was already having her first cup of coffee on the back porch. The fiery ball crept over the marsh in streaks of fire, turning the sky a thousand shades of purple and pink. She knew it was a sign that this was going to be the best school year she'd ever had.

Why was this so different from every year? This feeling of excitement and hope was exhilarating, but Harper couldn't explain it. She'd been trying since she leaped out of bed. She pondered this while she was humming along with an absent tune in the shower. Finally, she'd come to the conclusion that Jude Renfro was the unknowing, grand architect of her mood. Perhaps it was only subconscious, but the thought that she would see him today set Harper's heart aflutter. Sure, she was looking forward to meeting her new students and starting the year off with a clean slate, but seeing Jude would definitely be a bonus.

Harper reached into her closet and flipped through her rack of "teacher clothes." When she wasn't working, her wardrobe usually consisted of blue jeans and some variety of black t-shirt. She examined each item, turning her nose up and moving on. She'd never felt comfortable in the khaki pants and colorful tops that most of her colleagues wore. They never seemed to fit just right over her child-bearing hips and generous bosom. Today, Harper wanted to look her best. She told herself it wasn't for Jude, but she also knew that was a lie.

She agonized for several more minutes before finally deciding on vintage black pedal pushers and a button-up, fitted blouse adorned with tiny roses, skulls, and paisleys. She painted herself a pair of Bettie Page eyes and smoothed her hair. "You'll do," she said to her mirror with a smile.

Harper was not one of those crunchy granola types that believed in fate and signs from the Almighty, but it seemed that the universe was definitely talking to her as she flipped on the radio in her car and an old Affluenza song blared through the speakers. She sang along, pulling to a stop at the light.

Out of the corner of her eye, Harper could see the person in the car next to her. A wave of mischief, or maybe just a coffee rush, came over her. She reached down and cranked the dial on the stereo, turning the music up to earsplitting levels. Her coffee cup became a microphone as she belted out the song and danced in her seat. She flipped her hair like an expert heavy metal groupie and turned to the window, rolling it down.

"Blood red lips paint a schizophrenic smile," she sang to the person in the car beside her.

She was singing so enthusiastically that she didn't realize the car beside her had turned and another took its place. When Harper opened her eyes, she realized that she'd been making a fool of herself to none other than Jude Renfro. Her face must have flushed a thousand shades of red and purple. She wanted to slide down and become one with the seat covers.

Harper's brain was desperately trying to find a way that she didn't come out looking like a complete moron. Maybe he didn't recognize her. After all, they'd only met once for about ten minutes. Guys like Jude met thousands of people every day. He couldn't be expected to remember one little insignificant kindergarten teacher.

Harper straightened and pressed the button that would automatically roll up the window. She dared to steal a tiny glance, and Jude was smiling. One of those incredible, toothy smiles that reached all the way to the crinkly bits around his eyes. When he realized that Harper was looking at him, he waved and gave a thumbs up. She could only smile nervously and wave. Fortunately, the light changed, and she was able to speed away before she made even more of a fool of herself.

By the time she pulled into her parking spot, she'd all but forgotten the singing incident. A preoccupied mind did come in handy every now and then. Harper was thinking about how she was going to fit in all of the day's activities. It was only the first day of school, and she already had to meet with Mrs. Nettles that afternoon to talk about a committee to plan the Fall Carnival. She hoped that the principal wouldn't expect her to have a plan written out yet. Harper wasn't exactly a planner anyway. She had always been a bit of a global thinker, leaving list making and organization to others like her incredibly organized assistant, Jax.

Jackson DuBose was probably the most organized person Harper had ever met. He kept a list of tasks for each day and was never without his cellphone and its organization and productivity apps. Others had doubted when the school hired him, barely out of high school. Whoever heard of a male kindergarten assistant? But in their three years together, Jax had been the best assistant that Harper had ever seen. He was energetic, loving, and had an excellent rapport with their little ones. Especially the boys with no father at home.

Jax opened the door just as Harper started fumbling with her keys. She immediately dropped her bags and threw her arms around his neck, hugging him tight. "I'm so glad to see you!" she said.

"Oh, you're just saying that because I opened the door for you," he joked.

"Well, maybe a little."

The truth was that Harper had been afraid that Jax wouldn't be joining her this year. The district cuts had originally included all of the kindergarten assistants except for one floater that would be shared between the four classrooms. And given that Jax didn't have seniority, they had assumed the worst.

"The room looks great. Sorry I couldn't be here to help," Jax said.

"No problem. You deserved that vacation." Harper began unpacking her bags full of first day goodies, keeping one eye on the clock. The monitors would start bringing the children down at eight, and Harper wanted to have everything ready to go. "I'm just glad you're here."

"No doubt. The district kept us guessing right down to the last second." Jax twisted his braids into a wide hairtie.

"They were lucky you hadn't found something else."

"I wasn't looking," Jax said, squatting down to get a stack of drawing paper out of the cabinet. "Of course, Mia Goddard did send me a couple of nosy emails."

"Mia Goddard?" Harper narrowed her eyes. Mia Goddard was the snotty headmistress of Highgate Academy, the private school that was currently strangling Sojourner Truth Elementary.

"Yeah, apparently she'd heard that our district was cutting assistants and wanted to know if I'd be interested in working for them."

"Well, are you?"

Jax laughed and shook his head. "Not a chance. Besides, I don't think that the lily-white powers that be over at Highgate would be too keen on a male kindergarten assistant that was not only black, but also gay."

"Then they'd be morons. You're fantastic at your job regardless of your sexuality or your ethnicity. Which is why I keep telling you that you should go back to school and get your degree so you can have a classroom of your own."

"Well, if I did that, you'd be stuck with no assistant."

"This is true, but I'm willing to sacrifice the best assistant a girl could ever have so that you could be making more money."

"I'm not interested in more money…"

"Maybe not, but…" Harper took the paper from Jax and smiled. "Sometimes I feel guilty for not pushing you harder to get certified. You have a real gift, Jax. These children need someone like you."

Jax embraced Harper tightly and kissed her cheek. "You're a sweetheart for saying so. I feel like I am making a difference here."

"Of course you are, Jax."

"And besides, if I left, who would help you with this insane carnival idea?"

"Oh, you heard about that?"

"Sweetie, everyone's heard about that. The way you stood up to Jackie and made an impassioned plea on behalf of our students…"

"The impassioned plea was Nicole."

Jax laughed. "Whatever. I think it's a great idea, but it will take a lot of planning and support."

"Yeah, I'm supposed to be meeting with Nettles this afternoon to talk about that very thing. So, I can count on your help?"

"A team of wild beer trucks couldn't keep me away."

Children began arriving in droves promptly at eight. Most of them bounced in with their parents as if they'd been waiting for this day their whole lives. They giggled and shouted with glee as they swarmed over all the new toys. Others seemed unsure but quickly came around when Jax led them over to the tables stocked with drawing paper and fat crayons.

Harper was so busy that she didn't have much time to think about the fact that the Renfros hadn't managed to make it to school yet. Maybe her little spasm at the stoplight had forced Jude to rethink allowing his child to go to the public school on the island. Maybe he'd thought she was a little too strange to be a kindergarten teacher. It wouldn't surprise her. Harper had been accused of weirdness ever since she was a child. No one could believe she'd chosen to become a teacher. Or perhaps Mia Goddard and her band of robo-teachers had managed to get to Jude and convince him to send Kit to Highgate. It wasn't uncommon. Harper had lost at least four kids from her original class list in the month since picking it up from the office.

"Come on, Kit. We talked about this."

Harper stopped short as she stepped outside her classroom door. Kit Renfro stood at the door with his father kneeling in front of him. The little boy's cheeks were rosy and streaked with glistening tears. His unruly curls stood out all over his head in a dark halo that highlighted his green eyes.

"I don't want to go to school, Daddy," Kit sobbed.

"Well sometimes we have to do things we don't want to do," Jude said. "But I promise you'll have lots of fun if you give it a chance."

"What if the other kids don't like me?"

"We talked about this, Kit. Why wouldn't they like you?"

He shrugged. "I don't know. Because I'm new. Because I never been to school before. Maybe they'll think I'm not smart. Maybe they'll make fun of me 'cause I don't have a mommy."

"Look, Kit. There's always some kids that are assholes. You just have to ignore them. Be yourself and everyone will love you."

"But what if I can't?"

The kid was clearly gearing up for another crying jag. Harper had seen it a thousand times before. Separation anxiety caused perfectly reasonable kids to devolve into screaming, weepy banshees in seconds. That was not the way Harper wanted to start her day.

"Hey, Kit," Harper said, peeking out into the hallway. She didn't want them to know that she'd been standing there listening to every word. "Everything okay?"

Jude stood up, a desperate expression on his face. "We're a little shy this morning. I don't know what happened. He was so excited when we got in the car."

"Well, of course we're shy, silly," Harper said, ignoring Jude and squatting down to Kit's level. "It's the first time ever at school. That's always a little scary. There's new people and a big school and new rules. Am I right?"

Kit nodded, wiping his runny nose on his sleeve. "I don't want to go to school."

"I completely understand. But you know, everyone's in there waiting for you." She sat down on the floor beside him.

"Really?" Kit asked, his eyes going wide.

"Oh yeah. And I'll tell you a secret, most of them are pretty scared too."

"They are?"

"Sure they are," Harper said. "You think people are born knowing how to be in kindergarten?"

"I guess not. But why would they be waiting for me?"

"Because I bet that right now, there's some kid in there thinking, 'Gosh I'm scared. I wish somebody would come in and be my friend.' Not only that, but I've got so many games for us to play today, and we can't start without you."

Kit looked between Harper and his father, still unsure. He nibbled on his lower lip as if considering what she'd said and trying to make up his mind. After several moments of contemplation, he turned to Harper. "You don't look like a teacher."

"I don't?"

He shook his head. "They usually wear dresses and big earrings."

"My ears aren't even pierced," Harper said, pushing her hair aside to show him. "And I don't have a lot of dresses."

Kit pointed at one of the skulls on her shirt. "Teachers don't got skulls on their clothes either."

"You must have known some really boring teachers." She winked at Kit and stood up, offering her hand. "Speak friend and enter."

Kit gave his father a look of apprehension, but eventually decided that there was no way he was getting out of this and took her hand. Just before they reached the door, the boy turned to wrap his arms around his father's knees. "You promise you'll be here when I'm done?"

"I'll be right here waiting at two. Promise." Jude knelt and let the boy embrace him in earnest. He pressed a gentle kiss on Kit's curly crown and they sang lightly together.

"I'll be seeing you when the day turns to night and we'll dance together 'til the morning light."

Harper's heart gave a flutter as she recognized a line from Affluenza's last single. It was one of her favorite songs and to hear him singing it to his little boy was almost more than her ovaries could stand.

"Okay, Miss Winslow," Kit said, taking her hand once more. "We can go in now."

Before they could get into the classroom, Jude tugged at Harper's sleeve. She stopped and gestured for Kit to go inside to where Jax was waiting with a big smile.

"Hey, Miss Winslow…"

"Call me Harper, please," she said, suddenly feeling extremely bashful herself. "Everyone does."

"Harper, then. Thank you for that."

She shrugged. "What?"

"Taking care of Kit like that. He's been kind of an emotional wreck this morning. He's never been to school before."

"Oh, it was nothing. Most of the kids on the island have never been to school. Crying kids is kind of par for the course here at ye olde kindergarten hall. They're just afraid of being away from their moms and dads. Perfectly normal."

Jude nodded. "Yes, but for a second I was really worried that I wasn't going to be able to convince him to stay."

"I guarantee by the time you get to your car, he'll be playing with the others like he's known them for years."

"I hope you're right." He went into his back pocket and pulled out his cell phone. "Here, let me give you my cell number just in case you need me to come over."

The soft, blue glow of his cellphone illuminated his flawless skin, and Harper could see the smattering of freckles across his forehead. His full lips moved silently while he scrolled through an endless list of contacts. "Sorry, I have to keep myself as a contact so I know my phone number."

Harper giggled. "I do the same thing." Her hand instinctively went to her pocket where her own cell lay heavy against her thigh. She wondered if she should give him hers. Was that appropriate? She hadn't given her cell number to any of the other parents. If they wanted to talk to her, she had a strict policy that they call her at school. She'd made the mistake of giving parents her home number during the first year. After a couple of late-night phone calls, she'd learned her lesson.

"Here, let me give you mine too. You know, just in case you get worried."

"Oh great. Thank you. I promise not to trouble you with a constant stream of obsessive dad texts."

"No worries. You will definitely not be the only parent to be concerned about their child's first day of school."

He leaned in close to see her cell number, and Harper caught a whiff of his scent. Heaven. The man smelled like heaven. A combination of leather, old cigarettes, and aftershave. Harper had to stop herself from sniffing him like a dog as he carefully typed in her number with his thin, nimble fingers. She couldn't help wondering what those fingers might feel like as they trilled along her ribcage.

"I really appreciate this."

"What?" she asked, snapping out of her fugue. "I mean, you're welcome. I want Christopher's transition to be as smooth as possible. I know it isn't easy."

Jude offered a sideways grin. "You're really not like most of the teachers I've met before."

"They're usually pretty stand-offish. We try to be a bit more welcoming at Sojourner."

"It's a great help. Really." He offered her his hand, and she took it, meaning to give it a friendly shake, but instead holding it as she looked up into his endless dark eyes.

"Just um… doing my job," she said, finally dropping his hand before it could get more awkward. She wanted to say more, but the only words that would come to mind were, *"I want to have all your babies."* And Harper didn't think that would be appropriate. Thankfully she heard something crash and a cacophony of giggles.

"I should probably get back there. Since I'm in charge." Before Jude could say anymore, Harper turned and marched back into the classroom.

Chapter Five

Jude tried to make himself busy, but he wasn't having much luck. Looking around the room he could see that there was plenty to do, but he couldn't stop thinking about Kit. Had Miss Winslow been right? Did Kit run into the classroom, make a million friends, and completely forget about his worries? Or was he sitting in the corner, head down on his desk, crying? Jude kept thinking that any second his phone was going to ring, and it would be the school insisting that he come and pick the kid up.

He knew it was his own anxiety. He and Kit had been on their own for so long that with him not being here, there was this void left behind, and Jude had been trying all morning long to fill it with the thousand chores he'd created. They'd lived at The Willows for a little more than a week, and there were still boxes everywhere. He'd told himself that it was because he was waiting on the rest of their furniture, but it was really just procrastination of the highest order.

He stared at the boxes stacked neatly by the window in the dining room. They taunted him. Everything from the apartment in Boston still there, all sealed up neatly. All that baggage that he would have to deal with. All those boxes marked "Shelby."

"Okay, Renfro," he said to himself. "Let's get this party started. Jeeves, play High Fidelity playlist." A grinding guitar riff sounded, and music began to play all over the house. He had at least gotten the sound system set up. Some things were more important than others.

The kitchen was first on his to-do list. Mostly because it was the one room in the house that didn't need a complete decorating overhaul. He ran hot water into a bucket and poured in a generous splash of pine-scented cleaner. The black and white tile floors needed a good clean and a couple of layers of shiny wax. He sang along with the music as he pushed the mop back and forth and tried not to be intimidated by the size of the place. Their apartment in Boston had been pretty big for an apartment, but nowhere near the monstrosity that this place was.

His arms and shoulders began to ache with the exertion, but he felt good. Doing something physical helped take his mind of the melancholy and worry that had come over him. He blocked out everything else and just listened to the music and the soothing rhythm of the mop as it swished over the slick tile. Soon, he began to sing with the music, using the mop handle as a mic stand. All the old moves came back as he serenaded the kitchen. He let his voice go free, and it was a bit rusty, but the range was still there. There was that familiar sensation of the vibrato in his chest as the refrain built. The sweat began to bead at his hairline, and he was breathing hard. He opened his eyes, imagining a thousand screaming fans hanging on his every word. A cute girl on the front row stared up at him adoringly. He looked down and began to sing just to her. His eyes were fixed on hers and her features swam into focus. It was *her*. Harper Winslow grinned up at him, singing every word and matching his voice note for note.

The sound of his cell phone buzzing brought him out of his fantasy with a start. He shook the daydream from his head and crossed to where the phone was about to vibrate off the countertop. He took a deep breath and prepared for the bad news.

"Hey, this is Jude," he said.

"Hi, sweetheart." His mother's cheery voice blared through the speaker on his phone. The poor woman had a hearing problem so she was always shouting. "It's your mom."

Jude sighed with relief. "Hey, Mom. What's going on?"

"Oh, nothing. Just wanted to check and see how it was going down there in Dixie."

"I don't think they call it that anymore."

His mother chuckled, and he smiled hearing it. "You know what I mean. Anyway, is everything okay?"

"Of course it is," Jude replied, walking over to the mop to finish while they talked. "I'm sorry I haven't called you, but things have been hectic."

"Oh, I know. Your father said that I shouldn't bother you, but I wanted to be sure you and Kit were okay. You know, I don't look at the Facebook."

"I know. You could always try Instagram."

"I mean, I guess people were always stupid, but why did we have to give them a public forum to unleash their stupid on the rest of us."

"I dunno, Mom," Jude said, trying not to laugh. Elizabeth "Betts" Renfro was what some might refer to as "crunchy granola." She despised social media, was vigilant about GMOs and organic food, and binge-watched episodes of *Democracy NOW!*. His father, on the other hand, just wanted to be left alone with his guitar and a case of good beer. "How's Dad?"

"A pain in my ass," she replied dryly. "But he's fine. He's playing with the rest of those old fools in the Fall River Harvest Fest this weekend."

"That's awesome!"

"He doesn't need to be out there in the heat all day, but you can't tell him anything."

"He'll be fine, Mom."

"So how is Kit?"

"Great! His first day of school is today."

"Wow, isn't it a little early for that?"

"They start earlier down here, apparently. Anyway, he was a little apprehensive at first, but his teacher seems really... really nice."

"Well I can't wait to hear all about it." His mother paused, and Jude could hear her trying to decide how to say something. "Jude, I know you know this, but... your father and I are so proud of you."

"I know..."

"A lot of men would not have risen to the challenge of raising a child on their own. Especially when they'd lost their wives like you did. Not to mention having the kind of career you had. Walking away from your dreams, putting your life on hold—I know that wasn't easy, son, but you're doing such a good job. Shelby would be so proud of you both."

Jude could feel his cheeks burning at such high praise. He'd never taken compliments easily. "Thanks, Mom. I don't think I could have done any of it without you and Dad."

"We're always here for you, sweetheart. Well, I won't keep you. I know you have a million things to do down there, but if you wouldn't mind sending us some pictures of this gorgeous new place."

"If you would look at the Facebook account I started for you, there are tons of pictures there."

"Hmmph," she grunted. "I'd have to wade through a bunch of political garbage and half-naked pictures before I found them. No thank you."

Jude was nodding. He'd heard these arguments so many times before. "I'll send the pictures to your e-mail so your eyes won't burn out of their sockets."

"Thank you. I'll call back tonight and talk to Kit. I want to hear all about his first day of kindergarten."

"Yes, Ma'am. Love you and Dad."

He hung up and checked his phone for any missed calls. So far, so good. And he hadn't heard any emergency vehicles screaming toward the school. That was one good thing about living in a tiny island town; if something was going on, everyone knew it.

In another hour, the kitchen floor was sparkling and had a fresh coat of wax. He looked around the kitchen, pretty proud of himself. The room had been decorated in a retro style by whoever the last owner had been. The walls were a pale aqua with a bright white wainscoting. In the center was an island topped with a glittery white laminate top and stainless sink off to one side. Matching countertops ran down one wall set off by a tiled backsplash that looked like the floor Jude had just finished scrubbing. With some new appliances and some vintage stools, maybe some tattoo flash artwork, it would be perfect. Shelby had always said that the kitchen was the heart of any house.

Jude went to the dining room and began hauling all the boxes marked with a K into the kitchen. Maybe if he actually got one room of the house finished before going to get Kit he'd feel like he'd accomplished something. Glancing at his phone, he checked the time and saw that he had two hours left. Maybe a little less. He wanted to be standing at the door when the bell rang.

He hadn't quite come around to the fact that not only was he anxious to see Kit, but also Miss Winslow. He'd always heard that there were some people you instantly felt a connection with. It was a kind of strange magic that couldn't be explained. When he saw Miss Winslow at the school the other day, he'd felt that connection.

It was like the electric hum when you turn on an amplifier, low but so powerful you could feel it in your chest. When she'd handed over her cell phone earlier, their hands touched, and Jude would swear that he'd felt a tiny jolt as their hands made contact. He hadn't felt that way in a long time, and he was eager to feel it again. Of course, he could never act on any sort of attraction to her. After all, she was his kid's teacher. If things went bad between them, where did that leave Kit? Jude would like to think that Miss Winslow wouldn't take it out on a five-year-old, but you could never tell. He didn't know a thing about her.

Except, of course, that he had been thinking about her steadily since meeting her three days ago.

He shook off the thought and started unpacking boxes of plates. As he stacked them in the cabinet, he could hear Shelby's voice complaining that he really should put shelf-liner down first. Then advising him on where to put things so as to be the most efficient. He smiled, remembering how she always had a place for everything and an endless justification of why her way was the right one.

Jude went through one box after another, making quick work of getting the kitchen in order. After an hour, he looked up and realized that the mountain of boxes in the dining room had shrunk considerably. He was just about to get himself a congratulatory beer out of the fridge when his phone began to buzz again, this time a text.

"Good lord," he sighed. "Just one more hour." When he picked up the phone, he fully expected to find a text and accompanying photographs of how his child had set fire to the classroom and then hijacked a school bus.

HARPER WINSLOW: *Just letting you know that Kit is having a great day. Didn't want you to worry.*

A wave of relief washed over Jude, followed by a flutter that she'd actually thought to text him. Sweet.

ME: *Thank you so much, Miss Winslow. I really appreciate it.*
HARPER WINSLOW: *You're very welcome. Kit's a joy!*
ME: *Thanks…*

Jude paused. He wanted to keep the conversation going, but what would he say? Oh God, now she could probably see the little blinking dots indicating that he was still typing.

ME: *I'm really glad he's having a good time.*

As soon as he finished typing, he threw the phone down and walked away. He didn't want to know if she was responding. If she did, then he would be compelled to reply again, and on and on until they were having a full-on conversation. He wasn't sure if he was ready to have a full-on conversation with her. Despite Jude's musical career, he was quite shy, and he didn't want to make an idiot of himself.

Jude puttered around the house for another hour and finally decided he couldn't take it another minute. He'd just go on over to the school and wait. Maybe even surprise the kid by showing up at the classroom. See for himself just how well he was adjusting.

And just maybe come up with a reason to check out the lovely Miss Winslow.

Chapter Six

The first day of school was always an exhausting exercise in terror. Harper loved it. She loved getting back to the kids and into a routine, but the stress of getting everyone home was almost more than she could take. Kindergarteners were notorious for not knowing how they were supposed to get home, and there was always one left over after the bell rang. Once she got everyone shuffled off to the car pickup line, the bus line, and the daycare van pickup line, all she wanted to do was lie down in her classroom with a cool rag on her head. Not to mention that she still hadn't quite processed her less-than smooth encounter with Jude Renfro. Unfortunately, today she had a meeting with Ms. Nettles about the Fall Carnival. But maybe that was for the best. She wouldn't have time to let the embarrassment catch up to her.

Jax stood back, trying not to laugh as he watched Harper rummage through her desk frantically. "What are you doing, Harper?"

"I brought a notebook especially for the purpose of planning this event, and now I can't find it." It was probably lost under this mountain of emergency contact forms, bus assignment charts, and cheerful, crayon drawings of her and Jax that the kids had done during free time.

"Oh, you mean this one?" Jax produced a thick spiral notebook with the words "Fall Fundraiser" written across the front in Harper's careful block printing.

"Yes," Harper said, taking it.

"Am I to assume that your flustered mood is related to a certain parent?"

Harper didn't look up but continued searching through the wreckage of her desk for a pen. "I'm not going to dignify that with any sort of response."

"Well, he's pretty cute if you ask me."

"I didn't."

"Oh come on, Harper! I saw how you were looking at him when he came to pick up Kit this afternoon. You were beaming like a schoolgirl."

Harper shook her head and shoved the notebook and pen down into her shoulder bag. "I was being nice."

"I detected drooling."

"I was not drooling."

"Drooling?" The two of them gasped, startled by Nicole standing in the doorway. "You must be talking about the handsome Mr. Renfro."

"God, not you too!" Harper jerked the door of her mini-fridge open to retrieve a can of soda. "He's a nice guy, and he's new in town. I'm just being nice. Besides, his kid is precious."

Jax leaned into Nicole conspiratorially. "I can report that Mr. Jude Renfro came to the classroom to pick little Christopher up. I can also report that Miss Winslow giggled no less than five times in his presence. I can further report that they exchanged cell numbers this morning…"

"To make him feel better about leaving his only child at school for the very first time!" Harper interjected. "Look, we all know that Jude…"

Jax nudged Nicole. "Jude. They're on a first name basis."

"Mr. Renfro, then. We all know that he's pretty dreamy. I mean, what's not to love? Arresting eyes, amazing hair, a smile that could sail a thousand ships, and he's exceptionally talented. And a good dad."

"Sounds like she's been thinking about this for a while," Nicole snickered.

"But," Harper continued, ignoring Nicole. "He's also the parent of one of my students. I couldn't date him even if I wanted to."

"Oh please," Jax said. "That's so nineteenth century. News flash, Harper: you can wear trousers to work now."

Harper smirked. "It's still not exactly appropriate. Don't you agree, Nicole?"

The older woman seemed surprised that she'd been called on. "Well, as long as you were discreet about what was going on, I reckon it would be all right. Of course, if things went south, that might make your working relationship awkward."

Harper started to reply and paused, not knowing what to say. Were they really even having this conversation? "It doesn't matter anyway because there's nothing going on," she said finally. "He's a nice guy with a cute kid in my class. I'm the teacher. End of story." She hoisted the messenger bag over her shoulder, nearly upsetting a pencil cup. She stared down at her watch and gasped. "And now we're late to the meeting."

Nicole chuckled and followed Harper out, waving to Jax.

Harper made a point of not talking to Nicole as they made their way through the halls toward the office. She didn't want to answer any more questions about Mr. Renfro. Had she been so damned obvious about her attraction? And if she was, how on earth would she be able to get through the school year without making a fool of herself?

The two women rushed into the office, knowing that they were at least five minutes late, which might as well have been an hour to Andrea Nettles. The principal was a stickler for punctuality from both her students and staff, but when Harper opened the door to the conference room, the other woman just smiled and indicated seats for Harper and Nicole.

"Sorry, Mrs. Nettles," Nicole lied. "Poor Harper had a straggler stuck in transportation limbo."

"No worries," Mrs. Nettles said. "After all, it *is* the first day of school. I'm just glad you got here. I was starting to think you'd reconsidered heading up this committee." Just then the door opposite opened as someone entered from the other side.

Harper's heart leapt into the back of her throat, and she began coughing like a tuberculosis patient as she realized that the person coming in was none other than Jude Renfro.

"Hi. Sorry I'm late; I had to get my kindergartener settled in with the sitter." He reached out to shake hands with Nettles.

"You could have brought him with you," she replied, smiling and gesturing toward a chair on the other side of Harper.

"What's Mr. Renfro doing here?" Harper asked with a nervous smile.

"I thought we might need some parental involvement. And Mr. Renfro was kind enough to volunteer."

"I work from home," Jude said. "I heard Mrs. Nettles talking about the carnival in the office this afternoon, so I thought I'd offer my assistance."

"Oh…well…"

"How very kind of you!" Nicole interrupted, her bubbly enthusiasm saving the day. "We can sure use the help." She kicked Harper under the table.

"Yes! Absolutely. We can use all the help we can get."

"This meeting is going to be fairly brief and informal," Mrs. Nettles began. She nodded to Nicole, "Here's our committee for the fundraiser, Ms. Thompson and evidently you're already acquainted with Ms. Winslow."

Harper felt an awkward giggle bubbling up from her throat, but she swallowed it down as they shook hands again. "Yes."

"So today we need to talk about all the things we'll need to have in place before the fundraiser, starting with a date."

Nicole was the first to speak. Thank goodness, as Harper didn't think she'd be able to say anything intelligent with him sitting so close. "I was thinking that our fundraising goals aren't going to be met with just one event." Nicole pulled out her notebook and began flipping through it. She was so damn organized! "I took the liberty of pulling some of the figures from last year's efforts."

"Which didn't do very well, to be honest," Nettles sighed.

"Exactly," Harper said. "I believe the traditional methods of selling wrapping paper and expensive chocolates aren't going to work here on the island."

"Why?"

"It's obvious, isn't it?" Harper said. "The population in Crawford's Landing is mostly working class or people who are just here for the summer. The people with disposable income leave in September and the people who actually live on the island either can't afford or have no need of expensive Christmas wrap."

"But people that live on the island aren't the only ones buying, right?" Nettles asked.

"We have to assume that these kids are only able to sell to their friends and family that live here in Crawford's Landing," Nicole said. "And that our little market gets saturated."

"So you need to come up with different things that can be exclusive to the kids at Sojourner," Jude said.

"That's why I thought doing things that the parents could do with their kids would be more effective. Events and things of that nature."

"Things you could market to people off the island en masse."

"And that people would be willing to pay for," Nicole finished. "Which is why I think Harper's carnival idea is brilliant."

Harper felt the color rush into her cheeks. Being called 'brilliant' was not something she was used to. And she always felt shy when others singled her out, even if they were complimenting her.

Jude grinned. "That *is* a brilliant idea. Kids love a carnival."

Harper pulled out her notebook and flipped to the page where she'd begun doodling ideas. "I made a list of all the 'must haves' for the carnival. Things like food, space, games, and entertainment. Supplies…"

"We'll definitely need to come up with a budget," Mrs. Nettles said. "After all, we're trying to raise money, not spend it."

"Well the truth is, we'll have to spend a little to make it," Nicole said. "But there are lots of businesses on the mainland that might be willing to donate some of those items."

Jude tapped his lower lip with the tip of his finger, deep in thought. "I've got some friends I can call. Maybe they'd be willing to make some donations to offset the expenses. There are some people in the music industry who still like me."

"That would be so helpful. Thank you." Nettles smiled, startling Harper. She'd been working at Sojourner Truth Elementary for ten years, and she didn't think she'd ever seen Andrea Nettles smile. She didn't even know the woman had teeth. Maybe she wasn't the only one quickly succumbing to Jude's generous mouth and infectious smile. "We also need to consider other things we can do to raise funds. Just a carnival isn't going to do it."

"The carnival is just the start," Harper said. "I propose that we also apply for grants and do other drives in tandem."

Nettles nodded. "You're absolutely right. But I'm worried about how the grants will be funded. The school system is actively trying to close us down."

"What for?" Jude asked.

"It would be less expensive to bus our kids to elementary schools on the mainland," Nicole said. "The state gives us money based on how many kids we have enrolled, and our enrollment has dropped exponentially in the last five years. Keeping the lights on here for so few students is a drain. Or so they claim."

"The only option for our kids to stay on the island for school is Highgate."

"Highgate?"

"The private school down the road," Nicole said. "The high tuition prohibits most of our children from going there."

Jude shook his head. "So much for every child being given a public education."

"Ah, the law says that education must be provided, not that it has to be easy," Harper said.

"Where should we have this thing?" Nicole asked, trying to drag them back to the topic at hand.

"I was thinking that since the cafeteria opens up onto the courtyard, we could have it there. That way we'll have the kitchen and a large space that's both indoors and outdoors." Mrs. Nettles pulled out a folder that had the measurements of the room written down. "We can clear all of the tables out except for the ones we want to use for food. Or maybe food trucks?"

The more they chattered about the specifics, the more excited Harper became about the carnival. Not only was she certain that this was going to be a successful fundraising event, but the children were going to love it. Her pen flew across the paper as she made notes of their ideas and questions she would have to seek out the answers to. For someone that was so global and creative, Harper loved a project. Something she could throw herself into.

The four of them sat there for the better part of an hour making notes and brainstorming about the carnival. She and Jude slipped into an easy conversation. Miraculously, she had almost forgotten how attracted to him she was. After a while, Harper's little notebook was full of ideas. She glanced down at her phone and noted the time. It seemed impossible that they'd been sitting here talking this long.

"I'm going to make some calls this evening and try to get some estimates," Mrs. Nettles said, pushing back from the table. She was obviously trying to get out of there. "Why don't we agree to meet each week? Is this time good for everyone?"

The three of them looked at one another and eventually nodded.

"It's perfect for me, actually," Jude said. "Kit has a music lesson at this time. I can be here right after I drop him off."

"Then it's settled." The walkie talkie at Mrs. Nettles's side screeched angrily as someone on the other end called for her. "Oh… that's me. It was nice meeting you, Mr. Renfro. And thanks so much for agreeing to help us out."

"No worries," he said. "Kit and I are part of this community now."

She shook hands with Jude and hurried out of the room, mumbling into the walkie.

"I better run too," Nicole said. The wink she tossed Harper's way did not escape her attention. "I have a middle schooler waiting."

Harper suddenly found herself alone in the conference room with Jude. The silence was deafening. What was she supposed to say to him? Should she just make up some excuse to get out of there as quickly as possible? Or maybe…

"Kit said he had a great time in class today," Jude said, startling Harper out of her thoughts. "He was all smiles when I picked him up."

"I'm so glad," Harper said. "He's an awesome kid. You should be proud of him."

"I am," Jude said. "I can't thank you enough for being so sweet this morning. I didn't think I was going to be able to leave him. I barely got him in the car, but this afternoon it was almost like he didn't want to leave."

Harper smiled and began gathering her things. "I've been doing this a long time. Kids his age are always scared at first, but eventually they come around."

"Well, whatever it was, thank you."

He was so close. She could feel the warmth emanating from his body against her bare arm. Harper had dated men before, but she'd never encountered one that made her insides literally quake. She was drawn to him.

No, she couldn't allow herself to get involved. He was a student's father! If she let herself fall for him, if things ended badly, it would be awkward.

The tempest of self-doubt and what-ifs made Harper even clumsier than usual. When she turned to grab her shoulder bag, the contents spilled out all over the floor. Her cell phone hit the table with a sickening thud. "Shit baskets!" she exclaimed, going down on her knees to pick up her scattered toiletries.

Jude knelt to help her, chuckling under his breath. "What was that?"

"Oh... sorry..."

"Shit baskets?" he asked, handing over her cell phone.

"A colorful expression passed down from my grandmother." After a long pause, the two of them burst into peals of laughter. "Of course, she was also fond of sayings like, 'look at the ass on that tomato.' So really, she was kind of a senile old lady." They were still gasping for breath when Jackie opened up the conference room door and stared down at the two of them like they were idiots.

"Everything all right in here?" she asked with that tone of disapproval she usually employed when speaking to Harper.

"We're good," Harper squeaked. The older woman nodded and backed out of the room. Her hasty exit only made them laugh harder.

"Don't forget your phone," Jude said.

Their eyes met, and suddenly all of Harper's laughter died away. His eyes were more amber than she remembered, with little flecks of gold around the edges. She knew in that moment that she was helpless to resist the attraction she could feel between them. And for the first time in her adult life, she was sure that he felt the same.

"Thanks," she said, reaching for the phone. Their fingers brushed against one another, and Harper could feel a nervous giggle bubbling up from her belly. Fortunately, she was able to swallow it with a cough. "For that. And for uh… helping out with the uh… you know. The…" *Dear God, she was stammering like a schoolgirl!* "The uh…"

"Carnival?" he asked.

"Yes! That." She started to get up but misread her proximity to the table and smacked her head hard against it. "Ow!"

"Oh no! Are you okay?" Jude asked, taking her arm and helping her to her feet.

"Of course…" she said, despite the fact that her vision blurred slightly. "My head's pretty hard."

"Shit… you're bleeding," he said. "Here, sit down."

"I'm fine, really."

"No, you aren't," Jude said. "Let me see." He knelt in front of Harper and brushed her hair back from her brow. She probably had an enormous goose egg forming in the center of her forehead, but she didn't care. He was so close, nose to nose almost. God, he smelled like Heaven. "Wow, you must have hit your head on the edge. Should I get the nurse or something?"

"Oh, I'm sure it's just a scratch." She reached up and brushed her fingertips across the gash right at her hairline. She pulled them back, and they were covered with blood. "A very... bloody..." Suddenly Harper felt very faint. She tried to stand up but fell into Jude. Her head was spinning, but she wasn't sure if it was from the blow to her head or the proximity of his body. She knew she should be concerned about her own physical well-being, but she was distracted by the muscular arm that held her upright, and the hardened chest against her own.

"You are not fine," he said. "We need to take you to the emergency room."

"Don't be silly..." she said. "If I'm still feeling bad tomorrow, I'll see the doctor."

But Jude obviously wasn't taking no for an answer and held her tight as he led her toward the door. Harper got the distinct impression that if she had refused, Jude would have carried her out to the car.

"Well if you're insisting," she said, "there's an urgent care just down the road. That will do."

Chapter Seven

An hour later, they were still sitting in the lobby at the urgent care facility with a pack of ice on Harper's head. She wasn't really sure why. The place was deserted except for the two of them and a couple of giggly receptionists behind the counter. She remembered why she rarely ever went to the urgent care, but it was probably better than going all the way to the hospital ER on the mainland where they would charge her an arm and a leg just to give her an aspirin and an ice pack.

"Sorry," Jude said as he came back from the courtyard out front. "I had to call the sitter and let them know I'd be late."

"It really isn't necessary. If you have to go…"

"I wouldn't dream of leaving you here alone," Jude said. "Besides, your car is back at the school. Not to mention that Kit has already fussed at me for breaking his teacher."

Harper chuckled then winced as the wound on her scalp throbbed. "He's very sweet, but I'm hardly broken. Truth be told, I'm kind of a klutz. Chances are I would have hurt myself anyway."

"Don't tell me that," Jude said. "I'll be reluctant to leave you." He looked directly into her eyes as he said this, and Harper could feel her cheeks go up in flames.

His innuendo hung in the air between them and finally all Harper could do was giggle nervously. "Don't be ridiculous. I'm fine."

Before he could respond, the nurse finally appeared to call Harper back. She was thankful. What could she say? He probably didn't mean it the way it sounded. Either that, or he was just kidding. An innocent joke, right? Or maybe a little harmless flirting. Men often flirted with women they could tell liked them. Especially guys like Jude. He'd been a celebrity. Flirting with sweet little fangirls was a marketing tactic and nothing more. Old habits died hard, and Harper was just another fangirl.

She was still thinking about it when the nurse led her into the examination room and had her sit down on the table. The nurse was making small talk, but Harper was barely listening. She couldn't get Jude Renfro out of her brain.

"Your husband looks so familiar," the nurse chirped, wrapping a blood pressure cuff around Harper's arm.

"He isn't my husband," Harper replied. "Why do you need to take my blood pressure? I hit my head."

"Oh, it's just standard procedure," she replied with a smile. "I could swear I've seen him before."

"Maybe he just has one of those faces," Harper said, gritting her teeth as the cuff began squeezing her arm.

"Maybe," she said. The nurse kept squashing that rubber ball and inflating the sleeve until Harper was sure that her skin was going to burst open under the pressure. "I know," she said. "He looks like the guy from that band. That band… oh what was their name? They were on the radio every five seconds, but then they just disappeared?"

"Affluenza?" Harper shrieked, wondering if the blood pressure cuff was just going to snap her arm off at the elbow.

"Yeah, that's it. He looks like that guy." Mercifully, the nurse read the little dial and scribbled down Harper's blood pressure, letting the air seep out of the cuff. "A shame about them. I really liked their music."

"I did too," Harper said, working her arm around in circles in an attempt to get the blood flowing again.

"I saw them play on their last tour," the nurse continued. "They were so good. I really thought they'd be the next Rolling Stones, playing gigs into their seventies. It's a shame about what happened to them."

"What do you mean?" Harper said, replacing the ice pack against her forehead. "Bands break up every day. Nothing lasts forever, right?"

"I guess, but I read an article that said the lead singer's wife died suddenly."

Harper's interest was piqued. "Oh really?"

"Yeah, they never went public. He'd been on tour with the band, and he got a call that she was sick. Apparently, she had some kind of attack and died before he could get to the hospital. Probably a brain aneurysm or something. Tragic really. They had a small child too, so everyone assumed that he quit the band to take care of the kid. Isn't that the sweetest thing?"

Harper nodded. "Really sweet."

"I think I crushed on him harder after I heard that. But anyway, the kid won't be small forever. Maybe someday they'll make a comeback."

"One can only hope."

When the doctor came in, he asked her a bunch of questions about how she hurt herself, if she ever lost consciousness, if she was feeling sick—all the standard questions. She responded with all the right answers, but her mind was a thousand miles away. So that was why Jude had moved himself and his son out here. He was still grieving for a dead wife, gone too soon. Suddenly, Harper felt guilty for all of those warm, fuzzy, schoolgirl-like feelings she'd been having for him. How could she flirt with someone who'd lost his soulmate so tragically?

"I don't think you have a concussion, Miss Winslow, but you'd better take it easy tonight."

Harper snapped out of her thoughts. "Oh, that's good," she said with a nervous chuckle. "I knew it was silly to come in. Just a scratch."

"Better safe than sorry, I say. The scalp does tend to bleed a lot with the slightest trauma, but you can never be too careful with head injuries. Take some over-the-counter acetaminophen when you get home. Be sure to call us if you start to feel nauseated or lethargic."

By the time Harper got back out to the lobby, she felt worse than she had before. Just seeing his stupid face there, smiling and waiting for her to come back, was enough to break her heart.

"So, what did the doctor say?" Jude asked.

"Oh, you know. The usual. I whacked my head on a table. No concussion."

"Well, that's a relief."

Harper nodded, handing her credit card to the receptionist. "I seem to recall telling you it was nothing. If I ran to the hospital every time I hit my head, I'd have to get a job there."

Harper signed the receipt and started out the door. She didn't know why she was rushing away from Jude. He'd driven her here, so there was really no getting away at this point, but she felt this urgency to get away from him. As soon as possible. Maybe she should even talk to Nettles about getting Kit moved from her class. Harper refused to be the "shady lady" seducing her students' fathers.

"Hey! Slow down!" Jude called, sprinting after her. "What's your rush?"

"Oh... well, I just... you know... I hate doctors' offices. And don't you have to get back to Kit?"

Jude unlocked the car door and held it for her. "Well, sure, but he's with the neighbor. She won't mind keeping him a little longer."

"Who is the neighbor?"

"This nice older lady," he said, climbing in beside her and fastening his seat belt. "Miss Goddard? She lives across the street from me."

"Mia Goddard?" Harper said, making no attempt to keep the alarm from her voice. "That old battleax is taking care of Kit?"

"Battleax? She seems really nice."

Harper huffed. "I'm sure she does. You're just her type."

"What type is that?"

"Rich."

Jude laughed and started the car. "Rich is relative."

Harper shook her head and stared out the window as they started out of the parking lot. "Perception is all that matters. Mia Goddard is the headmistress at Highgate, the private school that is currently choking the life out of Sojourner Truth Elementary. She'd love to get you over there."

"Me? What difference would that make?"

Harper shook her head. It was starting to ache. "Goddard and her team of teacher Barbies are looking to draw all of the kids out of the public school system. You might have noticed that we're a tiny school anyway and the district is trying to get rid of us."

"What will happen if you close?"

"They'll bus all the kids that don't fit the 'Highgate mold' out to the mainland to the schools that are already overcrowded. Some kids will likely be on the bus for two or three hours a day."

"The 'Highgate mold'?"

She rolled her eyes, wondering if he was being serious with his question. "You know—rich. There's no bussing to Highgate. Parents have to volunteer at least five hours a week. Working class people, like the majority of the people that live on the island, don't have five hours a week to volunteer. They might not have access to a vehicle to take their kids to school. A lot of the people that live here year-round don't even have jobs through the winter. And then there's the astronomical tuition."

"So you think Ms. Goddard is trying to butter me up to send Christopher to Highgate?"

"Definitely."

Jude chuckled, pulling up beside her car in the school parking lot. "Who knew sweet little ladies could be so devious? At any rate, she's barking up the wrong tree."

"Oh?"

"Kit already has a wonderful kindergarten teacher. I don't think I'll be pulling him out, try as she might."

Harper caught his eye, noticing the mischievous gleam. He really would have to stop being so incredibly sweet if she was expected to stop lusting after him. "That's really nice of you to say…"

"I'm not just being nice," Jude said, holding her gaze. "Kit is quite taken with you. Ever since his mother's death, he's very cautious around people, but he warmed up to you immediately. And uh…I'm pretty taken myself, if I'm being honest."

Harper couldn't stop herself from staring. She knew that no matter what, this was one crush she wasn't going to be able to resist. Even if it was forbidden. "Well, Kit is pretty special," she said, her voice sounding so far away to her ear.

The blare of a car horn made Harper gasp. "I suppose that's my cue to uh… get out of the car. Someone sees us hanging out in your car after hours, well, it's the sort of thing small towns love."

Jude grinned. "Well, perhaps we should make the most of this gossiping opportunity."

An inappropriate burst of laughter bubbled out of Harper before she could stop herself. "I think that would be very unwise." She pushed open the car door, and her head throbbed. "Ow…"

"Are you all right?"

"Yeah, just feeling that bump now. The doctor said I wasn't concussed or anything."

"Maybe you should let me drive you home."

Harper shook her head a little too urgently. "No, I'm fine. Really. I've put you out far too much already today."

"I don't mind. I like putting out."

Damn it. He did it again. Harper's face was going to be permanently red if he didn't stop with the innuendo. "No, I couldn't let you do that," she said.

"Seriously, I could take you home now and come and get you in the morning on our way to school."

"Don't be silly. I only live a couple of miles away."

"Well, at least let me follow you. Just to be sure you get home safely."

"But then you'll know where I live." Harper winked and shoved open the car door. "We have to have some mystery left in our relationship. Besides, I make it a point to never let parents know where I live."

"This town is miniscule. Everyone already knows where you live."

"Still… I should go. On my own."

Harper closed the car door and gave a wave before hurrying into her own. The heat between them was a bit too much to bear. She wanted out of there before he could offer another protest. And before she could change her mind.

Harper was more than a little self-conscious as she searched through her purse for keys. He was sitting back there in his car, waiting for her to drive off. Waiting in his sleek, shiny black Jaguar while she was praying that her ten-year old Camry would start without hiccupping black smoke out of the exhaust pipe. That would be slightly embarrassing.

Thankfully, the car started without incident, and she drove away. He waved, and she beeped twice. As his car disappeared in her rearview mirror, Harper thought that Jude Renfro could be a real problem for her professionalism.

Chapter Eight

Jude and Kit fell into a comfortable routine as summer turned to fall. The house was a work in progress, but at least the furniture had arrived. Each day, Jude would take Kit to school and put in a couple of hours painting walls or scraping old wallpaper. He was enjoying the physical labor. Not to mention the joy of seeing the house taking shape exactly the way he had hoped.

After a quick shower and some lunch, he'd sit down in front of his computer and get to work. Not that he needed the money, but having a job was what had kept Jude sane over the last three years. He was working as a freelance journalist, interviewing musicians and industry people—most of whom were old friends. He'd had articles appear in various magazines and online blogs, and he was pretty proud of the work. But it didn't give him the same rush as performing.

But this was his favorite part of their new normal: the after-dinner quiet of the evening. It was a ritual he'd started a while back to get Kit to go to sleep at a decent hour. After dinner, the TV and all other electronic devices went off, and the two of them just wound down.

Tonight, Jude sat on the sofa plucking out a few chords while Kit read a book. In the last few weeks, Jude could hear the music again. It had been such a long time since he'd even felt like picking up his old Gibson, but suddenly, for no reason at all, he was hearing new melodies in his head. At first, he thought maybe they were songs from his past, but he couldn't place them. One riff in particular just wouldn't leave him alone, like an insistent earworm. He played it over and over, hoping that he would remember where he'd heard the song before, but so far no luck.

"Dad, what's this word?" Kit clamored on to his lap, pushing the guitar to the side. He brought the enormous picture book up, gently scraping the edge against his father's chin as he pushed it in his face.

"Which word?" Jude asked, holding the book at arm's length and trying to focus on the blurry words.

With much grunting and squirming, Kit finally managed to wedge himself into the crook of his father's arm and settled down in his lap. He pointed, "This one."

"Oh please, Kit. You can read this word."

"I can't get it," he said, but the smirk on his face revealed that he hadn't tried.

"Okay, let's sound it out like Miss Winslow showed you." He put his finger on the first letter, 'p.' "What sound does the 'p' make?"

"Puhhh," Kit said, exaggerating the pop of the letter.

Jude chuckled. "Okay, so get your mouth ready and make the p sound. P-p-p-p." They made the sound together and Jude made a big show of wiping the kid spittle off his cheek. "Say it, don't spray it, kid."

"You sprayed it first, Daddy," Kit giggled.

"So the beginning is p-p-p."

"Like in puppy!"

"Exactly. Now look at the end. It has an 'e,' but—"

"The 'e' is silent." Kit made fishy lips and put a finger in front of them. "Ssshh…"

"Right, but the 'r' right beside it isn't. So what sound does 'r' make?"

"Rrrrrr…"

"Okay, so the beginning is 'puh,' and the end is 'rrrr.'"

"But what about the middle?"

"What about the middle. What do you see?"

Kit thought for a minute and then pointed to the 'c.' "There's a 'c.' That says 'cuh,' like in cat."

"So let's put it together." Jude helped him slowly pronounce the word. "P-ic-t-ure."

"Picture!" Kit exclaimed. He pointed to the words as he reread the sentence. "This is a picture of my dog, Spot."

"Very good," Jude said, giving his son a high five. "You can read almost as good as me now."

Kit gave a proud, toothy smile. "Miss Winslow's a good teacher."

"Oh yeah?"

"Yep. She never yells at us, and she lets us play games, and she reads really good stories."

If he hadn't already been so attracted to Harper, he would be at hearing how much Kit loved her. After Shelby died, Jude had avoided any long-term romantic entanglements. Partly because Shel had been the love of his life and therefore, irreplaceable. But he didn't want Kit to get attached to someone who could never live up to such an impossible standard. But hearing how Kit talked about her, Jude could feel himself falling for his Miss Winslow. Despite not knowing her too well, Jude was confident that Harper Winslow could live up to any standard he could possibly set.

"So you think you'll stay in school, then?"

Kit nodded, flipping the pages in his book again. The next page showed a big, cartoony picture of the aforementioned Spot. "I don't think Spot is a very good name for a dog."

"Why not?"

"All dogs have spots. It isn't very unique."

Jude burst into laughter. Kit looked at him as if he'd lost his mind, his enormous eyes so serious that it only made his father laugh harder. "Unique? Where did you learn that word?"

Kit shrugged. "Miss Winslow taught it to us. She says unique means not like anybody else."

"She's absolutely right." He wrapped his arms around the little boy and squeezed gently. "So what do you think would be a good name for a dog?"

"Captain Fluffington," he said, like he'd been thinking about it for years.

"That's definitely a unique name," Jude said.

"I know." He paused and then shifted on Jude's lap until he was turned around looking at him. His eyes lit up. "We should get a dog!"

"You think so?"

Kit nodded. "We have a big house with a big yard. And dogs are awesome. Noah Riley in my class has a dog, and he knows how to shake your hand. Isn't that amazing, Daddy?"

"Wow, that is pretty awesome."

"Dogs are smart and nice and...," His words trailed off in a yawn. Jude glanced at the glowing numbers on the clock and realized that it was quickly approaching Kit's bedtime.

"We'll talk about it later, kid. But now it's time to get PJs and climb into bed."

"But I'm not tired," Kit said, rubbing his eyes.

"Oh yeah? Your eyes look like BBs." Jude stood up, hoisting Kit onto his hip and starting toward the stairs. Despite his gentle protests, the kid was wiped and immediately laid his head on his father's shoulder.

"What are BBs?"

"They're tiny metal balls."

"My eyes aren't metal." Jude started to put the book about Spot the dog down on the side table, but Kit let out a whine. "Noooo... finish the book."

By the time they got up the stairs, Kit's eyelids were heavy, and his head was lolling back and forth. He was just conscious enough to protest when his father dared to choose the wrong pajamas from his drawer.

"No... I want the Star Wars PJs...," he whined, pointing to the corner of his room where said pajamas were lying in an aromatic pile of dirty clothes.

"No way," Jude replied. "Those bad boys are going to walk down the stairs and get themselves into the washer." He threw the dinosaur pajamas on the bed and shooed Kit over.

"I don't like the dinosaurs," he complained as Jude knelt and pulled his shirt off. "They're all scratchy."

"Really? Well you've never said anything before. And I made sure to snip the tag off when we bought them at your insistence last month." He was slightly amused at Kit's obvious defense against sleepiness. He couldn't exactly fault the kid. Jude was always cranky when he was tired.

Kit gasped suddenly. "Oh no!" Big, salty tears welled up in the corners of his eyes, and he skirted past his father to bolt down the stairs.

"Kit! What's the matter with you?" He followed his son down the stairs and into the living room. The kid made a beeline to where his backpack lay open on the sofa. He started pulling things out and throwing them over his shoulder.

"I left it," Kit said, his voice quavering. When Jude reached him, he turned and threw his arms around his father's neck and began to sob.

"Kid, what's wrong?" Jude tried not to sound alarmed, but the child's sudden crying jag had him worried.

"My hoodie! I left it at school."

Jude almost laughed, relief opening up his chest. "Your hoodie?"

"Yes, the black one with the skeleton man on it."

"Okay. It's okay, kid." Jude hugged the child, trying to remember that he was five and extremely tired. "No reason to go to pieces."

"But it's my favorite. What if somebody took it?"

"Then we'll get you a new one."

"What if we can't find another one?"

"Then, we'll find another one sort of like it. Really, it isn't a big deal. Now come on, let's go back upstairs and get into bed." He pushed aside the unruly curls sticking to Kit's forehead and wiped away the tiny tears collected on the little boy's cheeks with a swipe of his thumb. "This is not a catastrophe."

Kit sniffled and nodded, letting his father pick him up and carry him upstairs to bed. He was nearly asleep before Jude tucked him under the covers and turned on his lightsaber night light.

Chapter Nine

The first couple of weeks of school passed by so fast, as they always did. Hot, summer days on the island quickly became crisp autumn mornings. The summer people had finally abandoned their cottages for the season, and the beaches were almost desolate. In Harper's yard, the leaves had already begun to turn so that the sun shone fiery shades of gold and red through the windows.

It was Harper's favorite time of year. It always had been. She'd been raised on Crawford's Landing, and the wild sea was part of her soul. It was why she'd never left, despite her mother's urging. Her mother had raised Harper on her own after her father, a commercial fisherman, had been killed in a boating accident. Louise Winslow had pushed her daughter to excel in school and go to college so she wouldn't end up cleaning hotel rooms for the rest of her life. And Harper had been an exceptional student. Everyone expected that she would go on to teach in the city or continue with graduate school. But Harper wasn't interested in that. She'd wanted to teach those kids like herself that felt trapped in such a tiny world.

Now, sitting on thirty, Harper had just assumed that everything would stay the same. She had gotten used to the idea of being an old maid schoolteacher who never had anything exciting happen to her. It wasn't that she was unhappy. Far from it, but the thought that she would someday run off to some glamorous life became more of a ridiculous fantasy with each passing year. Then, just when she'd given up all hope for something more, in walked Jude Renfro.

Now as she sat here on her lumpy, old sofa, grading papers by the flickering of the television set, her mind wandered to Jude. Over the last couple of weeks, their exchanges had been brief and casual. In fact, she'd been actively avoiding him. Regardless of what Jax and Nicole might say, Harper doubted that a "by the book" woman like Andrea Nettles would look too kindly on Harper throwing herself at the parent of one of her students. The truth was, if Harper saw too much of Jude, the more she'd want to see him again, and then things would just get awkward.

There was also the glaring reality that Jude was a musician. A retired musician, but a musician nonetheless. And those guys were not known for being what one might call reliable. If the tabloids could be believed, guys like Jude blew through relationships like a Carolina hurricane. They fell in and out of the beds of supermodels and actresses with alarming speed. It was more than likely that if Jude had any real interest in her at all, it was merely to have a warm body to fall on top of while he was stranded out here in the middle of nowhere.

More importantly, Harper had fallen completely in love with Christopher, or Kit as he preferred. He was an exceptionally bright and kind child. His sensitivity and outgoing nature had won him over with the rest of the class. He was loved by all of them, and he loved them in turn. He hadn't had another episode of hesitation since the first morning and was now walking into the classroom completely on his own. Every morning he greeted Harper and Jax with an infectious smile, and in the afternoons, he hugged them as if it were the last time they'd see one another. Getting involved with Jude might jeopardize that special relationship she'd forged with the boy.

Or maybe she was just scared.

Harper sighed and threw her folder aside, startling her enormous tabby, Matthew. It figured that the perfect man with the perfect kid walked into her life and she was too chicken shit to do anything about it. That had always been her problem. Harper didn't consider herself to be a great beauty. In fact, her mother, God rest her soul, had instilled a healthy dose of insecurity in Harper from an early age. *"Ninety pounds is trouble,"* she remembered her mother saying when she stepped on the scale at barely twelve years old. *"Are you really going to wear that?"* Or *"You have such a pretty face."* That one was Harper's favorite. As if the rest of her was a dumpster fire. She never thought she was wearing the right clothes. She couldn't ever get her hair to do what she wanted, so most days she just threw it up in a ponytail. Then there was her clumsiness, her loud, unladylike laughter, her near-obsession with Star Wars. All of these things made her feel awkward around the opposite sex. Sure, she had dated a little bit, but nothing serious.

All of this being said, she just couldn't get Jude Renfro out of her mind. It wasn't the way he looked. Okay, so it wasn't *just* the way he looked; it was more than that. Over the last few weeks, Harper had observed that Jude was intelligent and kind. He laughed easily and was loved by all the children. During their committee meetings, his excitement was infectious. He'd even managed to convince a few more parents and teachers to help them. He was just so... awesome.

"What's wrong with me?" she shouted, throwing herself against the back of the couch. How could she keep avoiding him when all she wanted to do was see his face?

Her cell phone answered with the insistent buzz of an incoming text. Harper glanced over at the clock. It was nearly ten. Most of her friends didn't text this late on weeknights unless something was wrong. "Probably some kind of sales thing," she said, finishing off her glass of wine and resolving to leave it until morning. It buzzed again, scooting across the table until it nearly fell to the floor. Harper caught it and the message notification flashed across the screen: Jude Renfro.

Harper's heart fluttered. Her belly flipped over, and she could hear the blood rushing through her veins. Her hands trembled as her fingers swept over the screen to open the text message.

JUDE RENFRO: *Are you awake?*

Harper glanced over her shoulder as if she expected someone to pop out of the linen closet. Was Jude really texting her, or was this yet another of her shameful fantasies brought on by too much wine and the tedium of grading papers?

ME: *Sure. I'm a teacher, not Amish.*
JUDE RENFRO: *Don't say disparaging things about the Amish. I hear those guys know how to party.*

Harper giggled. Not only did he text in complete sentences, he used words like 'disparaging' in normal conversation.

ME: *Did you need something, Mr. Renfro?*
JUDE RENFRO: *For starters, for you to stop calling me Mr. Renfro. Makes me feel old.*
ME: *If you were really concerned about feeling old, you'd stop texting in complete sentences. Mr. Renfro.*
JUDE RENFRO: *Touché, Miss Winslow.*

The butterflies in Harper's stomach made a hurried flight toward locales further south. She could just imagine the way his full lips formed the words, Miss Winslow.

ME: *I say again. What do you want? :)*

Oh, dear Lord in Heaven. Had she really just sent a smiley face?

JUDE RENFRO: *First, I think Kit left his hoodie on the playground.*
ME: *I know he did. It's in my washing machine even as we text.*
JUDE RENFRO: *You took it home?*
ME: *It was covered in mud.*
JUDE RENFRO: *Now I really feel like a shitty father. I hate laundry.*
ME: *No worries. So what was the second thing?*
JUDE RENFRO: *I got a rental place to donate some things for the carnival.*
ME: *OH WOW! That's fantastic! What are they going to donate?*
JUDE RENFRO: *They're sending me a catalog, and we can pick out a few things. The only catch is that we have to take things that aren't already rented for that day.*
ME: *We can totally make that work!*
JUDE RENFRO: *Great. When can we get together to look at the catalog?*

His words glowed bright blue on her phone. Harper rubbed her eyes, thinking that maybe her vision had blurred. Had he just asked her to go someplace? Together?

JUDE RENFRO: *Well?*

Oh God. He was expecting her to answer. A million questions tumbled around in her brain, and those butterflies were slowly crawling up her throat.

ME: *My classroom is being used by the after-school program tomorrow. Maybe the conference room?*
JUDE RENFRO: *I was thinking outside of the school. There's a coffeeshop downtown. How about there?*

Before she could change her mind, Harper found herself typing Sure! into her phone. She hit 'send' before she could change her mind.

JUDE RENFRO: *Excellent! Is 4:00 good for you?*
ME: *I'll be there.*
JUDE RENFRO: *See you soon…* The tiny dots after his words continued to blink, indicating that he was typing something else. Harper watched them for a bit. They would blink for a couple of seconds, then go away. Then blink. As if he were typing something, then thought better of it. Finally, *good night, Miss Winslow.*

Harper threw her phone down on the coffee table. She stared at the thing as if it might be a dangerous insect. Had she really just accepted a date with Jude Renfro? Surely some kind of lust demon had taken over her brain and caused her to have a case of temporary insanity. He was the parent of one of her students, for Heaven's sake!

"No," she said to herself. "It isn't a date. We're working on this project together, so naturally we'll have to be together to make it work. It's perfectly innocent."

Then why didn't she feel innocent?

She felt like the naughty lady of Shady Lane. Just texting with him about his child's hoodie had felt like she was committing some immoral act. And then there were the heated fantasies she'd been having lately. Daydreams that began with him picking her up from work in his shiny Jaguar and whisking her off to a glamorous weekend in Paris. And others that weren't so juvenile. Some that weren't juvenile at all. In fact, they were downright adult, and Harper knew that they were completely inappropriate daydreams to have about a student's father.

Harper threw her folder full of papers aside with a heavy sigh. Taking up the bottle of wine, she emptied it into her glass. "Bottoms up, Matthew," she said, then chugged the whole thing fast until dribbles of red wine slid down her chin. The cat twitched his tail as she slammed the glass down on the table.

"Sorry," she mumbled, scratching him behind the ears. He offered a disapproving meow and jumped down.

"No. I'm not going to feel guilty about this," Harper said. She stood up and grabbed the empty wine bottle and glass. She was only slightly unsteady on her feet. Apparently, finishing off a bottle of wine wasn't a good idea on a school night. "Great. We can add drunkenness to my offenses as a kindergarten teacher." She wondered if Jude was sitting on his couch having the same thoughts. Likely not. In Harper's limited experience, men weren't programmed that way.

Limited experience was a nice way of describing Harper's love life. All through high school she'd dated Alan Wingate. He'd been a cute boy in the marching band with dark eyes and floppy hair that she'd known for most of her childhood on the island. He was her first boyfriend, her first kiss, and her first grown-up date in a car. They'd even gone to the prom together. Everyone assumed that they would get married and raise a house full of chubby-cheeked kids with Harper's sparkling personality and Alan's talent for music. Then, the night of their graduation, Alan broke the news that not only did he not want to be Harper's boyfriend anymore, but that he had a boyfriend of his own. She remembered her friends being devastated on her behalf, but Harper didn't really mind. Alan had been a childish habit that she'd been putting off breaking for quite a while. Not to mention that Harper was always happy to see others finally being able to live their truth and bore him no ill will. She particularly delighted in seeing the pictures of Alan and his partner on social media-- living happily in Charleston with their Boykin spaniel and an adorable toddler.

Then, in college there had been Reign. Actually, his name was George, but he insisted everyone call him Reign. He'd been so beautiful with his long, inky blue-black hair and violet contacts. He was an English major that frequently hung out at the local coffeeshop, a long clove cigarette perched between his fingertips as he wrote sad poetry about dead leaves and heartbreak. Harper had admired him for the entire fall semester before finally getting up the courage to approach him. To her surprise, he'd accepted, and the two of them began a fiery affair that lasted nearly two years. Reign had taught her everything about love and sex. Everything about their relationship had been intense. Then suddenly, for no reason at all, it ended. One minute he was there, the next minute gone. Again, Harper wasn't bitter. Looking back on it now, she realized that she was better for having known him.

But that was it. Beyond those two men on opposite ends of the male spectrum, Harper had never had another long-term relationship. Sure, she'd had her fair share of dates, but in the end, they fizzled out. None of them ignited that passion she craved.

"This is ridiculous," she said to Matthew who sat at her feet, cleaning his paws. "I barely know the guy."

It was true. She knew nothing about Jude Renfro except what she'd read in the tabloids years ago. What was his favorite color?

His favorite meal? His middle name? These were questions that one should know about a person before becoming romantically involved. Not that she was anywhere close to being romantically involved with Jude. It was just a cup of coffee and carnival planning. What could possibly be the harm in that?

Chapter Ten

Harper was still having doubts as she parked on the street in front of Common Grounds, Crawford's Landing's answer to Starbucks. Looking around, she was painfully aware of just how small their little town was. The shopping and historic district always seemed to be bustling with activity at this time of day. Sojourner Truth Elementary was just a couple of blocks down, and the high school was on the other end of the main road. With school just having let out, there was a lot of traffic. People bustled here and there into shops getting last minute items for their dinner or shopping after work. Kids wandered up and down the street, enjoying the sunshine and stopping into the Dairy Kitchen for a snack or ice cream. All these people and their curious eyes. Not to mention their loose tongues. There was no way that Harper was going to escape without being seen. In a town like Crawford's Landing, privacy was at a premium.

With a deep breath, Harper grabbed her bag from the seat beside her and pushed the car door open. She stepped out, her eyes cutting left and right. The coast seemed to be clear, and she started across the street to the coffee shop.

Common Grounds was by far the coolest place in Crawford's Landing. The brick sides of the building had been painted a bright teal color and purple awnings shaded the scattered, mismatched café tables out front. Graffiti-style letters painted over the door announced the name of the place in bright rainbow colors. Harper's friend Sondra Robinson had opened it three years before in a dilapidated building on Main Street. She'd completely redone the place with her own two hands, and now it was the gathering spot for all the locals.

The cool air felt good on Harper's face as she made her way inside. While it was the first of September, the thermometer insisted it was still high summer. She made her way to a table at the back, glad that there didn't appear to be many patrons just yet.

"Hey there, Harper."

Harper was startled as she looked up into the face of Sondra's son, Trae. "Oh my gosh!" she cried, standing up to embrace him. "My favorite student! I haven't seen you in forever. How have you been?" Harper asked, sitting down again.

"I'm good," Trae said. "Home for the summer, so I thought I'd help out my mom. I'm trying to convince her to expand the place a little."

"How so?"

"Maybe get a band to come in every week, or even an open mic night. Something to get butts in the chairs and give this town something to do at night so people don't have to cross the bridge."

"That sounds great. A place for the locals to hang out. I approve."

"Yeah, I wish she was as excited as you. You know how Mama doesn't like change too much."

"True, but I know she's excited to have you home."

Trae shrugged. "I don't know about that either. She says I'm giving her a hard time."

"About?"

"Beefing up business. Not getting out. Being chained to this place twenty-four-seven. I told her the other night she needs to blow the dust off her dancin' shoes. Maybe join one of those dating websites."

Harper giggled. "Somehow I can't see your mom on an online dating site."

"Never gonna happen." Sondra Robinson walked up to the table and set a cup of coffee in front of Harper. That was the best thing about having a regular place. Harper didn't even have to order, and Sondra or her staff could bring her just what she was craving that day: a regular coffee with lots of cream and sugar most days, an Earl Grey with milk and a pump of vanilla on rainy ones. "I've had my share of weirdos and deadbeats."

"Every guy on dating sites isn't a weirdo," Trae said. He sighed and rolled his eyes as if they'd had this conversation a million times.

"Maybe not, but I'm not in the market research business," Sondra said, shooing him back toward the kitchen with a dishtowel. "Now go get some of those light roast beans out of the pantry like I asked you a half hour ago."

"You see how she treats me?" Trae said with a wink. He gave Harper's shoulder an affectionate squeeze and disappeared behind the counter.

"Good help is so hard to find," Sondra said, sitting down in the booth opposite Harper. "That boy is gonna drive me to drink."

Harper grinned. "He just wants you to be happy."

"I am happy," Sondra countered. "He's always harpin' on me to get out of this place and do more, but this place is my dream. I love it. I love my work. There's nothing wrong with that, is there?"

"Of course not," Harper said. "As long as you love it. Look at me. I'm not dating anyone, and I'm perfectly happy. I have my work and that's totally enough."

Sondra smiled. "Mmmhmm."

Something about the way she agreed made Harper think that her friend was merely humoring her. "What?"

"Oh, nothing. I mean, you're right of course. You can be happy without having a man in your life. Or a woman. Or any sort of partner."

"Right. Some people are just meant to be single."

Sondra leaned in conspiratorially. "The difference is, I had a long and wonderful marriage with Trae's father. We had our ups and downs, sure, but he was the love of my life. When he died, I thought I'd never get over it. But I did, and now I realize that this part of my life... it's finally for me."

"That's great, Sondra. I'm so happy for you."

"Thanks, but you're missing my point."

"Which is?"

"Which is—I don't want you to miss out on some of the best parts of your life because you're afraid."

Harper's jaw dropped, and then she gave a nervous chuckle. "I'm... I'm not afraid, Sondra. Why would you think that?"

"Harper, I been knowin' you since you was a little bitty girl, and in all that time I've watched you be afraid of what people think about you. People in town, people at the schoolhouse, your mama—all these people that have ideas about who you ought to be and what you should be doin'. But nobody can tell you who you are but you. You're a wonderful teacher, but that's not all you are. Take some time for you." Sondra's gaze shifted to the open door of the shop behind them.

"Yeah, she's over there, man."

Harper looked up to see Trae pointing out her table to Jude. He looked over the heads of the other patrons until he saw where Harper was sitting in the back of the dining room. He nodded to indicate that he'd seen her and started toward the table. It was like a slow-motion scene from a cheesy movie as he moved toward them. The late afternoon sunlight that streamed through the window glittered in his dark hair and sparkled in his eyes. His strides were long and sure, and Harper couldn't help noticing the way that his jeans clung to him in all the right places as he walked.

"Hey, Miss Winslow," he said, holding out a hand for her to shake. "Sondra, nice to see you out here and not on your feet for once."

Sondra smiled, and Harper could tell that she was almost as taken with Jude as Harper. "Somebody has to do all the work around here." She stood up and gestured for him to sit down. "Speaking of, can I get you something, Jude?"

"Trae got me," Jude said.

"All right, you two." Sondra gave Harper a knowing glance before she walked away. "Just let me know if I can get you anything."

Jude sat down in the booth opposite Harper. At first, she didn't want to look at him. She just knew if she did that she'd either start giggling uncontrollably or get up and bolt for the door. *This is ridiculous,* she silently scolded herself. *You've only talked to him a thousand times. Why should this time be any different?* Because it was. This time they were in a public place together that wasn't school. This felt like a date.

"Thanks for agreeing to meet me here," Jude said. "It's just easier when I drop Kit off for his piano lesson."

"It's no problem," Harper said. "Common Grounds is a great place."

"Yeah, I like it. I always hang around in here while I'm waiting for Kit. It's a great place to write. Sondra was the first person I met in town."

Harper nodded. "She's a great lady. You know, she was my babysitter when I was a kid."

"Oh really?"

"Mmhmm. I thought she was the most fabulous person in the world. She was sixteen, and her family lived across the street from us. So, when my mom had to work nights, she'd come over and stay with me. We used to have so much fun. She taught me to dance and put on makeup and hot roll my hair." *Hot roll your hair? What the heck year was this?*

"She is pretty fabulous. Any woman who gives me free coffee refills is fabulous in my book."

At the mention of coffee, Trae appeared with a tray laden with a French press, a coffee cup, and all the trimmings. "Mama said to bring y'all these muffins too." He set a plate with two pumpkin cream cheese muffins, still warm from the oven, between them.

"Oh wow," Harper said. "Sondra's famous muffins. She must like you."

"I think she just feels sorry for me. You know, the lonely bachelor. Clueless father." Jude pulled the tray closer and popped the lid off the press. Using a spoon, he stirred the grounds a little before replacing the lid and gently pushing the plunger down into the pot. He looked up, and their eyes met.

"You don't seem clueless."

"Don't be fooled by my French press abilities." He poured a cup of the dark brew and held it out to her.

Harper wrinkled her nose. "No thanks."

"Don't like coffee?"

"Oh, I like coffee," she said. "But that looks more like pluff mud."

Jude laughed. "I promise it doesn't taste like it."

Harper reluctantly took the cup and added cream and sugar. She sniffed at it as if trying to make sure that it was actually coffee. She sipped a little, expecting it to be piping hot. Instead, it was pleasantly warm, and the flavor, while stronger than she was used to, was hardly bitter. "Mmm," she said, setting the cup down. "Not bad."

"I know it makes me look like hipster scum, but it's the only way to get my coffee as strong as I like it. Darker roasts just taste burned."

"You should try getting decent coffee in a teachers' lounge. Most of the women I work with really just want hot water." She took another sip. "And they complain whenever I make it."

"I have the feeling that coffee isn't the only thing you differ with your colleagues on."

Harper raised an eyebrow, wondering if she ought to be insulted. "What makes you say that?"

Jude shrugged. "You just don't seem like the 'teacher lady' type."

"And what exactly is the 'teacher lady' type?" she asked, making little air quotes.

"You know...," he stammered. "Ladies that wear sweater sets, matching earring/necklace combos."

Harper giggled and thought about the drawer full of sweater sets at her house. "Oh, now down here you have to pair those sweater sets with capri pants and fifty-dollar flip-flops."

Jude nodded. "And frosty lipstick." He snorted his coffee as he said this, and both of them burst into uninhibited laughter. "I had a teacher in the fifth grade that wore this blinding frosty pink lipstick."

"I think I had that lady too. I bet she constantly smeared it on her lips, practically to the tip of her nose."

"Yes! And I remember she had pictures of all her cats lined up on the windowsill behind her desk."

"You think that's bad? I had a piano teacher that kept the ashes of her dead cocker spaniel on top of the baby grand."

Their laughter was comfortable. Almost relaxed. Harper could feel all of the anxiety she'd been carrying around since the previous night slipping away from her. It felt good. She had friends at work, but Jude was pretty perceptive in his analysis of her. Most of her friends that she'd felt really "got" her had all moved on to brighter horizons. There wasn't really anyone left in Crawford's Landing that she could laugh with this way.

"So, you play piano?" Jude asked when their giggles died down.

"God, no. Not in years, anyway. I don't think I can even read music anymore."

"It would come back to you," he said, pouring himself another cup of coffee. "You just have to get your hands on the keys again."

Harper smiled, shaking her head. "I don't think so. I'll leave music making to the experts." She gave him a pointed stare, then looked away as their eyes met.

"I wouldn't call myself an expert," Jude said. "An expert probably wouldn't make so many mistakes."

"Where is that written?" Harper chuckled. "That's how you become an expert. Making mistakes."

"Then I should be a damn genius."

"Some of us think so anyway," she said, taking a big gulp of coffee to hide the blush that was surely rising in the apples of her cheeks.

"You're too kind."

"Hardly," she said. "Affluenza was the only thing that kept me sane for a while. I bought the first album at a time in my life when I really needed something to hold on to. I was in college, not really sure what I wanted to do with my life, and then my mom had a massive heart attack."

"Jeez..."

Harper shrugged. "She'd had a weak heart since I was in elementary school. Had her first attack and bypass when I was twelve. She was okay after that, but then when I was a sophomore in college, she had another attack and just kind of went downhill from there."

"I'm so sorry, Harper," Jude said.

"It's fine. I mean, it isn't fine, but it is what it is. My dad died when I was young, so my mom had been my whole world. And she was one of those people that had all the answers, right? When she was gone, it was like... I didn't have a compass anymore. I was floundering. I had gotten a year behind at school because I was constantly out with her through that last illness, and I wasn't even sure I wanted to go back. I had no idea what I was going to do. I was super-depressed, but then... a friend introduced me to Affluenza. I know it sounds cheesy, but your music — your voice — it was like a salve for my soul. For the first time, I felt like somebody understood how I was feeling and was saying that it was okay. It helped."

Harper stared down, suddenly interested in the pattern on Sondra's tile floors. Had she really confessed something so personal to a virtual stranger? And in such a ridiculously asinine way. Out of the corner of her eye she could see the door to the place standing open as Trae brought in some boxes. How long would it take for her to bolt from the room? Of course, she sounded like a crazy person, so Jude might be the one to bolt. Instead he reached forward and grasped her hands.

"Wow... thank you, Harper." His jaw was agape, and his eyes were sparkling. "That's probably the nicest thing anyone's ever said about my music."

"Oh please," Harper said. She rolled her eyes and sat back. *Joke's on me*, she thought. He was teasing her.

"No, really. When I write music, I always hope that it will help someone. Or inspire them. Or make them feel something, but no one's ever said it. I mean, not in a sincere way." He pulled her hands closer and kissed the backs of each one. "Thank you." He kissed her hands again, and Harper held her breath to keep from gasping. Her belly rolled over, and her heart beat like it was going to burst out of her chest and dance across the table. Then she could feel girlish giggles bubbling up from her stomach, and she had to bite her lip to keep them from escaping.

"Umm... so...," she said when she was able. She pulled her hands away, unable to take the warm, rough skin against hers for a second longer. "You brought some catalogs?"

For more than an hour, they passed the catalog back and forth, discussing the ins and outs of bouncy houses and ball pits, calculating prices and the most effective use of space. All of these things seemed dreadfully important, or should be, but Harper was a thousand miles away. She nodded in all the right places and offered opinions, but right now she didn't give a flying fig about the carnival. All she could think about was replaying the moment he'd leaned in and kissed the backs of her hands. His lips had been so soft against her skin, sharply contrasting his calloused fingertips. His warm, peppermint breath so close that she could feel it against her cheek.

"Well, this looks great," Jude said, turning the notebook around so she could see what he'd written. "That was easier than I thought it would be."

Harper smiled and shook her head. "Don't get too excited yet. We have to get this past Andrea."

"Don't think she'll go for it?"

"We'll have to work out a budget. Like every good bureaucrat, Andrea is all about the money. We just have to prove to her that we can do this without spending more money than we'll bring in. After all, it is a fundraiser."

"True. But we're getting the games free." Jude glanced past her and his eyes widened. "Oh... no. Damn."

"What?"

He immediately began gathering his stuff and shoving it down into his shoulder bag. "Kit's piano lesson. It let out fifteen minutes ago. I'm late."

"Oh!" Harper exclaimed. "God, I'm sorry. I was just rambling on and on."

"No, it isn't your fault. I lost track of time too."

Harper noticed that he left his pen lying on the table under the edge of the plate that held the few remaining crumbs of Sondra's muffin. "Don't forget...,"

Just as she reached for the pen, Jude did too and their hands touched. Their eyes met for just a fraction of a second before he pulled away, but that strange electricity was there again. "Uhm... well, I better get going. Kit gets nervous when I'm not there right at five."

"Yeah, you better go," Harper said, still holding his gaze. "But I'll see you in the morning."

"Definitely." He gave a nervous chuckle and pushed his hair back from his face. Those lovely dark curls slid through his fingers, and Harper had to put her hand in her pocket to keep from reaching out to touch them. "And I'll try to get everything typed up. Maybe we can corner Mrs. Nettles after school."

Harper nodded, biting her lip. "Sounds great." She broke the connection before he did, afraid that she would say something ridiculous if she didn't. "I'll see you tomorrow then."

She watched him walk away. When he got to the door, Jude turned and gave a little wave. Harper waved back, hoping he hadn't noticed her ogling each and every stride.

As soon as he was gone, she sank back into the booth, holding her head. This was terrible, she thought. Now, not only did she have to deal with the uncomfortable longing she had for him, but now she was almost positive that he felt the same.

Chapter Eleven

"Do not put that in your mouth, Ezra!" Harper shouted across the playground. The boy in question looked back at her and waved. He had a big smile on his face that seemed to suggest that he had every intention of licking the rock as soon as her back was turned. "Drop it," she said, motioning that he should put it on the ground. Finally, he obeyed and dropped the rock, running off to the jungle gym.

"That kid is going to be the death of me," Harper said with a sigh as she sank back down on the bench she was sharing with Nicole. "Lately everything I say seems to go in one ear and out the other."

"Ah, the hardheadedness of autumn," Nicole said. "The honeymoon is over; now they just want to test us to see how much they can get away with."

"I know. It's amazing that any of them make it to October."

"They're cute. It's the only thing saving them."

They sat in silence watching the kids play. Harper was using their recess break to daydream about Jude, mostly. She'd been doing that most of the time for the week since their meeting in the coffeeshop. They met with Mrs. Nettles and got their plans approved, but she hadn't seen Jude much since, and she was starting to wonder if the chemistry she'd felt between them had only been in her mind.

"So, when are you going to tell me about your date?" Nicole piped up.

"What?"

"I was going to wait for you to bring it up, but the suspense is killing me."

Harper could feel her cheeks going up in hot red flames, and nervous laughter bubbled out before she could stop it. "I have no idea what you're talking about."

"Yes, you do," Nicole chuckled. "Otherwise you wouldn't be giggling like a schoolgirl. So spill it. Tell me everything."

"There isn't that much to tell. We sat in Sondra's coffeeshop and planned the carnival. In fact, you've seen everything we talked about. It wasn't a date."

"That's not what I heard."

"Oh? What did you hear?"

"Well you know, Sondra and Trae go to church with me. You and Mr. Hollywood were all they could talk about."

"Oh God...," Harper hid her face in her hands, completely mortified. If Sondra and Trae were talking about it, everyone else in town probably was, too. No wonder Jude had been scarce lately. Crawford's Landing was not a town known for discretion. Just like most small towns, idle news was idle gossip. "What did they say?"

"Just that the two of you sat together laughing and talking for over an hour. And that you looked pretty comfy."

"We weren't comfy," Harper protested. "We were sitting across the table from one another. And so what if we have a lot in common? It wasn't a date."

"Heads up!" Jax shouted right before leaping over the bench to knock away a football that was flying toward their faces. "Sorry, ladies," he said, picking up the football and throwing it back into the swarm of little boys in the field beside them. Harper could see little Kit Renfro at the center of it all. His blondish curls bounced around his head in a sweaty mess, but he was having the time of his life. His happiness was contagious, and Harper smiled just looking at him.

"So what are we talking about?" Jax asked, flopping down on the bench between them.

"About how you are teaching those little boys to kill one another out there on the field," Nicole grumbled.

"Come on now, Mrs. T. They're mostly just throwing the ball and trying to catch it. I promise I won't let them tackle." Nicole gave him a pointed look that didn't allude to much confidence in Jax's ability to keep the boys from hurting themselves playing tag football.

"I'll just go remind them to play nice," Harper said, starting to her feet.

"Oh no, no, no," Jax said. He grabbed Harper's hand and pulled her back to the bench. "You have been avoiding telling me all week about your date with Mr. Hollywood."

Harper's jaw dropped, and she glared at Nicole. "You snitch!"

"I didn't say a word," Nicole chuckled.

"No, she didn't," Jax said. "I heard it from Trae Robinson." Harper couldn't be sure, but she suspected she saw a little gleam in Jax's eyes when he mentioned Trae. Not that she could blame him. Trae was quite a catch. "So what's up? You and that dead sexy Jude Renfro dating or what?"

"Or what. And I'll thank you not to call him that. His child is right there."

"You think his child doesn't see how just about every female in town salivates every time he comes in the room?"

"Whether he does or doesn't is irrelevant," Harper said. "I'm not salivating at him. He's the parent of one of my students, for Heaven's sake!"

Jax and Nicole exchanged knowing looks. "She's getting very defensive about this," Jax said.

"I noticed that," Nicole said.

"I'm not being defensive," Harper said. "I'm just trying to explain that my meeting with Mr. Renfro was nothing more than a planning session. We had coffee, looked at a few catalogs, and then parted company. End of story."

Harper could feel her ears getting hot and the blood rising up into her neck. She knew that under her sweater the skin had gone a splotchy pink as it always did when she was embarrassed or upset. With a soft huff, she stood up and walked to the edge of the playground where a high plastic border held back the rubbery synthetic wood chips that surrounded the jungle gym and slide. She couldn't believe that Jax and Nicole were giving her such a hard time about Jude.

Of course, the reason that she was so affected by their friendly jibing was that they were right. She did like Jude. A lot. In fact, more than was healthy for a woman in her position. Going on dates with her students' fathers was not exactly professional, and Harper had always prided herself on being professional in all situations.

They say that people, when witnessing an accident, always see things happening in slow motion. Like they're in a giant pool and the pressure of the water is holding them back. Harper saw Kit Renfro running backward to catch the football that had been tossed in his direction. He was looking up at the blue, autumn sky and watching as it fell slowly. He was so intent on catching it that he didn't notice how dangerously close to the edging on the playground he was.

"Kit! Look out!" Harper shouted, running toward where the boys were playing.

The small boy looked up at hearing his name, turning toward Harper. He almost got himself stopped, but his foot got tangled in one of the shoelaces that dangled dangerously from his bright red Chuck Taylor All-Stars. It slowed him up just enough that when he fell over the plastic barrier, he hit his mouth on the edge as he went down.

When Harper reached him, Kit was so shocked by the fall that he didn't make a noise. Until he saw the look on his teacher's face and saw the blood that dripped off his chin and onto his sweatshirt. Then he unhinged his jaw and began to scream like a werewolf had come out of the woods and proceeded to gnaw on his twisted ankle.

"All right, Kit. You're all right." She tried to stay calm even as the child assaulted her eardrums. She knelt down and tried to get a look inside his mouth as he was screaming. She could see that one of his top front teeth was missing, but there was so much blood that she couldn't see much else. By this time, a crowd of kindergarteners had surrounded them, along with Jax and Nicole.

"It hurts, Miss Winslow!" Kit shrieked.

"I know, love." Her words were almost distracted as she examined the child to determine if he was broken. "What did you hurt?"

He didn't stop screaming but pointed to his mouth and chin. Jax offered her a handkerchief from his pocket, and she used it to mop some of the blood from his face. A deep gash, probably from the screw at the corner of the playground border, decorated his chin and was the source of most of the bleeding. She gathered Kit in her arms and hoisted him up on her hip as she started toward the office. "Miss Thompson, could you use the walkie to call up to the nurse's office and let her know we're coming?"

"Of course," Nicole said.

Harper glanced over her shoulder and saw that Jax was already herding their class toward the door. She didn't have to worry about getting them back inside and ready for dismissal. Jax was an expert, and she had a flutter of love for her assistant.

When they reached the nurse's office, she was already occupied with a bee sting. She handed Kit an ice pack and gauze and had him sit down to wait. Harper considered leaving him in her capable hands, but when she made a move toward the door, Kit clung to her side and whimpered pitifully. "Stay with me, Miss Winslow?"

She glanced up at the clock and sighed. Dismissal was set to begin any second. But what could she do? The kid needed her. "Of course I will," she said. "Let me just call down and let Mr. DuBose know that I won't be back for dismissal."

"And can you call my daddy?" he said, his tiny voice shuddering.

"I'm on it," she said.

Twenty minutes later, Harper sat on the bench in front of the office with Kit in her lap. Upon examination, Nurse Abbot had proclaimed that while Kit likely didn't have a concussion, that he probably did need a couple of stitches in his chin. Luckily, the kid didn't really understand what that meant.

"Miss Winslow?" Kit asked with a sniffle.

"Yeah?"

"My face hurts."

"I know, sweetie. As soon as your dad gets here, he'll take you to the doctor."

"I don't like the doctor."

"Why not? Doctors are awesome. They help you feel better when you hit your face on the playground."

Kit shrugged. "But the doctor's always giving you shots and yucky medicine. I don't like them."

"Yeah, but sometimes we need their help." She snuggled him closer. "I promise you're going to be okay."

Harper saw Jude sprinting up the sidewalk from the parking lot. The look on his face was panic, and suddenly she felt a huge lump form in her throat. "Okay, Kit. Here comes your dad." He clung tighter to her and began to cry again. Harper felt a little like crying herself. Here he'd left his only child in her care, and she'd broken him.

"What happened?" he said, coming into the lobby. He sounded a little agitated but didn't seem frantic or angry.

Kit burst into tears and scrambled off the bench and into his father's arms. He let Jude pick him up and wept against his shoulder. Harper could feel her eyes burning the way they always did before she started crying. Sure, she'd had kids fall on the playground before, but they'd never required stitches.

Jude gently pulled the ice pack away from Kit's face, examining all of his wounds as he pointed them out. "I fell down, Daddy."

"Well, what did you do that for?" Jude asked with a grin.

"I was running real fast... and I wanted to catch the ball... and.... and... I didn't see the thing on the ground... and I fell over it." His shuddery gasps turned to fresh sobs, and he fell against his father's shoulder.

"His feet got tangled," Harper said. "His shoelace was untied, and it tripped him up. I tried to get to him in time, but... I was too slow...," She took a deep breath, suddenly horrified to realize that she was about to start crying like a ninny. "I'm so sorry, Mr. Renfro."

"It's really okay, Miss Winslow. Kids fall down." He brushed Kit's curls back from his face and placed a gentle kiss on his temple. "I'm surprised he hasn't injured himself before now."

"I swear I was watching him."

Jude laughed. "I know you were."

"She watches us real good, Daddy," Kit said. God, she loved that kid.

"She's an awesome teacher," Jude said. "The nurse says he might need a couple of stitches?"

Harper nodded. "Yeah. She's a little worried about the cut on his chin. And he knocked one of his teeth out." Kit opened his mouth and pointed at the new space in the front.

"Am I going to die, Daddy?" Kit whimpered.

"Of course not, silly. The doc will stitch you up." He let Kit slide down from his hip and held out his hand to Harper. "Thank you for calling me, Harper."

She shook his hand and tried to hide the tiny shudder that always accompanied contact with his skin. "Don't mention it." When she looked up, their eyes locked, and whatever she was going to say just flew right out of her head. "It was my pleasure."

He smiled and nodded, finally tearing himself away from her gaze and taking Kit's hand. "Come on, kid. Let's go put you back together again."

She watched as they walked down the hall and out into the autumn sunshine. As soon as they were gone, she sank back to the small bench and buried her face in her hands. Her heart sank as she realized that there was absolutely nothing she could do to stop it.

She was in love with Jude Renfro.

Chapter Twelve

J ude put down the paint roller gently, trying not to make any noise. He didn't want to wake Kit who was fast asleep in his bed after a visit to the Crawford's Landing emergency room. The nurses and doctors were super nice, and that was a pleasant change from most of the hospitals in Boston. For one thing, when they walked in there wasn't another soul in the waiting room. They took Kit right back to a room and fixed his chin and lip. Surprisingly, it only took two tiny stitches in his chin and one on his lip. And Kit had been so good. The kid was really a miraculous wonder. By the time they left the hospital at five, he was already giggling and fighting the pain medicine the doctor had given him. He didn't even notice how his father's hands shook signing the release form.

They always say that once a trauma is past, your brain blocks out the worst of it, and you barely remember anything but the relief of it all being over. Jude knew for a fact that wasn't true. He remembered the day Shelby died clearly. The band was doing a concert in New York City, and he'd gotten a call from his mother that she'd had to take Shelby to the hospital, and she was there with the baby. He'd gotten on a plane right after the show was done, but by the time he got back to Boston, she was gone. The doctors said the aneurysm had been probably been there for a while, and that it was a miracle it hadn't burst before. A miracle. In the three years since, he'd come to terms with the fact that he couldn't have prevented Shel's death. He'd forgiven himself for not being there when she took her last breath. But hospitals still wigged him out, and a little physical activity would help him relieve some of that stress. So he'd put Kit to bed and started painting his bedroom.

The rooms at The Willows were huge. That was one of the things he'd liked best about the house when he first saw the photos. Their apartment in Boston had been so cramped that he'd specifically asked the realtor to find a place with room to spread out. Since moving in, he'd been sleeping on a mattress on the floor in what would eventually be the music studio, but soon this would be the master suite. High, vaulted ceilings with exposed beams and a set of French doors on one side that led out onto a balcony overlooking the property where it faded to dunes and sea oats. A fireplace made of rustic stones adorned the adjacent wall. The whole thing was large enough for his bed and a small seating area that would be perfect for late-night reading. The only problem was the hideous pumpkin orange color that the previous owner had assaulted the walls with. When the sun shined through the windows, the room actually glowed. So, he'd chosen a soft grayish seafoam color to accent the dark wood beams.

He stretched his back, rolling his shoulders to release the tension that had been building through two coats of paint. Despite being mid-autumn, it was sweltering tonight. Some of his friends in Boston had said that they were already turning on their heat at night, but down here in South Carolina, the weather was throwing him for a loop. He pulled off his grubby t-shirt and used it to wipe the sweat from his shoulders and chest. He could probably use a shower.

And speaking of physical activity, he'd always felt that the best tension reliever was a good, down and dirty tryst with an eager partner. As he gathered his paint implements and began putting them away, Jude's mind began to wander to the lovely Miss Winslow again. He couldn't help wondering what kind of partner she'd be — eager and adventurous, or slow and sweet. He tended toward the former.

When he picked up Kit today, she was wearing a sundress that accented her curvaceous frame. She'd taken his breath in an instant. Sun-kissed, flawless skin, hair with little flecks of fire that glowed in the sunlight, and the way her eyes had sparkled with unshed tears. In that moment, she was so beautiful. Now, he was having all these feelings that he'd assumed were long dead.

Before he could completely disrobe and make his way into a cold shower, he could hear knocking on the front door. He glanced at the clock wondering who in the world it could be at seven o'clock on a Friday night. He sprinted down the stairs, taking them two at a time, not wanting the banging to wake Kit. He snatched open the door, expecting to shush whomever it was on the other side.

Harper was having second thoughts about coming to Jude's house. When he didn't answer her text messages or phone calls, that probably meant that they didn't want to be bothered. But she had to be sure Kit was okay. The poor kid had been bleeding pretty badly when they left, and while he said that he didn't hit his head, what the heck did a kid know? If he ended up with a concussion, Harper would feel terrible. If she hadn't shouted his name, then he might not have fallen. And what's more — if she hadn't been sitting on the bench daydreaming about his father, then maybe she would have told them to get a safer distance away from the playground equipment.

After the third knock, Harper had decided to go back to her car and try to call again tomorrow. Then she heard someone moving around inside, and in another second, Jude was opening the door. The bubbly 'hi' she'd planned suddenly died on her lips when she saw him. His longish black hair was down, but the top had been pulled into a messy knot at the back of his head. He was shirtless and she could see the firm musculature that he'd been hiding under those trimly cut shirts. The curves and sinews were highlighted by an impressive collection of tattoos that ran down each arm. Another one stood alone just over where his heart should be — a line drawing of Christopher Robin and Winnie the Pooh.

"Harper," he said. A warm smile broke out on his face.

"Hi," she said, her voice sounding squeaky and ridiculous. "Sorry I'm here so late."

"Don't be. I'm glad to see you." He stepped aside and held the door open. "Please, come inside."

"Thanks," she said. "I just wanted to check on Kit. I tried to call, but you didn't answer."

"Oh, sorry. My phone died at the ER, and sadly none of their resuscitating equipment could bring it back to life."

Harper giggled, then hated herself for it. "Understandable. I just knew I wouldn't sleep until I knew the kid was okay."

"He's fine. Upstairs sleeping off the drugs they gave him."

"Oh good, so he'll be---"

"Up at two a.m., yes. That was my thought."

Harper found herself watching him walk across the room. The way his muscles moved under his skin. She was fascinated by the gentle undulations and wondered how much he had to work out to maintain that kind of physical perfection. She was also struck by how comfortable he seemed, half-naked in front of her. It was as if he barely noticed that he didn't have a shirt on. "Uhm... anyway, I won't keep you. You were obviously in the middle of something."

"Just putting a coat of paint on the walls of the master suite upstairs."

She looked around at the house. The truth was, she'd always wanted to see the inside of this house. When she was a kid, people said it was haunted. It had been sitting empty since the sixties at that point and half the windows were gone, and the paint was peeled back from the constant abrasion of the salty air. Then, one of those 'Flip My House' types from up north bought it and restored the place. "Yeah, it looks great."

"It's coming along. The people who had it before took pretty good care of it, but their decorating skills left much to be desired."

"I'm not surprised. Anna Stonecroft was a hellbeast of the highest order."

Jude's eyes went wide. "No love lost there, I take it."

"She was just one of those casually racist white ladies that makes everyone's life a misery until she either moves away or dies."

"Wow. Harsh." He chuckled and grabbed a t-shirt off the laundry basket that sat on the sofa.

"Sorry. She's kind of a sore spot for me. We worked together, and she worked overtime to make my life a living hell." *Damnit Winslow! You're oversharing again.* "Anyway, I should go."

"No, you shouldn't," Jude said. "I mean, you could stay for a minute. I was about to make a cup of tea."

"Like hot tea?"

He smirked. "What other kind of tea is there?"

"Oh well, you know... you're in the south now. We drink our tea in a glass with ice and lots of sugar."

He grinned. "Oh, okay. Then can I put yours in a glass with sugar and ice?"

"God, no," she said. "The cold tea won't melt the sugar. Are you insane?" She winked and offered a mischievous smile. "Making iced tea is a coveted southern secret."

"Well, I tell you what. Why don't you show me? Then, we can hash out some of these carnival details?"

"Uhm...," Harper glanced at the clock. It was after dark. She wasn't sure that she should stick around at his house at night. But she really wanted to. "Point me to your stove."

"Yes, ma'am." He led her into the kitchen and gestured to the stove and the cabinet with the pots. "Did I say that right?"

"Absolutely," Harper said, pulling out a large saucepan. "Next we'll work on 'y'all.'"

"Yawl," he said, trying to imitate her drawl.

Harper giggled, nearly dropping the saucepan in the sink as she was trying to fill it. "Not quite so much 'w.'"

"Oh, so it's like you all."

"Right, just run the you into the all. Y'all."

"Y'all."

"Perfect. Of course, if you're speaking about five or more people, then it becomes 'all y'all.'"

"I'll try to keep it straight."

"You better. You know, if you can't get the conjugation right, we send you back to Yankeeville."

"I'll do my best."

Harper smiled and put the saucepan on the burner. She reached to turn it on, but when she turned the dial, it wouldn't budge. She tried it a few times and couldn't seem to make the damn thing work. "I can't get your burner to come on. Am I not doing it right?"

"It's kind of old," he said, coming toward her. He came in behind her and reached over her shoulder to help. He laid his hand on top of hers. "You have to push it in, and then turn it."

Harper looked back over her shoulder, watching him as he focused on getting the dial to turn. He was so close. She could feel the warmth of his arm, sticky in the humid air. She could smell the scent of his soap and cologne, heady and strong now in the heat of the evening. She closed her eyes and inhaled deeply, taking the leather and smoke scented heat deep into her lungs. "I...uhm....," Her voice cracked a little, and she felt her cheeks go red. "I think I got it," she said, turning to look up at him.

Jude didn't pull back, his eyes cast down with a gaze so heavy that Harper could feel herself crumbling underneath. The tip of his nose nuzzled against hers. His cheek was so rough as it brushed the corner of her jawline. Harper couldn't help leaning into the embrace, just slightly so their lips were so close that she could taste his breath. In another second, it would be too late. His generous mouth feathered across hers. It wasn't a kiss, just a slight caress.

"I'm not sorry," he whispered, feeling her mouth against his.

"Me either," she said. There was no turning back now, and she turned up her chin to accept his kiss. This time it was full on. His mouth covered hers, capturing her in a fervent kiss. She let her arms slide around his waist and utterly surrendered. His hands were in her hair, tangling the soft curls around his fingers. He made her feel so small, and she held him closer, wanting the kiss to go on and on.

The pot on the stove behind them began to bubble. A tiny splash against the burner made a loud sizzle, and Harper broke the kiss abruptly. "Oh... uhm...,"

"I'm sorry," Jude said, backing away. "I didn't mean to do that."

"It's okay," Harper replied. Her voice was crackly and her breath labored. It had been a long time since she'd had a good kiss, and Jude's was one of the all-time greatest. One of those you could feel down to the tips of your toes. "I was a willing participant."

"Damn... now... now things will be awkward."

Harper shook her head. "Not at all, Jude. It's..." She wanted to fan herself. Her body was hot, and she could feel the sweat collecting around her hairline. "It's fine. We can just... pretend it never happened." She turned and pulled the steaming saucepan off the stove. The jerky action caused some of the hot water to slosh over the side and splash Harper's hand. "Ouch!"

"Are you all right?" Jude said, reaching for her hand.

"It's fine."

"Let me see it." He took her hand and held it tight, despite her trying to pull away. He turned it over and there was a tiny red welt just on the back of it. His fingertips, calloused from years of playing guitar, brushed across the wound gently. Just the tiny friction of it gave Harper another chill. "You're probably the most accident-prone woman I've ever met."

"Really? That's saying a lot considering how many women you've met."

Jude looked up. "What's that supposed to mean?"

"Just that given your profession, you've probably known a lot of women."

He narrowed his eyes, and Harper could see a glimmer of annoyance there. Good. If he was angry with her then maybe she wouldn't want to kiss him so badly. "Let me get you some aloe leaf for that."

She pulled her hand away and grabbed her purse. She had to get out of here. The longer she stayed, the more she wanted to stay. The warm rush of wanting was frightening. She hadn't felt it in such a long time, and this time it was too dangerous to take the risk. "That's okay. It doesn't hurt, and I really should be going."

"Harper, you don't have to go."

"No. No, I really think I do. In fact, I shouldn't have come here at all. Me and my silly impulses. Anyway, I'll see you later."

"Harper, wait..."

"Good night, Mr. Renfro."

Before he could say another word, she rushed through the living room, stumbling over one of Kit's toys. She fell against the door and pulled it open before he could reach her. The cool ocean breeze was a welcome reprieve. She had to fumble with her car door a little before pulling it open. As soon as she closed the door, she stole a glance at the house. He hadn't followed her, but she could see his form silhouetted on the porch, watching as she ran away.

Chapter Thirteen

There might be something more lonely than a rainy Saturday, but Jude wasn't sure what it would be. Looking out of his back doors to the wild sea below, he was struck by the grayness of everything. Maybe it was his mood giving everything such a dull cast. Ever since Harper walked out, Jude had been as stormy as the skies over the ocean.

How could he have been so stupid? So impulsive? Now he'd ruined any chance he might have had with Harper. And he'd so wanted that chance to make a connection with another person. He missed it. Just when he'd decided that part of his life was done, she walked right in. Smart, gorgeous, funny, and his kid thought she hung the moon. She was exactly the kind of woman he was looking for, and this time he felt ready to open that new chapter.

So how could he have behaved so stupidly?

"Hey Dad," Kit bounded into the kitchen with his sketchpad and a box of crayons. "What are you doing?"

"Not much, Kid. Just staring off into space I guess."

Kit scrambled onto one of the tall stools lined up by the center island. This was one of his favorite spots to sit in the whole house.

Jude watched with amusement as he got himself situated and opened his sketchbook. "Dad, would you draw with me?"

"Of course I will," Jude said, sitting down beside him.

Kit tore a piece of paper out of the book and handed it to his father. "I think we should draw fall pictures."

"Excellent idea." Jude grabbed a black crayon and began sketching out a tree. "What made you want to draw fall pictures?"

"Miss Winslow has been reading us books about fall, and we made these cool trees in art class with this thin paper."

"Sounds fun."

"It was. We have lots of fun in Miss Winslow's class."

"Oh really?"

Kit nodded. "We play games and draw pictures and dance. We even put on a play about Where the Wild Things Are."

"Well, that's typecasting if I ever heard it."

"Did you know some of those kids can't read at all?"

"Yeah, some kids don't have anybody to teach them before they get to school."

Kit shrugged. Jude could tell he was really concentrating on his picture because the little boy was hunched as close to the paper as he could get, squinting at the lines as he tried to draw them perfectly. "I guess. Miss Winslow lets me help Anthony."

"Who is Anthony?"

"He's one of the kids who can't read. It's not his fault. His mommy ran away from home, so she couldn't teach him. He lives with his grandmother now."

"She ran away from home?"

"That's what he said. Anyway, I told him it was okay because I didn't have a mommy either."

"Well you do, she's just—"

"She's dead. I know." He said it so matter-of-factly that it took Jude aback. They hadn't really talked about Shelby before. For some reason, he'd always tried to shield his son from knowing too much. "Grandma says that she had an *an-or-sysm*."

"Aneurysm. And yes, she did."

"What's an *an-er-ism*?"

Jude's shoulders tightened. He didn't really want to talk about this with Kit. What if he broke down when he talked about Shelby? "It's like, a bubble in your brain."

"A bubble? Like when I blow bubbles?" He started coloring the trunk of his tree in fast, broad strokes of brown.

"Kind of."

"Did my mom have brown hair? I can't remember."

"She did. And big green eyes like yours." Jude smiled remembering Shelby's face. "In fact, she looked a lot like you."

"Really?"

"Oh yeah, she was gorgeous."

Kit didn't say anything, but Jude could see a soft smile on the boy's face as he continued drawing his picture. Then, "I think Miss Winslow is pretty."

A lump formed in Jude's throat and for a moment he was terrified that he was going to start laughing. "Uhm... yeah. I... uh... I think so too."

"I don't think she's married."

Jude laughed. "What do you know about being married?"

"Ezra at school says that mommies and daddies have to get married."

"Which means what?"

Kit shrugged. "I guess it means they can hold hands. Don't you want to hold hands with Miss Winslow?"

Jude nearly choked on his coffee. "What?"

"Miss Winslow. Don't you want to hold hands with her?"

The truth was, Jude wanted to do a lot more than just hold hands with Miss Winslow. He barely slept last night thinking about all the things he'd like to do with Miss Winslow. "I don't think…"

"C'mon, Dad. I see how you look at her. I think you want to hold hands with her."

"What do you mean, how I look at her?"

"Like you think she's pretty." At that, he turned the picture he'd been so diligently working on so that his father could see it. "What do you think of my scarecrow?"

Jude smiled at the childish figure drawn with colorful blocks against a field of yellow corn and a blue streak above. "That's fantastic, Kit. I love the colors."

"We read a story yesterday about a scarecrow who was lonely. All the kids played with him and then one day, they decided to make a lady scarecrow and then the scarecrow was happy."

"Sounds like a great book."

"I liked it."

"You know," Jude said, sliding off his stool. "Your picture gives me a great idea."

"You want to go jump in leaves too?"

"Yes, but that's not my idea. I think we should use our pictures to make flyers for the Fall Carnival."

"Oooh! That is a good idea."

"I know, right?"

"That's why you get to be the dad." Kit chewed on his lip and scrunched his eyes as he stared down at the pictures he and Jude had drawn. "But how will people know where the carnival is?"

"We'll have to add words that tell people when and where to come."

"How do we do that?"

"Leave that to me, kiddo. You just get to work drawing a couple more fall-ish pictures."

Kit spent another couple of hours drawing fall pictures of every description. Some with trees shedding their leaves, others with spooky Halloween scenes of witches and ghosts, but all of them would make eye-catching flyers. With a little tweaking and computer know-how, Jude was able to create some lovely samples.

"These look pretty, Daddy!" Kit exclaimed as he looked down at the flyers laying on the coffee table.

"Fall Crawl to benefit Sojourner Truth Elementary." Jude read. "Join us on October 26th from 4pm to 10pm for games, food, and entertainment. How does that sound?"

"I like it! When can we go and put them up?"

"Well, I think we probably need to run it by Miss Winslow first." That is, if Miss Winslow would ever speak to him again.

"Can we call her right now?"

"Sure," Jude blurted, not thinking if he should. He was just so desperate to talk to her again. He needed to explain himself and try to win back her favor. If for no other reason than to get over this awkwardness so they could work together. Maybe that was the solution — don't give her any opportunity to run away.

Chapter Fourteen

Spending a chilly, rainy day in Common Grounds was one of Harper's happy places. She had her laptop open to the coming week's lesson plans and a small pile of books on the table beside her, but she wasn't really working much. Mostly she'd been spending the last couple of hours staring out at the rain and thinking about her encounter with Jude. His arms around her waist, the smell of his skin, the softness of his lips as their mouths met—it was enough to make her mouth water.

But it wasn't meant to be. She had to keep a professional distance. That was like Kindergarten Teacher 101: keep your hands off the parents. In her head, she understood this, but she wished somebody would explain it to her heart. In her heart, she felt like Jude was the home she'd been seeking for years. She'd gone out on lots of dates since becoming an adult, but not one of those men had been quite right. Even though she barely knew Jude, something about him just fit. It was more than just a physical attraction.

A text alert jerked Harper out of her thoughts. Jude's name lit up on the face of her phone and her heart gave a flutter.

JUDE RENFRO: *Kit had a great idea for the flyers. Can we talk?*

Hmmm. So, he wanted to talk, but about the carnival, not their little indiscretion. Should she answer him? Intellectually, she knew she should probably just ignore the text and make up some excuse about her phone being dead all weekend when he questioned her about it on Monday. As he surely would.

ME: *Sure. What's up?*

Who was she kidding, anyway? She couldn't resist talking back, but this time it would be all business. Just carnival talk.

JUDE RENFRO: *I've got some stuff to show you. I don't really want to send it over a text. Can we meet?*
ME: *I'm at Common Grounds right now.*
JUDE RENFRO: *Kit and I will be right there.*
ME: *Fantastic. :)*

Had she really just done that? Had she really just told the one person she was trying to stay away from to come over to Common Grounds and meet up? *Idiot*, Harper thought. She couldn't possibly be this stupid and masochistic. But it was just carnival business. And he'd have his kid with him. What could possibly go wrong?

The thought had no sooner crossed her mind than the door opened, and Mia Goddard walked in. Instinctively, Harper ducked down behind her laptop and prayed that she wouldn't be seen. She hated being drawn into conversation with that woman. Mia always had a way of making people feel inadequate. Harper sneaked a glance, praying that Mia was getting her coffee to go. That was the last thing she needed—to be seen being cozy with a student's dad by Mia Goddard. Mia stood at the register talking to Sondra, that fake smile plastered across her painted lips. Most people on the island looked like perpetual beach bums, but Mia never went anywhere without lipstick and her enormous Gucci leather purse. It was as if she were boasting her wealth to everyone on the island.

Mia glanced into the cafe and evidently caught sight of Harper. Her smile widened, and she waved. Harper could think of nothing to do except return the wave with a big, toothy fake smile of her own. "Please don't let her come back here," she chanted under her breath.

"Harper, hello!" Mia floated down the aisle looking like the Queen of England in a Jubilee parade. "I almost didn't see you there."

"Hi, Mia," Harper said, allowing the woman to peck her cheek. "It's been a while."

"Indeed it has. Still fighting the good fight over at Sojourner Truth?"

"I guess you could say that."

"I'm so thankful that they still have some good teachers like you over there. So many are leaving for the mainland schools."

"Or the private ones," Harper muttered.

"I was rather afraid that you all wouldn't be able to operate this year. I heard about all those ridiculous budget cuts from the state. How on earth do they expect schools like yours to prosper with so little support?"

"Easy. They don't."

She clucked her teeth. "Such a shame, but perhaps the state feels that parents who are willing to pay tuition for their child's education will value it more."

"You mean only students that can afford it deserve an education."

"Of course not. There are the mainland schools to serve our more... underprivileged children."

"If the parents can't afford to buy their children school supplies, what makes the state think they'll be able to afford transportation twenty miles across the bridge to a school."

"I guess that's what *buses* are for." The way she said 'buses' made Harper's blood boil.

"So the children can get on buses before the sunrise and not get home until dark. Excellent plan." Harper's tone was dripping with sarcasm, but she didn't care. "Sorry, I'm a bit sensitive about this topic."

"As well you should be," Mia said. "It's a shame what they're doing to you all." Funny, she didn't look the least bit sympathetic. Her smile was more snake-like. "I do admire your passion. You know if you ever need a job, Highgate would love to have you, Harper."

Harper was gripping her fist so tight that she could see the tiny white half-moons forming on the heel of her hand. What she wanted to say was that she and her teacher-bots could take a flying leap off the Kissi Pointe Bridge, but she would refrain and maintain her professionalism. "Thank you, Mia. I'll keep that in mind."

"Miss Goddard." Sondra appeared behind Mia holding a bag of pastries and a cup of coffee. "Here you go. Sorry you had to wait, but the coffee is fresh."

Mia smiled that sickeningly sweet grin and took the items, practically plucking them from Sondra's hands with her long, claw-like fingernails. "No worries." She fished a dollar out of her purse and held it out to Sondra. "See you later, Harper."

Sondra stared at the money in her hand as if she wasn't sure what to do with it. "Did that heifer actually just tip me a dollar?"

"She did," Harper said. "The woman has lived here for three years and still probably assumes that you're a waitress."

Sondra shook her head. "A woman like that sees everybody as 'the help.' Especially if you're black. It never occurs to her that I own the place."

"She's an idiot. You can refuse to serve her."

"Nah. I just give her yesterday's burned muffins." She pulled a bit of paper out and pushed it at Harper. "By the way, look at this and tell me what you think."

Harper took the paper. It was a leaflet advertising an open mic night at Common Grounds every Thursday night. "Oh, wow! Trae talked you into it."

"Boy didn't give me much choice. He just had those things printed up and started handing them out. I told him he could do it as long as he came home to deal with it every week."

Harper smiled, noticing the beautiful artwork, obviously crafted by Trae himself. "These look great."

"Yeah, I have to say, the boy has talent. Anyway, please come out for it on Thursday. And bring as many people as you can."

"Of course! It looks like a lot of fun."

"Fun is one thing, profit is another." She winked and patted Harper on the shoulder.

Sondra turned to walk away just as Kit Renfro ran from the door and threw himself against her. "Miss Sondra!"

"Ooh! Hello there, Kitster. How are you?" She knelt down, hugging the little boy and planting a pink kiss on his cheek.

"I'm great. Can I have a chocolate chip cookie?"

Sondra glanced up at Jude, strolling up behind him. "You'll have to ask your dad."

"Can I?" he pleaded, looking back at Jude.

"Absolutely. Make it two. And a—"

"French press," Sondra finished. "And a glass of milk for your young'un." She winked at Harper and walked off to get their order.

"Hey Miss Winslow," Kit said, scrambling into the booth.

"Hey there, Kit," Harper said with a smile. She held out her hand and did the secret class handshake that they had devised the first week of school.

Jude stared at them like they had birds flying out of their ears. "Did I miss something?"

"It's our class's secret handshake," Kit replied simply.

"You didn't tell me about any handshake."

Kit gave an exaggerated roll of his eyes that made Harper giggle. "It's a secret. Duh."

"Oh, I see." Jude sat down on the bench beside Kit and pulled out the envelope with their drawings for the flyers. "How are you, Miss Winslow?"

"I'm very well, Mr. Renfro. Thank you for asking. You said on the phone you had some ideas for flyers?"

"Look what we drew," Kit said, and started taking the fall pictures out of the envelope. "I did these ones, and Daddy did this one with the tree."

"I like them," Harper said. "I especially like the big smile on the scarecrow."

Kit blushed. "I didn't want him to be a scary scarecrow. More like the one in the story."

"I see."

"Kit suggested that we use the drawings for flyers for the carnival. I scanned them into my computer." Jude pulled out the flyer samples. "I added the time, date, and contact information. Voila! We have flyers."

"These are fantastic," Harper said. "What a wonderful idea, Kit."

"You think they'll make people want to come to the carnival?"

"I really think they will."

Sondra came over with their order, setting it down in front of them. "Did you draw those pictures, Kitster?"

"Yes, ma'am," he said, cramming a piece of chocolate chip cookie into his mouth. "Those are the flyers for the carnival."

"Carnival?"

"Yes, the school is putting on a carnival to raise money for supplies and after-school programs," Harper said.

"That's wonderful," Sondra said. "Can we help?"

"You could put some flyers in here," Jude said. "The whole town comes here eventually."

"Of course!"

"Even better," Harper said. "You and Trae could have a booth selling cookies and hot cocoa."

"That would be wonderful," Sondra agreed. "Maybe you could get some of the other businesses to rent tables for the day, or they could donate a portion of the proceeds to Sojourner Truth."

"That's a great idea," Jude said. "I've already got some calls in to some places to make donations; we could ask if they would be interested."

"There are businesses all along this street that would love the advertising," Harper said.

"And I'm going to call my cousin Marcus. His print shop is down the street and I bet I can talk him into cutting y'all a deal."

She rushed off, and Harper immediately wished she'd come back. The weight of being close to Jude again started to press down, making her nervous. "Good work, you two. Sounds like your idea's a hit." She stole a glance upward, and her eyes met Jude's. God, he looked beautiful today. His hair, naturally wavy, was a mess in the humidity. His dark eyes looked a little sleepy. Perhaps he'd been as rocked by their encounter as she was. "This shindig may actually come together."

"Dad, I'm finished with my cookie. Can I go play the video game?" He pointed to the back corner where there was an old Pac-Man machine that had been modified not to require quarters. All the kids in town loved it.

"Yeah, just don't hog it. If someone else wants to play, you need to let them have a turn."

"Okay," Kit said, wiggling around until he managed to slide out of the booth and under the table to the other side.

Harper watched the kid run back to the game. He looked miniscule in comparison to the enormous machine, but he grabbed a stepstool and stepped up like a pro. She smiled at how the kid never came up against an obstacle too great. Everyone should have that kind of confidence.

"So about last night..."

Harper's heart fell into her lap. "Look, we don't have to talk about it at all."

"Oh, I think we do."

"No, we really don't," she said, trying to look away. But damn his eyes—they kept drawing her in. "It was a crazy little moment. We lost our heads for a second. But it's okay."

"I don't think it was crazy, Harper. I think you and I... I mean, you can't tell me you don't feel something for me."

Harper looked around to see if anyone was listening, then leaned forward. "Even if I did feel something," she hissed, "I am you kid's teacher."

"What difference does that make?"

"Dating a student's father isn't exactly professional. I have to remain a neutral party. And what if things went south? That would be pretty awkward."

"Why do you assume they would?"

"Why do you assume they wouldn't? Let's face it, Jude. Every relationship ends, either in break-up or death."

"That's cheery..."

"It's true. Chances are, we'd date for a while, you'd realize that I wasn't interesting enough for you, and walk away."

"Whoa, slow down. Why would you think that I would decide you aren't interesting enough?"

It was Harper's turn to roll her eyes dramatically. "Oh, come on. You're an international celebrity, and I'm a kindergarten teacher. You've travelled the world, and I've lived my entire life here on Crawford's Landing. The most interesting thing that's ever happened here is when the funeral home cosmetician murdered her would-be boyfriend ten years ago. I've never even been on an airplane."

"First, I *used* to be an international celebrity. The fact that you're a dedicated kindergarten teacher that my child worships makes you all the more attractive. And did you ever stop to think that maybe the reason I moved to a small town on an island was because I was looking for a different sort of exciting?"

"Even still. My job makes dating you pretty damn complicated."

"Only because you're making it complicated."

Harper sighed. "That is so easy for you to say."

"You're getting all worked up about preconceived perceptions that may or may not be true. What the hell are you afraid of?"

"I'm not afraid of anything."

"Sweetheart, even a blind man could tell you were lying." Startling her, Jude reached forward and took her hand, gripping it gently. "I'm not suggesting that you hop into bed with me— something that, I won't lie, has crossed my mind several times in the last few weeks. Just give it a chance." She felt that electricity again, dancing over the back of her hand where his thumb idly stroked.

"I dunno..."

He spotted the leaflet about open mic night still sitting by Harper's open laptop. "Look, why don't you come out to the open mic night on Thursday night? I'm supposed to play a little." Harper glanced over Jude's shoulder to where Sondra and Trae were standing at the cash register, both of them looking their way. Sondra had handed her that leaflet on purpose, knowing that Jude was going to play for them. "Then after maybe we could have a late dinner?"

"That's a little late for a school night..."

"What are you? Ninety? Come on. I promise to have you home by eleven."

The boyish way he grinned and those sparkling eyes were Harper's undoing. She couldn't refuse him, so there was no use in trying. Maybe he was right. Her own head was the only thing standing in their way. Maybe she should take the chance. "All right."

"Yeah?"

Harper smiled. "Yeah, sure. Why not? It's not as if half the town will be here."

"That's the spirit."

Chapter Fifteen

Jude stood in front of the mirror, glaring at his reflection. It had been four years since the last time he'd been on a stage, and even though it was just an open mic night at the only coffee shop in Crawford's Landing, he wanted it to be perfect. Every outfit he'd tried made him look like a washed-up has-been. Jeans and a t-shirt were too casual. A suit just made him look like a bad David Bowie impersonator, and apparently there was no in-between in his wardrobe.

"Dad, I don't want to stay with Miss Goddard. Why can't I go with you to Common Grounds?"

"Because this is an adult sort of thing, Kit. And why don't you want to stay with Mia? You like her, don't you?"

Kit shrugged. "I guess. She's just bossy."

"Bossy?"

"She'll probably make me play the piano. And she always fusses when I make a mistake. I can't help it. I'm just learning."

"I'll tell her you practiced today. Maybe she'll let you off the hook."

"And when I stay at her house, she won't let me sit on the sofa. She says that little boys are too messy."

"Well she's right about that." He winked at Kit.

Kit was not amused. "And she's got this mean old cat that jumps at me whenever I go to the bathroom."

"Why the bathroom?"

"He likes to hide in the closet beside the bathroom."

"Oh. Well, she's coming over here, so you don't have to worry about her cat. Besides, she won't be here until seven, and you need to be in bed by eight-thirty. So that's not too long." Kit said no more, so Jude went back to fussing over his outfit. He finally decided on a pair of slightly frayed, fitted jeans and a slim cut, black button-down shirt. He'd washed his hair in the shower, so now his black waves were fluffy—too fluffy for his taste. He kept running his hands through it, which seemed to make it worse.

He pushed his hair behind an ear and replaced the small stud in his lobe with a silver hoop. It was the only piercing that had survived Kit. After the kid pulled the first one out at three months old, Jude had decided that the collection of jewelry running along the cuff of his ear was a little much. He rolled up his sleeves to the elbows, exposing some of his tats. He was hoping it would make him feel more like himself. Like a rockstar.

"You look pretty, Dad."

"Usually men are handsome, not pretty. But I appreciate the compliment."

"Then you look handsome."

"You really think so?"

"Definitely." Kit jumped up on his father's bed and giggled when it bounced him around. "Is Miss Winslow going to come see you sing?"

"I think so."

"Good. I like her a lot, but I wish she were coming to stay with me instead of Miss Goddard."

"Well I'm not giving her up, kid. Sorry."

Matthew the cat peered up at his insane human from under a pile of discarded clothes. Harper had tried on everything in her wardrobe, and now she was thinking of calling Nicole and asking if she could come raid her closet. Every single thing she owned screamed "old maid schoolteacher." Except for last season's ragged beachwear. She didn't want to dress up too much and make Jude think she was trying too hard. But then she didn't want to be too casual and let him think she didn't care. It was a horrible catch-22.

"Matthew, none of these clothes are right. He's a musician, for heaven sakes. He's used to women wearing thongs and leather corsets, right?" The cat only replied with an annoyed Matthew-meow that sounded more like a squawk. "You're right. I've got to stop letting my perceptions wig me out." She looked down at the collection of clothes splayed across her bed. The days were still warm on the island, but the nights were chilly, so sleeveless wasn't an option. She considered the bohemian sundress, but it was entirely too dressy. Maybe something she could pair with jeans? She glanced over to the dresser where she'd laid a pair of skintight jeans that had never been worn. At the time she bought them, Harper had gotten them home and decided that they were too fitted for her. She'd been meaning to return them for months, but there they were in her closet. Now, they might be just the thing.

She picked up the jeans and held them out in front of her, examining them like a person who had never seen denim before. They were dark washed and faded in such a way that was meant to accentuate a woman's curves. Harper pulled them on and they fit like a glove. A very snug, clingy glove. She found herself doing a little dance trying to get them over her ample hips, but once she did, they buttoned comfortably. She turned around, almost afraid to look in the mirror, but when she opened her eyes she almost laughed in surprise.

"These are amazing, Matthew," she said, turning around to look at how they hugged her backside. "I never knew that ass was in there."

Once she'd found the perfect jeans, finding a shirt to match was no big deal. A fitted t-shirt and a leather moto jacket would go perfectly and give her the edge she'd been looking for. Instead of wearing her hair up, as was her usual, she decided to let the blonde hair fall around her shoulders haphazardly.

"I clean up pretty nice, Matthew."

The cat jumped down and rubbed against her ankles, mewing his approval.

"Glad we agree," she said, bending down to stroke his head gently. The cat butted his head against the back of her hand, almost reaching up for her touch. "You love me no matter what, Matthew," she said, picking him up. He purred and rubbed his face against her. "If only winning the love of humans was so easy. I could just put down a bowl of food, and he'd be here for good."

She glanced at the clock. Only seven p.m.. The show didn't start until eight. She supposed she could go ahead down to Common Grounds and chat with Sondra before things got started. Of course, that would seem desperate and sad. She also didn't want to arrive right at eight, because that could also be construed as over-eager. And what was she so eager for, anyway? She was just going to see him sing. Technically, she'd done that several times in the past when he was with Affluenza. So surely there wouldn't be any sideways looks at her presence.

So why did she feel like a dirty groupie?

Just before she could begin listing to Matthew all the reasons why this whole thing was totally innocent, her cell phone rang. Harper set the cat down and raced through the house to where her phone was slowly vibrating its way across the kitchen counter.

"Hello?"

"Hi Harper, it's Sondra."

"Oh hi," Harper said. "What's up?"

"You know those flyers y'all made, and we put all over town this week?"

"Yeah."

"Well somebody has been taking them down."

"What? How do you know?"

"Well, I went outside to sweep up the sidewalk before the event tonight, and I found a whole heap of them in the trashcan at the corner, and Trae said there were more in the can down the street."

"Oh no," Harper sighed. "Who would do something like that? We asked people if we could put them outside their businesses."

"Yeah, and I have a good idea whose tearing them down. I just walked a little ways up the street and everywhere there had been a flyer for the carnival, a flyer for another festival on the exact same date."

"What?"

"Mmmhmm. And guess where the other festival is."

"Where?"

"Highgate Academy."

Harper's heart was like a stone as she sank to the nearest chair. All that planning and scrounging for money and donations. All of it was at serious risk of being flushed down the toilet like a dead goldfish. "What are we going to do, Sondra? The carnival is in less than a month."

"I don't know, babe, but from the looks of this flyer, Mia Goddard is definitely trying to steal y'all's thunder. Inflatables, carnival rides, funnel cakes, and apparently a DJ and dancefloor."

"All the things money can buy for them," Harper said bitterly. "Why would she do that? Why are they deliberately trying to hurt our school?"

"I guess she figures if they're the only game in town, folks will be forced to send their kids to Highgate."

"Well the state is taking care of that faster than she ever could."

"I'm sorry, Harper. We'll figure out how to fix it. Are you coming to the open mic tonight?"

"I'll be there."

"Good, we can talk then. That is, if you and Jude are up for company."

"Goodbye, Sondra."

"I mean, I know how cozy y'all are getting."

"Good*bye* Sondra."

When Harper hung up, she wasn't nearly as enthused about tonight as she had been. The news that Mia Goddard and her teacher-bot army were actively trying to sabotage their event had made her so angry she could spit fire. How dare they try and take money away from children! It wasn't fair. And what possible reason would Highgate have to want to kill the public elementary school on the island? Harper couldn't imagine why, but she knew one thing—she was going to find out.

Chapter Sixteen

*A*utumn nights in Crawford's Landing were nothing short of magical. It was like the whole place was finally relaxing after the hustle and bustle of the summer season. Late fireflies twinkled in the golden trees. The world was all inky purple—not quite dark, but just past twilight. The "summer people" had gone home and the locals now came out to play. When Harper emerged from the car, she noticed that the streets were packed with people out enjoying the soft cool of the early October night. Couples walked hand in hand, families holding cones of ice cream laughed together, and others sat at tables arranged on the sidewalk in front of Nita's Diner. Soft music floated from the open door of the local bookstore. Halloween decorations had begun to appear up and down the street. That faint scent of burning leaves filled Harper as she crossed the street to Common Grounds, and in its wake, left a calm that was completely devoid of worries about the carnival. Now, all she wanted to do was see Jude.

Common Grounds was abuzz with activity, as Harper had known it would be. The coffee shop had been a popular spot since the day it opened; it was only natural that a little nightlife would draw a crowd. When she walked in, Trae greeted her with a warm hug.

"Hey, Lady."

"Hey, Trae. Wow, it really looks amazing in here." And it did. The tables had been rearranged to make room for a small stage area that had been erected in one corner. Low lighting complimented the candles that burned in the center of each table. The heavy scent of freshly ground coffee was strong, but underneath was a soft spice that evoked a sensual darkness so prevalent this time of year. "You guys have outdone yourselves."

"Thanks. I'm really hoping that this will be successful. You know how Ma is about changing."

"Yeah, but I think she'll come around. I mean, look at all these people."

"I know, right? You'd think there was nothing to do in the Landing after dark." Trae looked up at hearing his mother calling. "Uh-oh, something must have blown up."

"Go on. I'll see you guys in a while."

"Anything to drink?"

"Just a regular latte when you get a chance."

"I'll have it right out to you."

Harper started toward the back, ready to get a seat in the darkest corner she could find, until she heard familiar voices calling her name. "Harper, over here." She turned to see Nicole sitting at a table full of other teachers, including Jax. "Come sit with us."

"Hey ladies and gents," she said, sliding into one of the chairs beside Nicole. "Which one of you is going to sing?"

"What are you talking about?" Jax asked. "My voice is so bad I won't even sing in the shower. It would scare away the grippy ducks on the tub."

"Well, it is an open mic night," Harper said. "Aren't people supposed to get up and sing?"

"At a regular open mic, probably," Diana Fischer, a third-grade teacher, said. "But I hear that Sondra and Trae rounded up a special guest."

"Oh yeah?"

Nicole burst into laughter. "Look at white girl playin' dumb. You know very well who that special guest is."

"I do?"

Jax rolled his eyes. "Are you telling us that you didn't know Jude Renfro was going to perform? I mean, I figured that's why you were here."

"He might have mentioned something," Harper lied. "Not that he talks to me about it."

"Oh, whatever," Jax said. "I was talking to Alice Berryhill at the copy machine the other day, and she goes to the same gym as Mr. Renfro. She said that he gushed about you for twenty minutes the other day after spin class."

"I can further report," Nicole said, "that Mr. Renfro was seen sitting in this very establishment with Miss Winslow last Saturday afternoon."

"We were just talking about the carnival," Harper said, blushing hotly. "You guys are ridiculous, you know. Honestly, I thought small-town gossip was beneath you."

"Not a chance," the three of them answered in unison.

"I don't know what the big deal is," Jax said. "Why are you trying to keep it on the down low? If I was going out with a man that fine, I'd be posting it in the United Brethren church bulletin."

"We are not going out."

"Staying in then?" Diana murmured.

"No!"

"Now y'all," Nicole said. "Don't tease the girl. I think it's wonderful that you've met someone."

"Absolutely," Jax said. "You're too awesome of a person not to find a soulmate."

"Who's finding a soulmate?" Trae interrupted, walking up with Harper's coffee.

"Miss Harper here," Jax said. Harper detected a slight crack in her friend's voice. Immediately he sat up straighter and when he reached for his coffee cup, Harper would swear that his hand was trembling a little. "She's been getting quite cozy with Jude Renfro."

"Jax!" Harper squeaked. "I'm not getting cozy. We haven't even been on a date, so would you please keep your voice down?"

"Please," Diana said. "I can barely hear myself talking. I don't think anyone will notice."

"Uh-huh," Harper grumbled. "This is a small town, and news travels fast."

"Don't worry about it," Trae said. "Your secret is safe here."

"It isn't a secret. It isn't... anything. I am *not* dating Jude Renfro."

The room suddenly went silent, and Harper wanted to sink into the floor. Then, a small spotlight lit up the stage area, and Sondra walked out to the mic.

"Hello, Crawford's Landing," Sondra said, drawing applause from the crowd. "Thanks so much for coming out to Common Grounds's first ever Open Mic Thursday! We are so overwhelmed at the turnout. Thank you." The audience clapped again, and the rhythm matched the beat of Harper's heart. She didn't know why but knowing that any second Jude was going to take that stage gave her a rush of excitement. It was even more powerful than when she was a college kid, waiting for Affluenza to come out.

"This week, we have a special treat for you. We figured that you guys would be shy at first, so my son Trae suggested that we get a sort of opening act to play. Now, if you want to take the stage, there's a sign-up sheet at the counter. But first, Common Grounds is pleased to present Jude Renfro!"

The applause this time was nothing short of thunderous. Harper could even hear a few gasps, and who could blame them? Unless you'd been under a rock for the last twenty years, you knew Jude.

For just a moment he paused under the blue glow of the single spotlight, looking about as close to an angel as a man could get. Everything about him was ethereal—the glow of his skin, the sparkle in his eyes, and that crooked way he smiled. He walked across the stage area. His strides were deliberate and for the first time, Harper noticed just how broad he was. In a dark alley, he would be pretty damned scary. He looked a little unsure of himself as he raised the microphone. Was it possible that this rock god might be nervous?

"Hello," he said, tapping the mouthpiece. "I... uh... I'm Jude Renfro. In case you didn't hear the introduction that was literally five seconds ago." A small wave of chuckles seemed to relax him a little. "I don't know if you guys know, but I used to be in a little band called Affluenza." Several whoops and whistles came from around the room, and Jude smiled. "Oh good, there's a few. Cuz I have to confess that I'm totally relying on name recognition here." More laughter.

Without another word, he went straight into the first song, an upbeat acoustic cover of an old Affluenza song that Harper recognized. Evidently others did too because when he reached the chorus, the whole room started to sing along.

"He's pretty talented," Nicole said, leaning into Harper's ear.

"I know."

"My mama used to say that you shouldn't ever push somethin' away when God was handing it to you with both hands." Harper gasped softly and turned to look at Nicole. The other woman nodded knowingly and patted her hand. "Just think about it."

Jude played for an hour mixing old Affluenza songs with covers of songs he loved. In between he'd tell some stories about how songs were written or what inspired him. The nervousness that he'd obviously felt when he started had melted away. Harper could see the old rock star that she'd crushed on for years coming back to life. But this time, a chrysalis of fatherhood and life experience had given him wings more beautiful than before. He was no longer a frontman, growling into the mic and showing off his tattoos, but a singer-songwriter weaving poetry from threads of heartbreak, loss, and hope.

"Thank you all," he said from the stage when his set was done. "I haven't performed in a long time, and this was an incredible comeback show for me. So, thank you for that." The crowd applauded, and he gave a little bow. "I don't know if you guys know, but I left the music industry three years ago when my wife Shelby died. She had something her doctor called a sleeping aneurysm, meaning that it had been hiding out for years in the back of her brain, likely since birth. No one knew it was there. I had been on the road for months, her home with our new baby, and it was so sudden that I wasn't able to be with her when she passed. I felt so guilty for that. I just didn't think I could go on. But then, I realized that while Shel might be gone, I still had a little part of her with me — my son Christopher. So, my last song of the night is a little song that I wrote for him. It's called 'Windjammer.' I hope you — y'all — like it." His eyes locked on Harper, and she shivered under the weight of his gaze.

His fingers trilled across the strings of his guitar, finding each note perfectly. His grip on the neck of the instrument was tight, like it was the only thing holding him to the earth as he played. *"Dragged down by the undertow,"* Jude sang, his voice soft and gentle as the ocean breeze. *"Don't let me set too far adrift. Body aching with the waves of memory. I can no longer breach this rift. Between life and death, I'm lingering. Calling out her name. Pull me ashore, little windjammer. Carry me back to sane."*

As the song went on, Harper could feel the emotion laced through every line. Every note was a beat of his heart, thrumming in time with her own. The more he sang, the more she was falling in love with him. This time there would be no denying, no turning back. Whatever it cost them was a small price to pay.

When the song was done, the room erupted in a storm of applause and cheering. Harper stood up and gave a whistle. At first, Jude looked shocked at the reaction, then disbelieving. Finally, a smile lit up his face, and he was almost laughing with sheer joy. He'd never looked so beautiful. He gave a bow and walked off the stage. Caught up in the moment, Harper almost got to her feet to rush over, but then realized that the entire table full of people was staring at her. She smiled and leaned back in her chair, crossing her legs. *Good save*, she thought.

Jude disappeared into a crowd of people standing to congratulate him and say hello. Harper lost track of him for a minute but saw him slip out the back door. Suddenly, she was terrified that she had missed her opportunity. Was he coming back? She'd been sure that he'd seen her when he was on stage, but maybe he thought she didn't show. Harper grabbed her purse and started inching out from behind the table.

"Where are you off to?" Nicole asked.

"Oh, I'm just going to pop into the ladies' room. Maybe get a cup of tea."

They didn't question her as she started to make her way toward the back where Jude walked out. There was a narrow corridor behind the stage area that led to the restrooms and the back office. He wasn't there, but she could smell his cologne. He couldn't have gotten far, she thought.

"Looking for me?" Jude whispered from behind her.

She turned around, and he grabbed her around the waist, pulling her into the tiny office. Their lips met with a furious passion that had been building since the day they met. Jude's arms were tight around her waist, and she could feel the heat of his body as he pulled her against him. His tongue teased over the crease of Harper's mouth, urging her to let him inside. She obliged willingly, letting him take her breath away. She could taste a hint of peppermint as he pulled her lower lip between his and worried it gently with his teeth. The sensation was so damn sexy and sent shivers all over. When he pulled back, she didn't want to let go and held onto him.

"Yeah," she panted. "You're exactly what I was looking for."

"Well, you found me."

"Good." She wrapped her arms around his neck and leaned in to kiss him again. Despite everything her sensible brain was screaming, this felt right. Suddenly, all those obstacles she'd been worrying about for the last several weeks seemed to dissolve the second they touched. Her fingertips slid under the hem of his shirt and grazed the smooth flesh. She wanted to feel all of him. Every inch of his body would be a new, indescribable wonder for Harper to explore. It had been ages since she had sex, but she figured it was like riding a bike. She was more than willing to give it a shot.

"Wow, what... what is this all about?" he asked when he was able to breathe again. "I thought we weren't supposed to do this."

Harper shook her head. "Shut up. I don't want to think. My stupid head gets in the way of everything."

"Then don't think," he said, cradling her head and feathering another kiss over her mouth. "Just feel it."

"Let's get out of here." She grabbed his hand and led him out the back of the shop. Her heart pounded in her chest so hard that she could feel it in her ears. They ran across the road to where Jude's jaguar was parked under one of the quaint streetlamps. He pulled her around to the passenger door and held it open. She turned, cradled in his arms and gazing up into his eyes. His hair was damp with sweat, and his eyes glistened with desire. Harper pressed herself against him, urging him to kiss her once more. His large hands circled her waist, sliding around her back and down until they rested at the curve of her buttocks. When he kissed her again and pulled her tight into his body, she could feel the hard knot of his need pushing at her center.

Harper brushed her fingers through his hair, feeling the silky strands slide between them. She used the tip of her tongue to trace his cupid's bow, then suckled at his lip gently. Why did he have to taste so good? It was making it harder and harder to pull away, and no matter how much she tried to drown out the little voices in her head, they were still there.

"Wait," she said, putting her hands against his chest. Her head was swimming as if she'd had a beer instead of a latte.

"What's the matter?" he said, nuzzling his rough cheek against hers. He nuzzled under her hair and kissed her neck just under her earlobe. "Are you okay?"

"Stop a second," she said. This time she pushed him against the doorframe. "We can't... I can't do this."

"Why?"

"I just don't think I'm ready for this." Harper ducked under his arm and stumbled down the sidewalk a little ways. She had to get away from him, or she'd lose her resolve. "We can't just hop into bed together. I barely know you."

"You know me pretty damned well, Harper. I mean, I'm a simple guy." His expression was playful, and when he reached out to take her hands, she let him.

"I'm the most complicated person I know," Harper said. She pushed her hair behind one ear and began to pace. "People don't ask me to pick out birthday cards because I'll stand in the aisle debating one over the other for hours. And God forbid if you get behind me in the serving line at McDonald's."

"What are you saying? You've decided you don't like me?"

Harper's eyes widened, and she shook her head. "God no. I like you. I *really* like you. But our situation is complicated. I've been going back and forth on this all night, but the truth is, you're the father of one of my students. I can't jeopardize my teacher-student relationship with Kit because we got overheated."

"Why would you think that your relationship with Kit would be compromised?"

"Think about it. If things between us went badly, it would inevitably affect him. And then there's this town. This small, sleepy, gossipy little town would have a field day with it. There are people in Crawford's Landing who like nothing more than making a fuss. Even if Mrs. Nettles was okay with it, tongues would wag until she decided it wasn't okay."

"I think you're worrying too much."

"You haven't lived here your whole life. Trust me, I've seen it happen."

Harper searched Jude's expression for signs of anger, but there were none. Disappointment, perhaps, but no anger. "So, you're saying that I have to wait until June to be in love with you?"

Nervous laughter bubbled up from her belly. "Oh, come on now," she said. "You aren't in love with me."

"I really think I am."

"No, you aren't."

Jude grinned, and she wanted to slug him. How dare he bring that killer smile and mischievous cock of his eyebrow into this discussion? "I think I know how I feel, Harper." He twirled her around as if dancing, then embraced her again. "But if I have to wait for you, I will."

"You will?" She hoped that her face didn't betray the doubt. After all, he was a rock star.

"I'm not going anywhere, Harper." He tipped her chin higher

and pushed her hair away from her forehead. "You don't seem to understand. I haven't been able to play a single note in three years. Then I met you, and it all came back. You made me hear the music again, and now that I can, I'm not going to let you go. I'll wait as long as you want, but I should warn you. I never give up." He leaned forward, and Harper's mouth was already watering, but this time he kissed her forehead.

"I think you should know, I'm stubborn."

"I'm getting that."

"And if we're doing this...," Harper gestured around them. "Whatever this is, we have to keep it quiet. At least for now."

"So, you're ashamed of me?"

"No, but... I'm not sure how my boss would feel about our situation. I'm not saying we have to hide, but not flaunting it is probably for the best. Agreed?"

Jude looked thoughtful, staring up at the sky. "Let's go get that dinner now."

Harper had the feeling he wasn't going to be the best at keeping secrets.

Chapter Seventeen

Harper sat behind her desk, clutching her coffee cup with both hands. She remembered this morning why she never went out on school nights. Evidently as one got older, they didn't need to imbibe alcohol to be hung over the next day. Not that she would have done anything differently. Dinner with Jude had been spectacular. They hadn't gone anyplace special, just a local seafood shack down by the docks. One of those places with black and white photos of shrimp boats adorning the walls, and the floors were coated with a layer of crunched peanut shells and cooking oil. They'd shared something called "boat trash." It was casual, but Harper thought it was probably the best date she'd ever had. Jude had been so sweet and attentive. They had talked about everything under the sun until the tired looking waitress threw them out after midnight.

"Someone was up a little late last night," Jax said as he walked into the classroom and threw his shoulder bag down. "I'm going to assume that you snuck out the back with Elvis after the show."

Harper sighed and shook her head. "You make me sound like a groupie or something."

"Nicole and Diane started to worry when you didn't come back," Jax continued. "But I told them you were in good hands with the noble Mr. Renfro."

"You told them I left with him?"

"You *did* leave with him."

"But… I mean… it wasn't like that." Harper groaned and put her head down on her desk, tapping lightly at the wood with her forehead. "How do I get myself into these messes?"

Jax sat down on the corner of her desk, crossing his arms and staring down at her. "Girl, I'd be happy to have a mess like yours. Jude is sweet, smart, gorgeous. What exactly is your problem? And don't tell me it's because his kid is in your class."

"You seriously don't think that's a problem?"

Jax shrugged. "Not at all. Look, Harper. This is a small town. If we start making rules about not dating people because of proximity, we're going to have a problem."

"It's a little more than that." She sat up and rubbed her temples. "You know, Jax, when I'm with Jude, it's like… there's no one in the world but us. I can talk to him about anything. And he knows about everything—music, art, books—all those things I love that everyone else thinks are weird. And he's been all over the world. He's…"

"The man of your dreams," Jax said. "I get it." He took her hand and patted it gently. "Harper, I've known you for a while now. You are probably the most capable, responsible person I know. You took care of your mom when she got sick. You take care of these babies in here like they're your own. When you see a problem like, for example, the island school is about to close and leave all these kids with nowhere to go but a crazy expensive private school or a two-hour bus ride, you throw yourself into solving it. All these things you do for other people. It's time to do something for you. Just for you. Let somebody take care of you for a change, eh?"

Harper smiled, her belly fluttering. It was a lovely thought that she might finally have someone around. Someone she could vent to; that could help her carry the weight of the world. And God how she wanted it to be Jude. Jax was right. He was the man of her dreams. His love was something that happened once in a lifetime. She could feel it.

"Sounds nice," she said, taking another sip of her coffee. "I guess I'm just afraid that the other boot is going to fall."

"That's love," Jax said. "The risk is part of what makes it so exciting. Just don't let it scare you."

"You sound like Sondra."

Jax shrugged. "Sondra is a wise woman."

"She is." Harper paused. "Speaking of Sondra. What's going on between you and Trae Robinson?"

"What do you mean?"

Harper giggled. "I think you know exactly what I mean, Jackson DuBose. I saw the way you were making eyes at him last night."

Harper hadn't ever seen a black person blush before, but she definitely detected a flush of color in her friend's cheeks. "I have no idea what you're talking about."

"Uh... yeah right. You were totally making googly eyes at him. Not that I blame you. He's pretty darned cute."

Jax looked like a fish out of water, his mouth opening and closing as he tried to think of what to say. Luckily, his torture was short-lived as Nicole rushed in from across the hall.

"Oh, I'm so glad you're both here." She leaned over, hands on her knees as she panted. "As soon as I heard it, I ran all the way from the office."

"What's up?" Harper said.

"I was standing outside of Andrea's office filling out my attendance card. And I could hear her in there talking to some guy in a suit." Jax handed her a bottle of water, and she gulped it down.

"Who was the guy in a suit?" Jax asked.

Nicole shook her head. "I have no idea. I've never seen him before. But they were talking about a rural communities grant. Apparently, we're one of the candidates."

"That's great," Harper said. "How much is it for?" She wasn't going to get her hopes up. At least once a year some big wig in Charleston would decide to take a momentary interest in the public schools and give a grant that turned out to be a couple of thousand dollars that they could use to write off on their taxes.

"It's one of those big corporate things. I think I heard five hundred grand."

Harper and Jax gasped. "Are you kidding?"

"Not at all. Apparently, Andrea's been working on it since the summer."

"A half-million dollars? That could fund after school arts programs for a few years," Jax said. "Not to mention all the remediation stuff that we had to cut this year."

"That's fantastic," Harper said.

"Yeah, but don't get too excited." Nicole crunched up her bottle and tossed it in the garbage can. "It's between us and Highgate. They put in for it too."

"Highgate?" Harper asked, her eyes nearly popping from their sockets. She could feel her blood start to boil at the mere mention of the other school. "They're a private school. Are they even eligible?"

"Evidently," Nicole replied. "I didn't hear much of the conversation, but from what I can gather, the board of the foundation is visiting each school to see what kind of programs they're offering to their students. Andrea told the guy about the carnival. I think she's hoping we'll impress them enough to win the grant money."

That was it, Harper thought to herself. That's why Mia Goddard was trying so hard to sabotage their fundraiser. She wanted the money for her school instead of Sojourner Truth, despite the fact that they were moving money out from in front of their proverbial toilets to pee.

"Then that's what we'll have to do," Harper said, rising from her chair. Suddenly, all of the tiredness from her night out dissolved, and a fire started in the pit of her belly. "We're going to knock the socks off of those board members." Harper narrowed her eyes and took another swig of her coffee. "Mia Goddard has messed with the wrong school."

Chapter Eighteen

"Dad, these are going to be great!" Kit stood behind Jude, watching as he painted the finishing touches on a cartoon clown. "I think my friends are really going to like these games."

"Yeah, kid. I hope so. It will cut down on the cost for the school if we can make some of this stuff ourselves." He gestured to where he'd painted four other boards with funny Halloween characters: a black cat, a witch, a haunted house, and a jack o' lantern. Each of the boards had circles cut out in random places that would just fit a bean bag. "Especially the games for the little kids."

"Are we still going to have the bouncy house?"

"Of course," Jude said, putting his brush down and standing up. "What's a carnival without a bouncy house?"

"What about the popcorn?"

"Yes, we're going to have popcorn too."

"And the man that makes the balloon animals?"

"Yes, Kit. All the stuff Miss Winslow and I picked. The man at the party rental place said that we could have anything that wasn't already booked for that weekend, so I think we got the best of the lot."

"Hooray!" Kit squealed, leaping into his father's arms and climbing him like a tree. "This is going to be the best carnival ever."

"I think so, kid. Now help me paint the polka dots on the clown's suit."

Kit squatted down beside his father in that way that only small children can manage—crab-like and weightless. He took the big brush and began painting orange circles down the clown's chest for buttons. Jude watched, smiling as he noticed how Kit's tongue stuck out the side of his mouth when he concentrated.

"Dad," he said finally, pausing to admire his handiwork. "I don't remember Mom at all."

Jude's heart gave a little shudder. "Well, you were pretty young when she died."

"Do you think she would have liked me?"

"What kind of question is that? Of course, she'd have liked you. She loved you. You were her favorite thing in the whole world." Jude reached over and tousled Kit's hair playfully. "She liked you better than ice cream."

"Better than candy?"

Jude nodded. "Even better than warm peanut butter cookies."

Kit giggled. "That's a lot. Those are my favorite cookies."

"I know."

"What else did she like?"

Jude sat down on the grass and Kit crawled into his lap. "Well, she really liked the beach. And dogs. She was definitely a dog person. She liked roller coasters and scary movies."

"Miss Winslow likes scary stuff too. She's been reading us stories about ghosts. She told us this story about this lady who had an arm made out of gold."

"I think I know that story. Did somebody steal her arm?"

Kit nodded. "Yes! Her husband came and stole it out of her coffin and her ghost came back." Kit scrunched his face up and his voice was small and raspy. *"Where's my govolden aaarm?"* He dissolved into laughter. "Some of the kids were scared, but I thought it was really funny."

"You're kind of a weird child."

"I know." Suddenly his eyes lit up, and he gasped with excitement. "Can we have Miss Winslow over for dinner?"

Jude had to bite the inside of his lip to keep from laughing out loud. The speed at which Kit changed trains of thought was hilarious. Jude supposed it was a good thing that he'd already asked Harper out for that night. "Why do you ask?"

Kit shrugged. "I don't know. She's just my favorite. Can we?"

Before he could answer, Jude spotted Mia Goddard trotting across the road toward the house. Although it was the weekend, she was dressed to the proverbial nines with her hair perfectly coiffed and her enormous Coco Chanel sunglasses. "Mr. Renfro," she called with a wave.

"Hello, Miss Goddard," Jude said, nudging Kit aside and standing up to greet her. He scrubbed his paint splattered hands on his jeans. She always made him feel awkward. Like he was still a kid Kit's age, and she was the teacher. "Nice to see you." He started to shake her hand, but she surprised him with a dignified embrace.

"Lovely to see you both," she said. She opened up her purse and fished out a small, brightly colored pouch. "I think Christopher left this in my parlor yesterday."

"Hooray! I thought I'd lost all my pencils." He took the pouch and immediately unzipped the top, looking in to be sure all his pencils were there. "It must have fallen out of my bookbag."

"What do you say, Kit?" Jude said, nudging the boy with his hip.

"Thanks, Miss Goddard."

"You're quite welcome," she said, giving Kit's cheek a light pinch.

"You should go put those back in your bookbag so you don't lose them again," Jude said. Kit nodded and raced into the house. "Thank you for bringing it back, but you didn't need to go out of your way for Kit's stuff. I've told him a thousand times he should be more responsible with his things."

"Oh, it was no bother. I was afraid that if I waited until next week's lesson that it would get swallowed up in all the other things. My dining room is an absolute horror."

"Busy at school?" Jude said, trying to make conversation.

"Heavens, yes," Mia replied. "We're trying to get ready for this carnival, and it's a bit more work than I thought it was going to be."

"Oh really?" Highgate was having a carnival, too? When did this happen, and did Harper know about it?

"There's arranging all the games, selling tickets, lining up the food... so many things to take care of. Our planning committee has been working hard on it. I hope it's going to come together. The children are so excited."

"I'm sure," Jude said.

"And why shouldn't they be? We're having popcorn, funnel cakes, and cotton candy. I also found this self-service slushie station. The party rental places have such fun things. Did you know you can even get a small, kid-friendly roller coaster to set up? And then of course, there's the camel."

"A camel?"

Mia nodded. "We're getting two camels that the children can ride on and get their pictures made. And then there's the petting zoo… The whole Highgate campus is going to be a child's paradise."

"Wow," Jude said. He could already feel the lump forming in his throat. The Highgate carnival was going to be a thousand times better, he feared. He could bet they wouldn't have homemade bean bag tosses.

"Yes. But the only thing we're missing is entertainment."

Jude began gathering his paints, not wanting to hear what she was about to say. "Well, I'm sure those party rental places have clowns and such."

"I'm sure they do," she said. "But I was really hoping for something a bit less... childish."

"It is a carnival."

"Well, I know," Mia chuckled. "But there will be people there from Charleston. And all over the state."

"Oh, I see." Jude busied himself picking up the boards and stacking them against the garage door. He knew that Mia was going to ask him to perform at the Highgate carnival, and he didn't want to have the awkward conversation that would surely follow when he turned her down. She'd insist on knowing why, and the explanation might be enough to cause trouble for Harper.

"I was kind of hoping that I could convince you to perform for us on the mainstage."

He stopped, still bent over the pumpkin board. And there was the question. "Uhm... well Mia..."

"Now don't get shy on me. I heard that your performance at Common Grounds was excellent. And of course, given your rock star past, you'd sell us out for sure."

Jude laughed nervously. He could feel the warm color rising up over his shirt collar and into his cheeks. "Are you flattering me, Mia?"

"Is it working?"

"Uhm..." He laughed nervously. The other night had proved to him that there were few things in life he enjoyed more than performing. But performing at Highgate's carnival seemed like a betrayal. "When is this bacchanal happening?"

"In three weeks. The last weekend in October."

Jude noted the sly gleam in Mia's eyes. He'd always heard about small town dramas, but he couldn't believe the woman would have planned her carnival purposefully on the same date as Sojourner Truth's carnival. "Well uh...my family is coming down that weekend. To see Kit." His mother would be so surprised. "It'll be their first time in South Carolina. So, I'm afraid I won't be able to book anything."

Mia withered like a flower left too long in the sun. Her smile melted in an instant, and Jude once more felt like a child being scolded by the teacher. "What a shame. I was really hoping to get you over there to see our campus. And I have a friend that's dying to meet you."

"I'm really sorry, Mia. Maybe next time." He wanted to cut the conversation short. Suddenly he felt guilty for even talking to her. "Well, it was nice talking to you."

"She says the two of you know one another," Mia continued. "Mike Arliss?"

Jude started to make an excuse to go inside when the name stopped him dead in mid-breath, making him choke on the words. Michaela Arliss was probably the most sought-after producer working in the music industry today. She'd worked with everyone and knew even more. She made superstars out of YouTube personalities. An album produced by Mike Arliss was an automatic hit. She also happened to be the woman he'd lived with for two years before meeting Shelby.

"That's a blast from the past," he said. "I do know her. Mike's an old friend."

"She remembers you fondly, I think," Mia said. "Anyway, Mike's mother and I have been friends for ages. She has a house on Daniel Island, and we try to get together whenever she's in town. As luck would have it, Michaela is going to be here the weekend of the carnival. She seemed really happy to hear that you had moved to Crawford's Landing."

"Happy might be a strong word," Jude grumbled. The truth was, they hadn't parted on the best of terms. Sure, they had some great times together. And the sex was incredible, but Mike had wanted commitment. Jude hadn't had any desire to change the way things were. Their relationship, while intense, had been open in every sense of the word. Even then he'd known instinctually that Mike wasn't the woman for him.

"Well, I'm sure she'll be sorry to hear that you're unavailable. But perhaps we'll see you around town." As she turned to walk away, Jude was worried about the thin-lipped, serpent smile she'd given him. There was more to what was going on here, and he was starting to feel like a pawn.

Jude nodded. "Perhaps."

Kit hopped down the steps and over to where Jude stood. "Bye Miss Goddard," he said, waving at her as she went back across the street. The two of them waved again as she got into her car and drove away down the street. "That was nice of Miss Goddard to bring back my pencil case."

"Yeah, kid," he answered, bending down to pick up their paintbrushes. "Nice."

Kit babbled on about the carnival and the superhero costume he'd decided on for Halloween, but Jude was barely listening. Mike Arliss was a name he hadn't heard in ages. Did Mia know about their past together? Surely it wasn't a coincidence her showing up. Of course, if he ever had any desire to get back into the industry, getting reacquainted with Mike wouldn't be the worst thing. The old Jude Renfro, the pre-Shelby Jude, would have used this to his advantage to the fullest. Within a week he'd have bedded Mike, written a new album in a drunken stupor, and been in the studio recording. A year later, he'd be all over the radio and living back in New York.

But was that the life he wanted now? Was it the life he wanted for Kit? Of course it wasn't. He hadn't just changed his mind; he'd changed his heart. Once you change your heart, you can't go back.

Now all he wanted was a quiet, happy life by the ocean with his son. His music would always be there. It was in his blood, but it wasn't the most important thing anymore.

Then there was Harper.

In just a few months, she'd made room for herself in both he and Kit's hearts. Jude couldn't imagine living without her. Being with her was as easy as breathing. Since Shelby's death, Jude had felt this hole in the center of his chest. Kit filled up most of it, but there had always been a tiny wound that refused to heal. Since meeting Harper, that wound had started to close, and he could finally breathe. He wanted to write music again. He felt more alive than he had in years. He wasn't going to do anything to risk that now.

"Dad, are we going to call Miss Winslow?"

Jude smiled at his son and nodded. "Absolutely. But Kit…" He knelt down so that he could see eye to eye with Kit. "Let's not tell Miss Winslow about Miss Goddard asking me to play for her carnival."

"Why not?"

Jude shrugged. "I just don't want to make her upset. And I'm not going to play for Highgate, so there's no harm."

"You told me we shouldn't ever lie," Kit said, rubbing the sweat from his upper lip with his sleeve.

"You're absolutely right, kiddo. We shouldn't lie, but this is more like not telling everything we know."

Kit bit his lip. It was a gesture the child picked up from his father whenever he concentrated. "I guess so."

"Good." He and Kit high-fived and Jude picked him up, swooping him in circles until he was giggling wildly. "C'mon, kiddo. Let's go call Miss Winslow."

Chapter Nineteen

Harper was livid. She could feel the heat rising up from her chest and into her face. Any second her anger would break, and she'd find herself weeping angry tears that would completely destroy her makeup.

"Unbelievable." She crossed her arms and sat back against the car seat, fuming "What kind of a sicko harpy uses a children's fundraiser to make herself look better?"

"Evidently the sort that's willing to spend a fortune to do it," Jude replied. As he listed off the cavalcade of childish delights, Harper's blood boiled. "I can't imagine that the school would have that kind of money just lying around. Where do you suppose they got it? I mean, you know as well as I do that the stuff she's talking about is expensive."

"I wouldn't put much past her. She took down all of our flyers. It took me all day last Sunday to put them back."

"How do you know she's the one who took them down?"

"Who else would? And now she's planned her carnival on the same day, at the same time, and she's got Disneyland coming. She's obviously trying to sabotage us to get that grant. Not to mention more money from the state for having more students. It's the only explanation."

Harper sighed and crossed her arms peevishly over her chest. She'd never been one for vengeance, but right now she had the overwhelming urge to rush over to Mia Goddard's house and drag her out by those cheap Vera Wang knock off earrings.

Jude drove on for several minutes in silence. Harper could tell that he was trying not to set off her temper. He was holding something back, she knew it. Rather than press, she decided to change the subject. "So, what are we looking for?"

"My parents are coming down next week, and I realized that I have nowhere for them to sleep."

"Oh wow. I thought that was just something you told Mia so you didn't have to take Kit to her carnival."

Jude chuckled. "Well, it was, but then I figured I'd better invite them anyway."

"Such a boy scout."

"I know, right? But it's pretty difficult to perpetrate a lie with a child around. And they wanted to come down once we got settled anyway."

"So carnival weekend just worked out."

"Exactly. Besides, my mother is great with helping."

"We'll need every hand we can get, I'm sure."

Once they crossed the bridge, the traffic was insane. Harper was reminded why she never drove off the island unless she had to. Cars zipped past and changed lanes without so much as a glance. Jude seemed pretty unbothered, keeping up with the flow of traffic while he chattered away. He was calm and smooth as he drove. Harper liked that. A girl could tell a lot about a man by the way he handled a vehicle.

"Are we almost there?" Kit said from the back.

"Just about, kiddo," Jude said. "Why?"

"I'm thirsty."

Harper bent down into her purse and rummaged through, pulling out papers, her wallet, keys, a hairbrush, and all manner of odds and ends before coming up with a small, kid-sized bottle of water. "Here you go," she said, handing it back.

"Good God," Jude said. "How big is that purse?"

Harper giggled. "It's like a TARDIS. Bigger on the inside." She came up with a tiny bag of goldfish crackers and tossed them back to Kit. "I'm a teacher. I'm around kids a lot. I always have snacks."

"So that's why you always smell like cookies," Jude said.

"One of the many reasons I always smell like food."

"That must be why I like you so much." Jude reached out and took Harper's hand, giving it a secret squeeze. "One of the many reasons."

Jude pulled up to a furniture store. Out front was a huge sign that looked like a carved headboard. "A Roll in the Hay" was the name emblazoned across it. Harper glanced over at Jude, trying not to smile. She wondered if he'd chosen a store with such a provocative name on purpose. "Classy," she said, getting out of the car and turning to help Kit out of his seatbelt.

"What? I've heard this is the best place in town for bedroom furniture."

"A Roll in the Hay?"

"Yeah, doesn't that sound like the perfect place to buy a bed?"

"For your parents?" Harper was fully expecting there to be bearskin rugs on the floors of the display rooms. Perhaps a trapeze over the beds.

He came around the car and took Harper by one hand and Kit by the other. "Don't be such a prude."

Harper realized how wrong she was as soon as they walked in the place. The showroom was a sparkling example of modern décor. Bright white, marble floors clicked under Harper's low heels. Geometric furniture with hard lines were arranged in model bedrooms along the walls, lit with soft lighting. The place was packed to the gills with shoppers who wandered around with salespeople dressed like popstars—all black with little headsets.

"Come on, Dad," Kit said, pulling Jude toward the first model room. "I want to see the bunk bed rooms."

"Calm down, kid," Jude said. "Remember, we're here to find a bed for Nini and Grandpa."

"They can sleep on my bunk beds."

"Somehow I don't think they'll be into that, Kit."

Kit rolled his eyes and pulled away from his father. "But I want to look at the bunk beds."

Harper chuckled to herself. "What's that all about?"

Jude shrugged. "I don't know. The last few days he's been obsessed with getting bunk beds. Never mind that his bed is almost as big as mine, he wants a tiny little kid bed."

"Charlie Myers has bunk beds, and they're really cool," Kit said to Harper. Apparently, he'd decided that talking to his father wasn't getting him anywhere, so he'd turn his attentions to her. "The one on the top is so high that he can touch the ceiling."

"Really? Wow." She looked at Jude. "Charlie Meyers has bunk beds."

"Oh yeah?" Jude said. "Does Charlie Meyers frequently end up curled up on the floor beside his bed in the mornings because he fell out in the night?" He cocked an eyebrow at Kit, and the effect was so comical that Harper couldn't help laughing.

"I only did that once," Kit said dejectedly.

"A week," Jude added. "And trust me, kiddo, there's a lot further to fall on a bunk bed."

The three of them wandered around the showroom, investigating beds, sofas, and side tables. Jude pointed out a few that he liked, but Harper was quick to remind him that his parents weren't used to that rock star life. "Jude, this bed looks like it should be sitting in the middle of a party room at the Playboy Mansion."

"What? I like it. Black leather goes with everything."

"Uh, no, it really doesn't." She ran her fingers across the shiny, black leather headboard with the silvery grommets. "In fact, I can almost guarantee that these little notches back here are for handcuffs."

Jude threw his head back and laughed heartily, scaring a lady in the aisle behind them. "Don't knock it 'til you've tried it, right?"

"Yeah, I can't see you explaining that to your mom." Harper winked and let him thread her arm through his. He took her hand, lacing their fingers together. It was a bold gesture, and she had to fight the urge not to look around to be sure no one was watching.

"I like this one!" Kit had run down the aisle to where one of the showrooms featured a simple, modern sleigh bed in a deep mahogany. "This one looks like Nini."

"Wow," Harper said. The store had made it up with a colorful, jeweled duvet in a sort of Indian style. Very boho. "You must have a cool grandma."

"My Nini is the best," Kit said. "She's got crazy hair, and all her clothes look like this pillow." He held up the throw pillow with its embroidered mandala pattern.

"Interesting," Harper said.

Jude shrugged. "I told you she was a retired hippie. Very crunchy granola." Once more he squeezed Harper's hand, pulling her closer into his side. "I can't wait for you to meet her."

"I can't wait either. I'm sure she has all sorts of stories that explain why you are the way you are." Another wink and Jude pulled her into a tight embrace, kissing the tip of her nose. She could feel those impossibly long eyelashes of his, brushing gently against her cheek. She rubbed her nose against his, and their lips met for a tiny second. All the tiny hairs on the back of her neck prickled, and she wanted more of him. She wanted to breathe in his scent and taste the smoky, sweet flavor of him.

"The bed's really high." Kit's voice gave them both a start. "I can't get up here."

Jude slid past Harper. "Don't climb on that, Kit." As he reached for the child, his foot got tangled in the quilt that had been so stylishly arranged at the foot of the bed. He fell forward, bouncing twice and nearly sliding off the edge as he rolled over. Harper couldn't help laughing as she tried to help him get up. The decorative rug underfoot was made with a slippery satin-like fabric and Jude couldn't gain purchase. As Harper grabbed his hand, the rug slipped, and he pulled her down on top of him.

"Oof," Harper grunted. She started to back away, but when she looked up, their eyes met. The warmth of his body coupled with the obvious strength of his arms around her made Harper's head feel swimmy. His breath was labored and soft against her cheek. She could feel the hard knot of his maleness shudder against her center. Harper's mouth was a desert, and every nerve ending stood at attention. For a moment, the rest of the world drifted away, and she believed that they could stay like this forever.

"What a small world."

Harper gasped when she recognized the voice of Mia Goddard. She scrambled off the bed and smoothed down her clothes as she turned, putting on a radiant smile. "Oh hi, Mia. Fancy seeing you here." Another woman stood with Mia. She was tall with a regal air about her and short, blonde hair. The woman was gorgeous, but she had a hard look like someone who had been smoking cigarettes since the second grade.

"Indeed," Mia said. "I didn't think Sojourner ever let you leave the island." The woman's tone was dripping with disdain. She turned her eyes to Jude and Kit. "And with such agreeable company."

"Oh, every now and then they let me out," Harper said. She offered her hand to the other woman. "Hi, I'm Harper Winslow." She ruffled Kit's hair. "This cutie is Christopher Renfro and…"

160

"Jude," the woman said, dropping Harper's hand and moving her and Kit aside. Harper cut her eyes at the woman as she stumbled. "It's been ages." Without any pause or ceremony whatsoever, the woman grabbed Jude by the face and pulled him in for a kiss. Jude's body language was clearly stiff, but he didn't push her away. "I'm so glad to see you."

"Wow, Mike. What a surprise." His gaze met Harper's as he made a point of pushing the other woman away. "Mia said you might be coming to Crawford's Landing."

"Yeah, I'm visiting my mom. You know she lives over on Daniel Island now."

"Mia said something about that."

"Do you always come to buy furniture on your vacation?" Harper asked, a sickly-sweet smile plastered on her face. Jude tried to reach back and take her hand, but she wasn't having it.

Mike chuckled and shook her head. "I'm just tagging along, actually. Mom had an appointment, so I decided to pal around with Mia today." She turned and hugged Jude again. "It's so good to see you."

"Is it?" Jude asked.

"Of course. You know, I was so sorry to hear about Shelby. That must have been terrible."

Finally, Kit, obviously tired of being ignored, insinuated himself between his father and Mike. "Daddy, I'm ready to eat."

"It was a bad time, but I think we're coping well."

"That's great," Mike said. "Of course, now we're all going to be pestering you to get back to writing music."

"Daaaad," Kit whined, not wanting to be ignored.

"Just a minute, Kit," Jude said, placing a warning hand on his shoulder. "I'm not sure I'm ready for that just yet. I just finished my first song in five years."

"Don't be so modest," Mia said. "I heard that your performance at Common Grounds the other night was nothing short of extraordinary."

"Hardly," Jude said.

"You've been performing?" Mike asked, hugging him tightly. "That's wonderful." Harper could feel her mood darkening. This citified harlot was flirting with her man without so much as the smallest acknowledgment of her presence. Not that Harper felt like she had much right to be jealous. After all, they'd only shared a couple of kisses. A few longing embraces.

"Just the once. I think everyone was being nice. I mean, they were there to support Sondra and Trae more than to see me."

"Don't be silly, Jude," Harper said. This time she took his hand and allowed him to draw her into his side. She gazed up into his face and admired the gentle arc of his throat. "Didn't you hear the way everyone cheered when you took the stage? And the song. Well... it was brilliant." Harper caught his eye, and he smiled. His grin was so boyish and endearing. How could she not be hopelessly in love? "Absolutely brilliant."

"Well, Jude," Mia said. "It seems you have a fan in Miss Winslow." When Harper turned, Mia's hawkish glare was narrow and piercing. A wave of understanding clearly made its way over her features, and Harper knew they'd been found out.

"I'm just one of many," Harper said, meeting Mia's stare with an ice cold one of her own.

"Oh, but I think you're particularly special, dear." Mia nodded toward Jude's arm resting against Harper's hip. "I can't say I'm surprised. Our Harper here is a wonderful teacher, as I'm sure you know already."

"Oh, you're a teacher?" Mike asked, finally acknowledging that Harper wasn't just a figment of everyone's imagination. "At Highgate with Mia?"

"No," Harper said. "I'm not at Highgate—"

"She teaches kindergarten at Sojourner Truth Elementary," Mia answered before Harper could finish.

"She's my teacher." Kit threw his arms around her legs and hugged Harper's knees. "And she's the best."

"I always thought teaching kindergarten would be awesome," Mike said. "Getting paid to play with little kids all day sounds like so much fun."

Harper's blood was boiling so hard that she was sure any second it would explode out the top of her head like a gory geyser. Not only was she openly flirting with Jude, but she assumed that all kindergarten teachers did all day was glue macaroni to construction paper and sing the alphabet song. "It's a riot," Harper said. She squeezed Jude's hand so hard that she could feel the bones along the back crackle.

"Anyway," Jude said. He obviously sensed that this woman's life was in danger. "Harper and I were just here looking for a new bed."

Harper's face blanched, and she laughed nervously. "For his guest room. His parents are visiting next week, and he needs a place for them to sleep."

"Oh yes," Mia said. "Jude mentioned they were coming down when I tried to convince him to sing at Highgate's Fall Carnival."

Harper started to reply, but the words caught in her throat. Jude hadn't said anything about her approaching him. "Really?"

"Mmm," Mia hummed. "I tried my best to get him to come and do a concert in the courtyard that evening, but he said that he was tied up with his parents."

"I was so disappointed," Mike chimed in. "I'd really like to hear your new song."

"Well, it's really rough..." Jude said. He shoved his hands down in his pockets and shifted nervously from one foot to the other. "I'm a little rusty."

"Nonsense," Harper said. She was gritting her teeth so hard that she could feel the ache in her jaw. Worse, she could feel tears stinging her eyes. "Jude sounded like old times the other night." She forced a small smile and turned around, walking toward another showroom.

Chapter Twenty

"Harper, I'm sorry. I should have told you." Jude tried to keep his voice down as he noticed Kit sleeping in the car seat behind him. Harper hadn't mentioned the conversation with Mia and Mike at the furniture store, but he could tell that she was peeved. "I honestly didn't think it was important since I told her no."

"Jude, you really aren't under any obligation to tell me anything about your life. In fact, if you wanted to play for Mia's carnival it wouldn't be any of my business."

"You know I wouldn't even entertain the notion of playing for her. You and I are in this together, remember?" Harper sighed and nodded. He reached down and placed his hand over hers. She didn't move it away, but she didn't look at him either, continuing to stare out the window into the darkness. Evidently, she hadn't decided to forgive him just yet. He couldn't say that he blamed her. Even Kit had tried to tell him. Omitting the truth was the same as lying. He'd been very careful to tell her about Mia's visit while leaving out the part where she'd asked him to perform. Not to mention conveniently forgetting about Mike.

"So Mike Arliss," Harper began. "Is that short for something?"

"Yeah, Michaela."

"She seemed pretty glad to see you."

Jude nodded. "She's an old friend from the industry. A producer. One of the best."

"Kind of a coincidence that she and Mia were together, don't you think?"

Jude shrugged, sliding to a stop at the light. He drummed his fingers nervously on the steering wheel. He didn't want to add his previous relationship with Mike to his repertoire of screw-ups tonight. "It's a small world, I guess."

"Oh, come on, Jude," she said, then winced at the volume as Kit stirred. "You can't seriously believe that Mia isn't doing that on purpose," she said, taking her voice down to a whisper.

He chuckled. "How would she know that Mike and I knew one another?"

"She's a nosy old biddy, that's how."

"I think you're possibly a little paranoid where Mia is concerned."

"The woman has tried to actively sabotage the carnival. She's never liked me, so she'd like nothing more than to watch me fall on my face at the expense of small children. If she could find some old music producer friend of yours to convince you to play at her carnival, then that would just be icing on her little cake of psychosis."

A tiny whimper sounded from the back seat, and Kit shifted, disturbed by their bickering. "Are we home yet?" he whined.

"Not yet, Kit," Jude said. "But almost."

Harper waited until Kit was snoring again before she continued. "Not to mention that Mike kept staring like you were something to eat."

"Don't be ridiculous."

"I'm being perfectly serious, Jude. That woman has the hots for you." She paused. "Not that I can blame her for that."

"Oh? You got the hots for me, Miss Winslow?" He pulled into the driveway at his house and turned the car off.

She giggled, releasing the seatbelt and sliding closer to him. "In a big, bad way."

Jude leaned into Harper. He wanted to kiss her, but not just yet. He wanted to give himself time to savor the scent of her perfume. It made his mouth water. His heart thrummed in his chest as he stopped just short of her mouth. Her lips were deep roses, almost black in the moonlight, and so full. Like a ripe fruit that he couldn't help wanting to taste. She was so close that he could feel her breath against his cheek.

"Well, aren't you going to kiss me?" she asked, gazing at him from under feathery lashes.

"I don't want to go too fast. I want to hold back until I can't stand it anymore."

"Self-torture, then?"

"In a manner of speaking." He pushed his hands through her hair and crushed her lips to his. Once contact was made, his body relaxed, and the world faded until all he could feel was her body against his. Their mouths moved together, perfectly in sync as if they'd been made for one another. She slipped her tongue between his lips, teasing him to play.

"Are we home yet?" Kit's sleepy question startled them and Jude pulled back fast. He smacked his knee on the steering wheel.

"Yes," Jude said, gritting his teeth in pain.

"Good. I'm sleepy, Daddy."

Jude got out of the car, running around to open Harper's door. She got out, and that spicy smell got to him again. He groaned softly in the back of his throat. His body felt sticky and hot, and that throbbing tightness had settled into his sex. He wanted to press her against the car and kiss her again, but Kit was waiting.

"Let's get you in bed," he said to Kit, unbuckling his booster seat. But was Kit really who he was talking to? "You look like a zombie, kiddo."

"Do I..." he yawned. "Do I have to brush my teeth?"

Jude picked Kit up and heaved him onto a hip. "Absolutely," he said, scrunching up his nose. "Your breath kind of smells like a zombie."

"Daddy..." Kit giggled, snuggling against Jude's shoulder.

"Well... I'll just be going then," Harper said. She started toward her car, but Jude stopped her with a gentle grip of her hand.

"Why don't you stay?" he asked. "It's still pretty early for us adults. And uhm... you could get a look at that guest room. We ordered the bed, but I could use some help with colors."

Harper chewed her lip nervously. She looked everywhere except his eyes as she considered. Jude could feel his own belly flip-flopping. It wasn't as if he'd asked her to go to bed with him. Just a few more hours of her company was all he wanted. It shouldn't be a big deal.

"Sure. I mean, if you need some help with the guest room. And you did promise to show me the games you guys made for the carnival."

"I did promise," he said. "And a promise is a promise."

Jude led the way up the drive to the house. He kept looking behind to be sure Harper was still there. As if she might change her mind and bolt for her car as soon as he turned his back. What in hell was wrong with him? He hadn't been so nervous about a woman since Shelby. He was a rock star, for Heaven's sake. He was used to practically combing women out of his hair, but Harper was different. He felt like he had to work for her affection, and she didn't accept slackers.

"Sorry the house is a wreck," he said, holding the door open for her. "It was kind of a mad dash earlier."

"No worries," Harper replied.

"Just make yourself at home while I run upstairs and deposit the kid."

"Okay."

"The remote is just there on the coffee table, so turn on whatever you want. And there's beer and cider in the fridge. And soda."

"Thanks."

"Just don't leave, okay?"

"Would you get out of here?" Harper laughed, tossing a throw pillow at him.

The weight of the near-unconscious five-year-old seemed insignificant as Jude jogged up the stairs with him. That teenager-ish excitement had come over him all over, and he wanted to get Kit in bed as soon as possible. He rushed into Kit's room and put him down on the bed. Kit was like a rag doll and sort of flopped over on the pillow. Jude chose a set of pajamas from the drawer and threw them down on the bed.

"Okay, kiddo. Let's put your PJs on."

Kit took one look at the blue pajamas with the dinosaurs on them and turned up his nose. "I don't like the dinosaur pajamas," he whined. "Get my skull ones." He was referring, of course, to the favored black set with the dancing skeletons all over them that were currently lying at the bottom of the laundry hamper in his bathroom.

"Forget it," Jude said. "Those things could walk in here by themselves."

"But they're my favorite."

"I know, but they're dirty. Wear the dinosaurs instead, okay?"

"But Daddy…" His words trailed off into an unintelligible whine. Jude ignored the argument as he shoved the t-shirt down over Kit's head. "The collar is itchy." Now the child had managed to conjure up some tears of protest.

"Kit, you're dead on your feet. In two minutes, you'll be asleep, and it won't matter which pajamas you're wearing."

"But I don't like them," Kit said with his chin trembling.

Jude sighed. He was trying to hold on to his patience, but it was slipping fast. The last thing he needed was to have a power struggle with an exhausted five-year-old. "All right, Kit." He reached into the drawer and pulled out an old Affluenza t-shirt. It had been Shelby's, but Kit liked to wear it as a nightshirt. He threw the offending dinosaur pajama shirt behind him and helped Kit into the t-shirt. "There, is that better?"

Kit nodded and started to slump back over. "Oh no you don't, kiddo. You need to brush your teeth and use the bathroom."

"But I want to go to sleep."

"Come on, please." He was at the point of begging. Harper was waiting downstairs. Jude could taste her kisses already. His imagination was already running wild with what the night might hold if he could ever get his kid to bed. "If you don't brush your teeth, they'll rot out of your head. And you know what happens when you don't use the toilet before you go to sleep." Kit grumbled, but he got out of bed and let his father lead him into the tiny bathroom. He was practically asleep by the time he got back to the bed and Jude tucked him in.

"Good night, kid," Jude said. He knelt by the bed and placed a soft kiss on Kit's forehead. "I love you all the way to Mars."

"What about Jupiter?" Kit asked.

"Further than that." Jude tucked Kit's favorite stuffed animal under his blanket. "Maybe even all the way to Neptune." He kissed Kit's nose again and brushed his hair back from his eyes. "See you in the morning."

"Daddy," Kit murmured just before Jude could make it to the door. "Will Miss Winslow still be here when I wake up?"

Jude's heart leaped his chest. God, how he wished she would be. "I don't think so, Kit."

"Well, tell her I love her too, okay? All the way to Mars?"

"Not Neptune?"

Kit giggled and rolled over. "Neptune's just for me."

Chapter Twenty-One

"**I**f I were a corkscrew, where would I be?" Harper clutched a bottle of chardonnay that she'd found in the door of Jude's refrigerator while looking for the aforementioned beer. At first, she'd thought that consuming alcohol when she was already in a compromising position might be a bad idea, but she couldn't stop her hands from shaking. Then, when she saw the wine bottle, she took it as a sign from God that she needed a drink.

Harper rummaged through a drawer that she thought she remembered having silverware. Of course, her memories of the last time she was at Jude's house were a blur. That first kiss had pretty much obliterated everything else.

"Eureka," she said, finally pulling out a complicated piece of stainless-steel machinery that could only be a corkscrew. It only took three tries to make it work. Once the bottle was opened, she looked through the cabinets trying to find glasses. She didn't want to snoop, but every cabinet seemed to be filled with anything but wineglasses. "Why would you have a bottle of wine and nothing to drink it out of?" she murmured, pulling down a Fred Flintstone juice glass. She was contemplating using it when she saw the stemmed glasses peeking from the top shelf.

She reached up to get one, but it was out of reach. She tried again, and her fingers grazed the edge, pushing it back further. "Damnation," she said, standing on the tips of her toes to grab it and having little success.

Harper sighed and looked around. He had a kid, maybe there was a step stool somewhere. "No such luck," she said to herself. Looking down, she noticed that the counter underneath the glassware cabinet had heavy drawers. She pulled the bottom one out and tested it tentatively with her foot. It seemed pretty sturdy and would give her just enough height to reach the glasses. She stepped up on it and reached for the glass. It was still pretty high, but she thought she could do it if she stretched. Just a few more millimeters...

"Don't fall!" Jude grabbed her around the waist and pulled her down from her perch. He did it with such ease, she thought. Harper had never been what one might describe as 'skinny.' The thought that her child-bearing hips weren't daunting to Jude made her belly flutter with desire.

Harper squealed as he pulled her into his arms and silenced her with a kiss. Harper melted as he held her tight, leaning into his kiss without hesitation. "You idiot," she giggled, pulling back. "You scared me."

"You're the one climbing on the furniture," he said. He stepped around her and pulled two glasses down from the shelf easily. "You could have just asked for help."

"I'm not really good at that," Harper said. "I'm pretty independent."

"I noticed," he said, taking the wine bottle and pouring them each a glass. "You're kind of a brat."

Harper shrugged, taking a sip of her wine. "I can't help it. I guess I've been on my own too long. No one to ask for help when you live alone."

Jude grabbed the wine bottle and started toward the living room, expecting Harper to follow. "Have you always lived alone?"

"Pretty much. After my mom died, with me being an only child, there wasn't really anyone around. But what can you do, ya know? We adapt." She flopped down on the fluffy couch beside Jude. The overstuffed cushions pushed her against his side. He didn't seem to mind, so Harper relaxed. To her surprise, he threw his arm across her shoulders and drew her body closer. She took a deep breath and slid her arm across his waist, snuggling.

Jude nodded. "I know what you mean. Of course, when Shelby died, there wasn't much time to think about being alone. Kit was always there."

"How old was he when your wife died?"

"Not quite three."

"Wow, so practically a baby."

"Exactly. And babies really don't care if you're falling apart." He smiled, but he went silent. Harper slipped her hand into his, and he clutched it gently, playing with her fingers. She glanced up into his face. His jaw was tight, and she could tell that the wounds from Shelby's death were still close to the surface. "It wouldn't have been fair to him. He was too young to understand what had happened, or why his father didn't want to get out of bed in the morning."

"Did you have friends or family to help with him?"

"Oh yeah. I ended up breaking the lease on my apartment in San Diego and moving us back to Fall River, right outside of Boston, to be near my folks. And at first, it was awful. I would drop Kit off at my parents' house and then go home and sulk. Just staring at the walls, or worse, sitting there in the attic with all of Shelby's stuff. But gradually, with my family's help and a kick in the pants from my dad, things got better. I started writing for a little online magazine in Boston, reconnected with some old friends—just started living life. Which I guess was good. I got a new career out of it. That little online magazine turned into The Pulse, which is now the biggest music blog in the country."

"I'm sure that was horrible," she said. "I can't even imagine losing the love of my life."

"It was terrible. I've never experienced grief like that, and I pray that I never will again." He leaned forward and took up his glass, taking a generous sip of the wine. "The good news is, I don't believe in soulmates." He brought her hand to his mouth and brushed his lips across the back. "Second chances happen every day."

Jude stared down at their hands as if examining the tiny lines and dents of her bones. Harper thought how beautiful he was, his eyes downcast beneath sooty lashes, the smooth line of his cheekbone. His nose might seem largish to some, but it fit his face perfectly. And then his mouth. The generous lower lip that invited her to kiss it. When he looked up, he caught her staring at him. He started to smile, but Harper leaned in, crushing her mouth against his. It was so sudden that he dropped his wine glass, but they barely noticed. She pressed herself against him, feeling his warmth and the hardened musculature beneath his clothes. It made her more eager to feel him, and she found herself climbing into his lap. He lay down, pulling her with him until they were prone on the sofa.

"You're just too much," Harper whispered, leaning down to kiss the crest of his cheekbone.

"Too much what?" Jude asked, bumping his nose against hers.

"Too much for me to resist. You broke me down. That wasn't very nice."

His arms circled her waist, and his hands slid under the back of her shirt. His warm palms rubbed slowly along her spine. She could feel the tiny calluses on the tips of his fingers from years of playing guitar. They scratched lightly, and she squirmed against him. "I can't help that you're so damn sexy."

"Oh, so it was me that seduced you?" Her voice quavered as his hands slid down and cupped her ass, pulling her body into his.

"Definitely. By doing nothing at all."

Harper pushed Jude's hair away from his face. She liked the way his hair felt like silk falling through her fingertips, soft and cool. She hovered over him, their skin just barely making contact. She wanted to kiss him, but she wanted to tease. It had been such a long time since Harper had felt wanted like this. She wanted to stretch it out and make it last.

Jude's fingers grazed up her sides. They trilled along her ribcage until finding the edge of her bra. He played at the edges of the fabric, tickling lightly. "You have great skin," he whispered.

"Wow, that doesn't sound creepy at all," Harper teased.

Jude laughed. "Sorry. That came out wrong."

"Yeah, kind of Norman Bates-ish."

Jude growled playfully and sat up with her straddling his lap. "You have lovely skin, Miss Winslow. I'd like to make it into a coat." As he said this, his fingertips worked at the top button of her blouse, opening it slightly so he could bite her shoulder.

Harper feigned horror and swooned. Jude used her dramatics to pull her closer, nuzzling against her neck. His lips, teeth, and tongue teased over her skin sending flutters along her belly and further down. In her most intimate spots, she felt feverish. Her blood was pumping so hard through her veins that she could feel it rushing under the skin, and her head felt light. The rush of lust was unfamiliar, but intoxicating. She found herself taking his hands and placing them on her body where she most wanted to feel them. Across her belly, sliding up to where her breasts strained against their prison. He seemed tentative at first, but with a gentle nudge, he was eager.

"Are you sure this is okay?" Jude asked. "I know you were..."

"Having an attack of good sense? I was, but…" Her words trailed off into a soft moan as the palm of his hand slid over the center of her breast.

"All gone now?" he whispered, gazing up at her as he worked at the buttons down the front of her blouse.

"Well, not all gone." Harper shuddered as the cool air hit the bare skin of her midriff. "I still think discretion is required."

"Then you mustn't be too loud," he said. His look was positively predatory, and Harper shivered once more. "I have neighbors."

"Mmmhmm… and a curious child."

Jude chuckled and pushed Harper's blouse over her shoulder and down her arms. "I'm not worried. Kit sleeps like the dead."

"You say that now." Harper gasped as he pulled the edge of her bra aside and nuzzled the curve of her breast gently. The rough stubble along his chin scraped deliciously across the soft skin. "Kids have a way of coming in… at the most inopportune times."

Jude slipped his hands under her ass and held on to her tight as he stood up. Harper gasped, startled that he was able to pick her up so easily. No man had ever even attempted such a thing. She wrapped her legs around his waist, holding on tight. "Then I say we take this someplace more private."

When she gazed down into his eyes, she could see longing and desire burning there, but also a sort of plea. She knew if she said yes that there would be no turning back, but she couldn't deny the swell of love she had for Jude. She'd never felt this way about someone before, and she wanted it to go on forever.

"Take me upstairs, then."

Jude didn't need to be told twice. He swept her into his arms and started up the stairs. Harper held on tight, already kissing his cheeks and chin. She could smell the light scent of his cologne of woodfire and citrus. It made her mouth water. She could taste his skin even before they reached the bedroom.

He set her down gently on his bed and stepped away from her. She could see him trying to steady himself. Evidently, he was as eager as she was. "Give me one second," he said. His voice was full of grit. "Just uhm… make yourself comfortable. I'll be right back."

Harper nodded, a little out of breath herself.

He turned and walked out of the room and as soon as he was out of earshot, she grabbed a pillow and screamed into it as she rolled around wildly kicking her feet in triumph. She couldn't believe that any of this was happening. If only the twenty-year-old Harper could see her now. She was about to do the nasty with a rock god. Was this even real or just another one of those fevered dreams she'd been having lately? If it was, she had no interest in waking up.

Jude's bedroom was different than she'd imagined it. Yes, Harper had spent a lot of time thinking of his bedroom during her most heated fantasies, but in those it was a mess of clothes, cigarette butts, and musical instruments. Looking around now, that couldn't have been further from the truth. The queen-sized bed was meticulously made up with a masculine duvet in shades of purple and gray. All of the furniture was a dark wood, including a set of bookshelves that had been built into two of the walls. There were books of all kinds from James Patterson thrillers to classic literature. A cozy little wood fireplace was tucked into the corner. Black and white art photos had been arranged in frames along the walls, and on his nightstand there were several photos of he and Kit together. One stood by itself. Jude and a gorgeous blonde holding a baby. Obviously, this was Shelby.

Harper picked up the photo and ran her fingers over the glass. This was yet another imagining she'd gotten wrong. She had assumed that Shelby was a Pam Anderson-type with big hair and fake breasts, but this woman was an earth mother. In the photograph, she was smiling unabashedly at the camera, showing off a crooked tooth and soft creases around her eyes. She had a scattering of freckles across her nose and not a stitch of makeup. Her hair was piled on top of her head in a hopeless messy bun. She looked like someone Harper would be friends with.

"I hope you would have liked me, Shelby," she said to the photo. "I promise to take care of your boys."

A rumble of thunder gently shook the windows, startling Harper. She set down the picture. Opposite the bed, the wall was dominated by a large set of French doors. She slid down from the bed, kicking off her shoes as she wandered over to the doors. She expected them to be locked, but they opened easily on to a balcony that ran the length of the back of the house. She stepped out just as a flicker of lightning lit up the dunes below. The storm was out over the ocean, and the sea breeze was wild. She could smell the salty ozone and it made her feel sexy. She leaned over the rail, watching the whitecaps dance in the water as the waves crashed hard against the sand.

"Ah, you found my happy place."

Harper turned, and Jude had returned. He'd taken his shirt off during his absence and as he came closer, Harper could feel herself staring. "Yeah, sorry. I was just curious about what was behind the curtain."

"No worries. Every place would be happier if you were there." He slid his arms around her waist and pulled her close. That intoxicating scent was back, and Harper could barely breathe. She slid her hands down his arms, feeling the hard muscle. They were so strong, and he was so big that she felt completely encased by him. It was such a lovely, comforting feeling, and Harper just melted against his chest.

"This place is so beautiful," Harper said. "You've worked hard on it."

"I wanted to have a home. I wanted Kit to have a home. That's the thing about apartments. They never really feel like home to me."

"Are you telling me that you want to make a small town like Crawford's Landing your permanent home?"

"Absolutely," he said, brushing her hair back from her forehead. "As long as you'll be here too."

"Well, uhm…" She gazed up into his eyes. They had gone deep and black with a fire behind them that was full of intent. "As long as you'll have me."

He didn't answer but crushed his lips against hers. His kiss was sudden and decisive as he cupped her cheeks in his hands. His tongue slipped over the crease of her mouth, and he suckled at her lower lip, pulling it against his teeth. Harper couldn't breathe, but she didn't care as long as he kept so close. When he pulled away, she whimpered and tried to hold on.

"You're a bit overdressed, aren't you?" he whispered. She nodded lazily, still drunk from his kiss. His hands went to her waist, pulling the t-shirt high to lift it over her head.

"Wait," she said, stopping him. "Do you want to do this out here?"

Jude looked around. "Why not?"

"Well, we're… outside."

Jude chuckled. "Nobody can see us."

"What about people on the beach?"

"If there are people on the beach at this time of night, they deserve whatever they get." He pulled up on her shirt again and discarded it. "Besides, the dunes are too high. If you're on the sand, you can't see over them to the balcony. I've tested already." He nuzzled against her throat and slid his fingers under the strap of her bra.

"Oh, so you've been planning this?"

"Possibly."

She giggled as he kissed along the curve of her breast. He sneakily pulled the fabric aside and kissed gently at smooth skin.

She leaned back against the wooden rail, using it for support as his hands and mouth made her weak at the knees. He wandered from one breast to the other, nibbling and licking at the prickly gooseflesh that had popped up all over. His eyelashes tickled her breastbone as he began to work his way down her body. She had a moment of panic as he reached her belly. Harper had never been a skinny girl with a washboard stomach. She was soft and squishy, and it had never bothered her before, but Jude was so hot and was probably used to supermodels and actresses.

His fingers traced patterns over her skin as he kissed around her navel and let his tongue flicker over her curves. "Your body is spectacular, woman."

"You think?" Harper said, trying to hide the quiver in her voice. "A guy like you probably isn't used to stretch marks and muffin tops."

He bit down on her skin playfully. "Shush. You're so beautiful, Harper. These curves are the stuff of dreams, babe. I can't wait to slide over all of them." As he said this, he tugged at the button on her jeans until it popped.

She took a deep breath and told herself once more to be brave. "Then what are you waiting for?"

Jude wrapped his arms around her thighs and stood up, lifting her off her feet. She giggled, staring down at him and threading her fingers through the silken strands of jet-black hair. She slid down slowly until she could wrap her legs around his waist and look him in the eye. "Don't rush me, woman. I want to take my time with you." He rubbed his nose against hers, nudging her to kiss him. Their lips met with a fevered urgency that got Harper's heart racing. The pulsing in her chest worked its way down to her center. She pressed her body against him tighter as he carried her back into the bedroom. "And I'm not wasting one more second."

Chapter Twenty-Two

Harper opened her eyes, and for a moment, she had no idea where she was. The room was dark, but she could just barely see the outline of the furniture around her. The window opposite revealed that it wasn't quite morning yet, but the sky had taken on that gray-blue cast that happens just before the first rays of the sun peek over the horizon.

When she stood up, she could feel the stiffness in her arms and legs from her exertions the night before. She sat back down on the edge of the bed and smiled like the cat that ate the canary, remembering the sensation of Jude's body on top of hers, the pleasant weight of it. The gentleness in his hands as they stroked her skin. The way he silenced her moans of pleasure with kisses that left her breathless. The rush of thoughts made her shudder, and she wanted him all over again.

The other side of the bed was empty, save for an indentation where his body had been. Harper brushed her hand across it and found that it was still slightly warm. She didn't hear him nearby. She pawed her way across the room until she found her phone lying on the dresser. The numbers glowed 4:27 in front of the picture of Matthew that served as her lock screen. His cat face was always judgmental, but he seemed to glare accusingly from behind the tempered glass. "What am I doing?" she murmured, going around the room and plucking her clothes from where they'd fallen in a haphazard path across the floor. "I'm a good girl, damnit." She pulled on the jeans and blouse, not paying much attention to whether she was buttoning everything correctly. She shoved her underwear into her purse and twisted her hair back into a tie she found on the nightstand.

"The best thing to do is just find Jude, say goodbye, and get the hell back to my house before anyone sees me." *Especially Kit.*

Harper stepped out of the bedroom and tiptoed carefully down the hall. The house was gorgeous, but she didn't want to take any chances on those fantastic hardwood floors creaking and waking the child. As she got to the head of the stairs, she heard soft music coming from below. At first she thought that maybe they'd left the music on last night, but as she got closer she realized that it was a live performance.

Down the stairs and past the den was a large room with fluffy carpet. At one end was a seating area with a couple of bookshelves, but the space was dominated by a dark wood baby grand piano. Behind it were numerous stands that held several guitars. On the other side was an enormous set of French doors that opened on to a patio that appeared to stretch the length of one entire side of the house. Harper couldn't help herself and wandered across the music room and onto the patio, where she found Jude sitting on a stool playing to the enormity of the ocean that stretched out beyond the dunes.

He was so caught up in the song that he didn't hear her approach. He sang into the wind, just vocalizations, but beautiful nonetheless. He wore last night's jeans, unbuttoned at the waist, no shoes, and no shirt. The darkness had faded to an inky purple, and Jude's form was highlighted by the pink and orange streaks that had just started to appear over the ocean. The shadows danced over the tattoos that wound around his arm, making them look alive. She didn't want to disturb him but crept closer until she was sitting on the porch at his feet. Finally, he paused and leaned forward to write something on a piece of paper that was lying under a rock on the rail of the porch. Harper made a small noise, and he jumped.

"Oh my God, Harper," he said, clutching his guitar to his chest. "You scared the hell out of me."

"Sorry," she said with a small giggle. "I didn't want to disturb you."

"No," he said, putting the guitar aside and offering her his hand. "By all means, disturb me." He pulled her into a tight embrace and placed a kiss just behind her ear.

"I just wanted to say goodbye before I left."

"You're leaving?" He sounded almost frantic, pulling back and holding her by the shoulders. "Why are you leaving?"

Harper laughed. "Don't worry. I'll see you later. I just didn't think it would be proper for Kit to see me here, hair disheveled and wearing last night's clothes."

"He's a kid. I don't think he'd notice."

"But I would," Harper said. "I don't want any awkwardness."

"What's there to be awkward about?" Jude asked, kissing her lips then each cheek. "I love you, Harper."

He said it. So casually and matter-of-factly that for a second, Harper hadn't realized what he said. Suddenly, her palms were sweaty, her pulse was racing, and she could feel her cheeks burning with heat. She couldn't help the weird, goofy smile that broke out on her face and a ripple of girlish giggles slipped out. "I…"

"It's okay if you can't say it yet," he said, looking down. "I know I let my emotions get the better of me sometimes, but I couldn't let you walk out of here without telling you."

He started to babble, making more excuses for his brazen admission, but Harper silenced him with a fingertip across his lips. "Shush," she said. "Of course I love you too. I think I have since the first time I laid eyes on you. But this is all so new. I'm a little frightened of it."

"Me too. After Shelby, I never thought I'd get a second chance. But here you are. I promise I won't waste it." He kissed her again, this time holding her tight to his body, as if he feared she might blow away in the gentle sea breeze. Their tongues mingled, and he stole her breath with the force of his longing. Harper whimpered softly against his mouth, nibbling at his lip and wanting more, wanting everything.

"You sure do make it hard for a girl to leave," she said when she was able to speak again. "But I really should go. Besides, they're delivering a bed today, and I know you aren't finished painting your parents' room."

"See, you already know me so well." He kissed her again, letting his hands slide down her back to play with the hem of her shirt. "You really could stay."

Harper groaned, biting her lip as he pushed his fingertips under the waistband of her jeans just slightly. "I tell you what. I'll go home, shower, maybe nap a little, and come back in my painting clothes with a pizza around noon."

"Or you could just shower here. With me. I have some clothes you could wear." He nuzzled into her neck before giving a playful bite. "I'll make us breakfast."

Harper ducked out of his arms. She knew if she stayed much longer that it would be too late. She would end up going back to bed and taking him with her. "I will not succumb to your evil persuasions."

"I'm an excellent cook, but I won't pressure you."

"Good, because you know I can't take it." She laid her head

against his chest for a moment listening to the rhythm of his heart. It seemed crazy, but she could almost feel it syncing up with her own.

Jude watched as Harper walked down the steps to get into her car. His heart sank a little. He didn't want her to leave. Funny how someone could become so entrenched in your life in such a short period of time. He held up his hand to wave as her sensible sedan rumbled down his gravel driveway and into the street. She was going to be back in a few hours, but they seemed like an eternity. He glanced down at his watch. It was barely five a.m. That might be enough time to finish the song before she got back. Or he could go and try to sleep a little more. That was probably the wiser thing, but he wasn't sure he could do it. He was so keyed up after last night.

Jude had had some great sex in his life. From wild and crazy to soft and slow, but last night with Harper had transcended the spectrum. Not since Shelby had he felt so satisfied and content. Just after he started to wake up after Shelby's death, he'd thought that the way to heal himself was to find comfort in the arms of another. Many, many others. Affluenza was still a going concern, so there'd been no shortage of groupies. The act itself had felt good at the time, but there had been something missing. It was a hollow act that did little to dull the pain. Making love to Harper had made him feel alive. She wasn't in love with some fantasy. He wasn't a fetish. God, it was so damn corny, but with Harper, he felt loved by another. That's what the new song was about. So far it was just a melody in his head; there were no words. He would have to find them, but he was confident they would come through.

Jude yawned and walked back inside. It was still early, but he could see the dim light of the sun coming up over the ocean. Maybe he'd just make a pot of coffee and watch a little TV. Kit would be up soon enough.

The strange feeling of being watched woke Jude a couple of hours later. When he opened his eyes, Kit was standing over him holding out his cell phone. "The phone's for you, Daddy," he said with a yawn. The kid had obviously been awoken from a sound sleep. All of his fluffy, curly hair was on one side of his head, and he was still clad only in his pajama shirt. "It's some lady named Mike."

"Mike Arliss?" Jude said. "What does she want?"

Kit shrugged and pushed the phone into his hand before flopping down on the sofa beside him. He nudged himself under Jude's arm and snuggled against him.

Jude glanced at the clock on his phone. *9:18*. Kind of early for conversation. "This is Jude," he said.

"Hey there!" Mike's cheery voice came through, clearing Jude's sleepy head immediately. "I thought the kid had forgotten to give you the phone."

"Uh... no. He was, I mean we were still asleep."

"Oh, sorry. I forget about that rock star life. Party all night, sleep all day, right?"

"Hardly," Jude replied. "I haven't partied all night in years. The curse of having a kid, I guess."

"I guess so," Mike said. "Probably why I never had any." She paused, and Jude could tell she was lighting a cigarette. He remembered the whiff of lighter fluid and that first drag in the morning. It was enough to make the corners of his jaw ache.

"What did you need, Mike?"

"No, no. The question is, what do *you* need?"

"Me? Not a thing. Unless of course you'd like to do an interview for The Pulse."

Mike laughed. She had a strangely girly laugh for someone who looked like she could crack walnuts between her knees. "Anytime, but that's not why I called."

"Do tell."

"Well, I'm curious. Why on earth are you interviewing musicians when you should be the one being interviewed?"

"What do you mean?"

"I mean that the industry has been without the brilliance of Jude Renfro for three long years. It's high time for you to come out of this hiatus."

It was Jude's turn to laugh. "I'm not sure if you noticed last night, but that five-year-old kid was mine."

"So? Lots of musicians have children."

"But most of them have wives." His mouth suddenly felt dry, and his belly began to flutter. "Or girlfriends."

"Well, you looked pretty cozy with... what's her name... Harper." She paused and he could almost hear her smiling. Mike's smile always had a sinister look, and with good reason. She was a schemer. There was always an ulterior motive behind every compliment. "Or maybe she wasn't your girlfriend."

Was Harper his girlfriend? According to her, they were supposed to be keeping things discreet. He didn't want to let the cat out of the bag if she wasn't ready to tell people. Then again, he didn't want there to be any confusion about his feelings for her. If it got back to Harper that he'd said she wasn't his girlfriend, she might think his interest ended once he got off.

"Jude? Are you still there?"

"Uh, yeah. No. Harper's just a good friend." He hated himself already.

"Oh, I see. Well, you might want to tell her that. She seemed pretty touchy-feely."

"Did this conversation have a point, Mike?"

"Make a record with me, Jude."

"What?"

"I want to do a record with you. Solo. All new stuff."

Jude couldn't help laughing. She couldn't be serious. "Why?"

"Because you're the most amazing singer-songwriter that I've ever known. Because I'm tired of doing bubblegum pop albums with spoiled, plastic teenagers. Because I think that the market is ripe for a big comeback from you."

"What about the rest of my band?"

"What about them? Jimmy Bose is playing guitar for Half-Caff Mocha Frapp and touring the world. Maxie Kasdan is a studio musician, and Aurelio Ramirez is writing music for Hollywood. Trust me, none of them is crying their eyes out every night waiting for Affluenza to get back together. Have you even spoken to any of them in the last year?"

"I had lunch with Jimmy last month," Jude lied. The truth was, his friends had all moved on. He couldn't exactly blame them. For the first year after Shelby, he hadn't been the best company. They had wanted him to jump back into the rock star life, but Jude had developed a hatred for that lifestyle. In his mind, Affluenza had stolen the thing he'd loved the most in the world. It was harsh, but he couldn't help it. "What are you getting at, Mike? I have to feed my kid."

"I'm trying to tell you that all of your bandmates have moved on without you. It's time you did too."

"I did move on. Maybe I like my life the way it is."

"Oh, get serious, Renfro. I know you. In the Biblical sense."

"What's that supposed to mean?"

Mike sighed. "You might be able to fool sweet little schoolmarms with your boyish charms, but not me. You live for the spotlight.

Mia told me about your little performance the other night at the local watering hole."

"Oh please, that was just me doing a favor for some friends."

"She recorded you singing that new song of yours. I heard how that crowd cheered for you. I mean, that's probably the first time they've had a show here in Dogpatch that didn't involve a guy playing a jug."

"Hey, I happen to like this town."

"I'm just saying that little spark of magic that you had ten years ago is still there glowing bright. And I really want to help you get back out there."

Jude paused, taking in her words. It was true that he missed performing. Writing and performing music had always been the one thing he felt completely confident about. Some might say it was the only thing that he was ever any good at. The exhilaration of performing in front of an audience, the applause… Looking down into someone's face and seeing that your words had touched them or made them feel something. It was the best thing in the world. On the other hand, he hadn't missed the crazy life: long hours, living out of a suitcase, being recognized everywhere he went. The constant party atmosphere and false friends. Not to mention that it wouldn't be fair to Kit. If he went back to performing, he would be a part-time father, at best. The kid would likely end up living most of his life in Boston with his grandparents.

"Mike, I just don't think…"

"Shush," she said. "Don't think. You don't have to answer me now. Just promise me you'll think about it."

"I…"

"Just consider it."

Jude shook his head. He knew he should refuse her outright, but there was another part of his brain that screamed YES. Almost just to see if he still had it in him. "Fine. I'll think about it."

"Excellent. You got my number. Just give me a call."

Chapter Twenty-Three

Harper drove around the block a few times to avoid not getting back to Jude's too early. She'd told him that she would be back at noon, and she didn't want to seem overeager. The truth was, she hadn't wanted to leave in the first place, but she didn't think she was ready to explain to Kit why his teacher was having sleepovers with his dad just yet.

The more she was with Jude, the more she wanted to be with Jude. Her grandmother had always claimed to have Second Sight, and she was always going on about how when you meet the person you're supposed to spend forever with, that God would send you signs. That you'd just instinctively know. Harper had the sneaking suspicion that these were the signs she'd been looking for. That Jude was the person she'd been looking for.

When she rounded the corner the last time, it was 11:55. *Close enough*, she thought. She wanted to giggle like a schoolgirl. Her heart was actually pounding with anticipation as she pulled into his driveway. Her palms were sweaty, and she couldn't stop smiling. Harper didn't think she'd ever felt this way about anyone before. All those signs were there.

As soon as she was maneuvering around the car with the big pizza box, Kit was rushing out to greet her. "Miss Winslow!" he exclaimed, throwing his little arms around her legs.

"Hey Kit," she said. "Think you could help me with this?" She handed him a picnic basket that was almost as big as he was. She couldn't help giggling as he struggled with it up the front steps and across the porch.

"This basket's really big, Miss Winslow."

"Well, I wanted to be sure we had enough food." She balanced the box from Zefferelli's Pizza on her hip while she wrestled her purse out of the car. She heard Kit shouting to his father and turned.

There was Jude. Standing on the porch, fresh from his shower, he looked like a god. His wavy black hair was still damp but fell perfectly. His plaid shirt was open, revealing that muscled plane of a chest that Harper could still feel beneath her fingers. His jeans were slung low on his hips, and she could see that sinful ghost of bone that framed his sex.

"Give me that before you drop it," Harper heard him say before he took the basket from the child in one hand and hoisted it over his shoulder. "Hey, pretty lady. Thought you'd never get back."

"Well, I had to run a couple of errands before I got here." When Harper reached the porch, he caught her by surprise and pulled her into a warm hug against his side. He kissed the top of her head, and she could feel the butterflies in her stomach kick into overdrive so hard she sighed.

"I'm glad you got here," he said. "What about you, kid?"

Kit nodded emphatically. "Can I show her my room?" he asked, taking Harper's hand.

"Absolutely," Jude said. "But first, let's eat." He led them into the house. She noticed that he'd picked up the clutter from the previous night and the place smelled like he'd just vacuumed the carpet with some of that room freshening powder.

"Looks like someone's been busy," Harper said, putting down the pizza on the kitchen counter.

Jude grabbed the pizza in his other hand. "Well, Saturday is our morning to clean anyway. Right, Kitster?"

"I made up my bed all by myself, Miss Winslow." The kid flashed her a smile, obviously proud of his work.

"That's great," Harper said. "But where are you going with that pizza?"

"C'mon," Jude said, beckoning her forward. She followed him through the kitchen and out a set of French doors. A few steps across the grass and a sandy path led through the sea oats to the beach just below.

Harper had lived in Crawford's Landing her whole life and until this moment she'd thought she'd walked every inch of coastline, but the beach behind Jude's house was spectacular. Wide with fluffy white sand. There were no swarms of tourists tripping over one another as they tried to find a tiny plot of unoccupied space. No neon high rise condos. No beach stores proclaiming "END OF SEASON! Nothing over $1.00!" No restaurants with giant shellfish looming over the entrance. Just miles of unspoiled coastline against a sparkling aquamarine ocean.

"What do you think?" Jude asked.

Harper's breath was taken by the view and for a moment she couldn't say a word. "Well..." she stammered. "It's ugly."

Jude narrowed his eyes and then caught the twinkle in hers. "I know, right? Probably why I got the house for such a bargain."

"I'm jealous that you get to wake up every morning to this. My apartment is several miles from the beach. On the marshy side."

Jude leaned in and kissed her cheek before whispering, "You can come enjoy my view any time you like, Miss Winslow." Harper blushed, a new wave of prickly chills rolling down her arms.

Kit grabbed her hand and began pulling her toward the beach. "Let's go find some seashells for my collection." Harper giggled and followed him down to the packed sand.

She glanced back at Jude. "Wanna come gather shells?"

"You two go ahead. I'll get our picnic ready."

Harper followed along behind Kit, watching him squat down over the sand in that way that only small children can accomplish. Despite it being late October, the air was warm, and Harper was glad that she'd opted for the denim shorts and flip-flops. Though she wasn't quite as brave as Kit. The kid had kicked his shoes off at the edge of the sand dune and was currently splashing through the surf to clean off his shells.

"Isn't that water freezing?" she called.

Kit shrugged. "It's warmer than the beach near my Nini and Pop's house."

"Where do they live?"

"In Fall River, Massachusetts."

"Oh yeah. The town where Lizzie Borden axed..." Harper suddenly remembered she was talking to a five-year-old. "...some wood."

Kit laughed and picked up a thick fragment of an oyster shell. "I know. Lizzie Borden took an ax, gave her father forty whacks." He held the shell up to her. "Look at this one Miss Winslow! That must be a big fish."

"I see," Harper said. She turned the shell over in her hand, examining the streaks of gray, blue, and purple. "Oh wow, Kit. See this sparkling stuff on the inside. There's still some mother of pearl."

"Mother of what?"

"Mother of pearl," Harper chuckled. "Oysters have mother of pearl inside their shells. If they get a piece of sand or grit inside, it irritates them, so they cover the grit with the shiny stuff to make it smooth. After a while, the piece of grit makes a pearl." Harper pulled her shirt back to reveal a small, pearl pendant.

"Oooh… that's pretty, Miss Winslow."

"Thanks. My mom gave it to me for Christmas a few years ago."

The two of them walked along the sand in silence for a while. Kit was so intent on his treasures that he didn't have much to say, but it was okay. She felt comfortable around them. Harper had the thought that she could fit in with this family nicely. When she was with them, she didn't begrudge Kit's presence or wish they were elsewhere. She just existed in the moment, and it was so freeing.

"Hey you two!"

Harper turned to see Jude jogging down the beach toward them. "Hey yourself," she said with a wave.

"Lunch is served." Taking advantage of Kit being down the beach with his shells, Jude grabbed Harper around the waist and pulled her into his arms. He pressed his mouth to hers, moving the tip of his tongue softly along the crease. She could feel herself relax against him, burrowing into the embrace as his fingers slid into the tangle of her hair. "I missed you," he said when he pulled back.

"I was only gone a few hours. Besides, I thought you had work to do."

"I can work with you around."

Harper giggled and wound an arm around his waist. "I'll have to try harder next time, then."

Jude whistled for Kit and led them all down the beach, back to where he'd set up a magnificent picnic on the sand. He'd laid out a large blanket for them to sit on. Their pizza, along with napkins, plates, glasses, and a sparkling pitcher of tea had been arranged neatly on the pallet.

"I want pizza, Dad!" Kit exclaimed, diving onto the blanket.

Jude caught the tea just in time before it toppled over. "Kit! Be careful."

"Sorry…" he said with a sheepish grin. "But can I have pizza?"

"Of course," Harper said. She scooped up one of the smaller pieces and put it on his plate. Jude added some grapes and apple slices, drawing a groan from Kit.

"All I wanted was pizza." Kit poked out his lip and crossed his arms over his chest as if he were considering putting up a fight.

"And I'd like for you not to have a bellyache later."

"I won't have a bellyache. I promise!"

"I don't believe you. But why are you arguing? You like grapes and apples."

"But I like pizza more." Kit emphasized his point by picking up the slice of pizza and shoving half of it into his mouth at once.

Harper tried to swallow her laughter at Kit's childish logic. "Well you can't really argue with that." When Kit shoved most of the piece in his mouth, he looked like a squirrel preparing for a long winter. When he pulled back there was a pepperoni slice stuck to his cheek. The visual was too much and soon Harper and Jude were gasping with laughter.

"Kit, that's not a nice way to eat." He pulled a small container of baby wipes out of the picnic basket. It only made Harper laugh harder.

"There's a picture for Rolling Stone."

"What?" he asked, using a wipe to scrub at Kit's squirming face.

"Rock god and international sex pot, Jude Renfro, carrying baby wipes."

"Hey, these things come in handy. They're like a portable shower."

"You keep a box of them in your glove compartment, don't you?"

Jude smirked. "Maybe."

"Dad!" Kit whined. "You're wiping my lips off!"

"Well if you wouldn't eat like the Tasmanian devil."

Kit finally allowed his father to clean his face and hands. As soon as he was done, the child must have decided that he'd better get while the getting was good and ran off toward the ocean. The two of them laughed as Kit squealed when the surf splashed over his toes.

"He's a great kid," Harper said. "You should be really proud of him."

Jude nodded. "I am. Trust me, no one is more surprised by how great he is than me."

"Why's that? You're pretty great yourself."

Jude snorted and looked down at the picnic blanket, tracing the little lines with his fingertip. "Yeah, but when Shelby died, I was kind of a mess. I thought I was ruining him for sure."

"Grief can make us do weird things, I guess."

He shrugged. "Weird, yes. I was pretty self-destructive though. Drinking too much, staying out late, a lot of meaningless sex."

Harper's smile faded. "Oh…"

Jude wiggled his eyebrows. "I threw that last one in to see if you were paying attention."

"Oh… good. I mean, why shouldn't you?" She took a nervous sip of her tea and looked out to where Kit was bent over the sand.

"If it makes you feel better, I didn't really enjoy it. I had a few flings, and all of them felt great in the moment, but afterwards I always felt worse. Sex is all about pleasure, and I wasn't looking for that at the time. In fact, I felt like I didn't deserve it. I mean, why should I be alive when Shelby wasn't? She was the kind one. She was the one who never met a stranger. The compassionate one that was always looking for ways to help. The world would have been a much better place if Shelby had lived. If I'd been the one to die, there just would have been one less self-centered rock and roll asshole in the world."

"Survivor guilt?"

"I guess. Anyway, it took me a while to get back to me. I hope I didn't leave any deep scars on Kit that will surface later."

"I don't think you did. He's sweet, funny, compassionate. He's always helping the other kids. The others see this and want to be better too."

"I'm sure you've got a lot to do with that." Jude reached for a handful of grapes and scooted closer to her. "Kit says you're a great teacher."

"He's probably a little biased."

"Mmm…" He lay back on the blanket and tucked one arm behind his head. "Didn't you know that kids always tell the truth?" He tried tossing one of the grapes into his mouth, missing entirely.

"Not always," Harper said.

She plucked the grape off the blanket and offered it to him with her fingers. He stretched to reach it, but she pulled away at the last second. He smirked and tried to grab it, but she shoved him back down on the blanket. "Don't be greedy," she said, adopting her best teacher voice. "You have to ask nicely."

"Oh yeah?" he asked, sitting up.

"Yes. Or no grapes for you, I'm afraid." She turned her nose up as she picked another grape off the bunch and popped it into her mouth.

Jude feigned an angry stare, fixing those enormous brown eyes on hers. Harper had never actually seen someone smolder, but Jude's eyes were definitely smoldering. "Please, Miss Winslow," he said. His voice was purring drone that made the butterflies in her belly flutter. "Please let me have one of your grapes." He crawled closer like a big cat stalking its prey.

"Oh, all right," she said. "Open your mouth."

Jude obeyed and opened his lips just slightly. Harper touched the cool surface of the fruit to the swell of his lower lip. He made no move to take it so she traced along the gentle bow and playfully bouncing it against his teeth.

"Don't you want it?" Her words were meant to tease, and the innuendo was not lost.

"Oh yes, Miss Winslow. I want it very, very much."

She tried to push the grape into his mouth, but he grabbed her wrist, stopping her. "I think it would be tastier from your lips."

Harper smiled and took it into her mouth. She leaned in, offering the fruit from her mouth. Jude accepted it this time, sliding his tongue along the seam. She didn't let him have it all at once, urging him to draw it from her mouth with his tongue. Finally, it was poised between them. Harper bit down and the grape flooded their mouths with the sweet juice. She giggled and tried to pull away, but Jude held her close, deepening their kiss until Harper couldn't breathe.

"Mmm…" Jude sighed as he pulled back. "That was delicious."

"Yeah? You want another?" Harper's voice was breathless and rough, more of a gasp. She was desperate to taste him again, and when he reached for her, she didn't protest.

Jude pulled her into his arms until she straddled his lap. He tangled his hands in the masses of curls that tumbled down her back. Knotting his fist, he pulled her into an insistent kiss. "I don't think I'll ever get enough of you, Miss Winslow."

"Oh, I dunno. You say that now. There are so many things about me that are annoying as hell. I leave my wet towels on the bed. I'm prone to leave glasses with two millimeters of milk in the bottom just lying on the counter. You just haven't known me very long."

"Long enough," he said. "I'm not a kid. I think I know how it feels to be in love."

Love. Had he really said love? With her? Mousey schoolmarm Harper? It had been so long since she'd felt loveable that the idea was foreign to her. Every relationship in her history pointed to her being the person everyone left when they got a better offer. Looking into his eyes, he seemed so sincere. She said a silent prayer that she wasn't just blinded by infatuation. Her heart was beating out of her chest, and her mouth was a desert.

"You didn't think this was about sex, did you? Well, not just about sex anyway."

Harper blushed. "Well, I hoped."

"Oh no," he said, placing a gentle kiss at her temple. "I intend to keep you around as long as you'll have me."

"Well, I definitely want you to stick around." She tipped her face up to his, closing her eyes against the sun that sparkled off the ends of his hair. He obliged her with a deep, soul-stealing kiss that she could feel all the way to the tips of her toes.

Behind them, Kit squealed as another wave broke against him. Harper looked up just in time to see the wave knock the child backward. He sat down hard on the sand. The tide was coming in, and this time there was another breaker just behind. It washed over Kit as he tried to get to his knees. He came up sputtering and shaking his head. "Kit!" Harper shouted, scrambling to her feet.

Jude got up in an instant and pushed past her, running toward the screaming child. He reached Kit in a matter of seconds and plucked him out of the water like a fish gasping for air. As soon as he was in his father's arms, the little boy crumpled against his shoulder and began to wail as if his heart were breaking.

"Kit!" Harper said, rushing to them. "Are you okay?"

Kit scrubbed his face against Jude's shoulder. "The big wave got me."

"You're okay, kid," Jude said. "I've got you now."

"Poor thing," Harper said. She placed a soothing hand on Kit's back, rubbing circles and trying to calm him

"I couldn't get up. Stupid waves."

"I know, sweetie," Harper said. "Sometimes the ocean is like a big bully."

"That's right," Jude said. "That's why you have to be careful and never turn your back."

"I was looking for shark teeth."

"Did you find any?"

Kit shook his head, his tears already starting to dry up. "Just some old shells."

"What?" Jude said, hoisting Kit on to his hip. "You almost died and didn't even find even one shark tooth?" He clucked his teeth. "Cruddy old wave."

Kit giggled. "Cruddy wave." He wiggled from Jude's grasp and slid down his side to the ground. He took his father's hand in one of his and Harper's in the other. Clearly his near-death experience had been forgotten as he led them down the beach.

It was such a nice day, Harper thought. The sort that reminded her why she never wanted to leave this place. The wide beach with its soft sand the color of champagne and the aquamarine sea beyond was a postcard from every dream of paradise. During the tourist season the beaches were so crowded that most of the locals in Crawford's Landing stayed away, but in October, the air was still warm enough to enjoy without the worry of a stray football or a runaway beach umbrella.

The three of them were walking along the sand, Harper and Jude swinging Kit through the air and laughing like loons. Like a family. The kind of family she'd always wished she had. When Harper's father was killed, her mother just sort of checked out. She threw herself into her work, and Harper was alone. Looking at Jude, it didn't escape her notice that despite the fact he could have done the same to Kit, he'd held on and made a new life for them. She had to admire that.

"Look, Dad! It's Miss Nettles from my school!" Kit pointed toward a tall woman in a large floral hat coming toward them. A tiny dust mop of a dog ran along in front of her, splashing in the surf.

"Oh no," Harper said. She dropped Kit's hand and began

dragging Jude back toward their blanket. "Turn around. Maybe she won't see us."

"What?"

"Andrea Nettles. My boss. That's her up ahead in the hat."

Jude looked up, squinting against the sun. "Oh, yeah. That is her."

"Yes, it is. Now come on before she sees us."

"What? Why? I don't get why we're running from her." As he said this, he dropped Kit's other hand. Like most children, Kit was excited and amazed to see a member of the staff at his school out in public, and he raced toward Andrea.

"Uh…" Harper stammered. "I umm… I just don't know what she'll say. You know, about us. She might not like it."

Jude laughed and held her hand tighter. "Who cares? Are you ashamed of me?"

"Not at all but…" She looked to where Kit was already chatting up Andrea and playing with the yappy French poodle. "I don't want to lose my job."

"You won't," Jude said, returning Andrea's wave.

Damn, now she'd seen them for sure.

"Thank goodness you were here, Christopher. I was starting to think that I would have to chase Oleander all the way to Hilton Head."

"Hi, Andrea," Jude said, offering his hand. She shook it warmly, and Harper could feel her eyes burning on his other hand which was clasped tightly in hers. "How are you?"

"I'm good, Mr. Renfro. Enjoying our lovely Carolina weather." She knelt down to where Kit was petting the dog. "And how are you, Christopher?"

"I'm good. Except for the part where I fell in the water."

"Oh no!" Andrea exclaimed, clutching her chest and feigning shock. "You fell in the ocean?"

Kit nodded. "I was trying to look for shark teeth, but a big wave came up and knocked me down."

"That must have been so scary," Andrea said, patting Kit's wet head. She stood up and smiled, turning her attention to Harper and Jude. Harper tried to drop Jude's hand, but he held on tight. "You two enjoying the beach?"

"Oh yes," Jude said. "I thought the beaches in Mass were pretty, but nothing like this."

Andrea nodded. "Indeed. And today is a perfect day on the island. Not too warm, but not too cool. And plenty of sunshine."

Harper could have sworn she saw the woman's eyes drift down to their clasped hands. She tried to unobtrusively step closer to Jude in an attempt to hide them behind her thigh. "We were just having a picnic," she said, almost shouting. "You know, to talk about the Fall Crawl."

"Last minute prep," Jude agreed.

"Ah yes," Andrea said. "Everything coming together then?"

"Definitely," they answered in unison.

"Things couldn't be better," Jude said. "I think it's going to be a roaring success. The response in town has been great."

"And the kids are all so excited," Harper said.

"I certainly hope so." For the first time in Harper's memory, Andrea looked worried. "The board of directors from Manticore will be there, as will members of the school board. I don't think I have to remind you both how important the success of this carnival is. Not just to the school, but to the town. If Sojourner Truth closes, the heart of Crawford's Landing is gone. We'll just be another tourist town along the Carolina coast. Holiday Inns and pancake houses will take over. We'll survive, of course, but it won't be the same. And as for our kids…"

"Don't worry, Miss Nettles," Harper said, placing a comforting hand on her shoulder. "We're going to knock it out of the park."

Andrea smiled and patted Harper's hand. "Of course we are.

You and Mr. Renfro have worked so hard. And you're a wonderful teacher, Harper. I believe you can do just about anything." She knelt down in front of Kit again. He was scratching the little yappy dog behind its ears and cooing. "It was very nice seeing you, Christopher."

"You too, Miss Nettles," Kit replied. "I like your dog."

"Well, you come play with him any time you like." She leaned in and whispered, "I bring him to school sometimes."

Kit's face lit up, and he looked back at his father, his mouth ajar. "You bring your dog to school?"

"Some days," Andrea said. "He even has his own pillow under my desk to sit on." She winked at Kit and stood up. She offered her hand for him to shake, but he threw himself against her shins and hugged.

"See you at school, Miss Nettles."

She ruffled his hair gently. "Not if I see you first." She whistled for the little dog who immediately fell in beside her. "Harper, I wonder if I could speak with you for just a second in private?"

Harper froze. Here it comes, she thought. Andrea had caught them red-handed. Their hand-holding, their kissing… Maybe someone had even seen her car parked outside Jude's this morning and alerted the principal that one of her teachers was sleeping with a parent—out of wedlock! Suddenly, little beads of sweat began to collect around the hair follicles on her forehead. She managed to conjure a smile that looked more like a grimace of pain and followed her boss toward the dune.

"Yes, Miss Nettles?" she croaked. She felt like a kid summoned to the principal's office.

"I just wanted to tell you," Andrea began. "You look so happy."

"Pardon?"

"At the start of the year, I feared that you were growing tired of us. That awful Mia Goddard had been sniffing around, asking questions about you…"

"About me?"

"Mmm... I got the distinct impression that she was looking to steal you away to Highgate. I know that she can probably offer you more than we can, but we need you at Sojourner Truth. In case you hadn't noticed, you and Nicole Thompson are two of the very few teachers that we have that are motivated to save us."

"Me? You think Mia Goddard is after me for Highgate?"

"It wouldn't surprise me. You're a wonderful teacher, Harper. I'm sorry if I never tell you what an asset you are to our students."

Harper started to reply, but the words got stuck in her throat. She couldn't believe that this was the same Andrea Nettles that she'd been working for over the last five years. She shook her head. "You don't have to worry about that. Me leaving Sojourner, I mean. I wouldn't want to be anywhere else. The teachers and the kids there are like my family."

Andrea nodded. "I'm glad." She glanced over at Jude who was throwing shells into the waves with Kit. "You know, you and Mr. Renfro make a good team."

"What do you mean?"

Andrea smirked, and Harper detected a slight blush to the older woman's cheek. "You work well together. It's an infectious energy you two have. And he just glows whenever you're around."

The nervous giggles that Harper had been holding back since Andrea walked up finally burst forth. "You think so? I hadn't noticed."

"Oh yes," Andrea said. She leaned in, fixing Harper with a knowing stare. "You know, sometimes when you meet the right person, everything just falls into place exactly the way it's supposed to."

"With the carnival you mean?"

Andrea chuckled lightly and nodded. "Yeah. The carnival." With a knowing wink, Andrea bent down and picked up her dog and walked off down the beach.

As Harper watched her go, she was amazed to discover that she hadn't been fired or reprimanded. No one had popped out from behind the dune to brand a scarlet A on her chest. She watched the woman walk down the beach until she was almost out of sight, her mouth hanging open. She was so flabbergasted by the situation that when Jude touched her shoulder, she nearly leaped out of her skin.

"Sheesh," he said, stepping back. "What was that all about?"

"Oh… sorry," she said. "She just… she just wanted to tell me what a great job we'd been doing with the carnival."

"Nice," he said, winding an arm around her waist and leading her back toward the water where Kit was still squatting at the edge. "But we knew that already. We have a bouncy house and everything."

Jude stopped and pulled her tight against him. Harper noticed how perfectly her body fit against his. They complimented one another. The hard muscle of his chest pressed to the softness of her curves. He took her hand, and she could feel the rough callused fingertips scraping against her smooth palm. When he wrapped his arms around her, she could smell the soft, masculine scent of him — the ocean breeze and the woodsy-smelling shampoo he used. It made her mouth water, and when he brushed his lips along her wrist, her body cried out for his.

"I think she knows about us," Harper whispered, her voice running dry. "And I think maybe she was trying to give us her blessing."

"Oh yeah?" he asked, sliding his cheek against hers and nuzzling at her earlobe. "How do you figure?"

"I'm not sure." Her body shuddered as he took the cuff of her ear gently between his teeth and nibbled. "She seemed so… warm. It wasn't like her at all. It kind of freaked me out a little."

Jude pulled back a little and cupped her cheek in his hand. He tipped her face up to his, leaning in until their lips met in a deliberate kiss. When he released her Harper stumbled backward.

If he hadn't been holding her, she probably would have hit the sand. "I'm glad she reassured you, but I have to say, Harper. Nothing, absolutely nothing could keep me away from you now."

Kit wandered back up to them. Evidently, he'd tired of trying to return the shells back to their natural habitat. He pulled the two of them apart and squeezed between. "I'm cold, Dad. Can we go inside now?"

"Well, it's not a surprise," Harper said, pushing the boy's wet curls from around his forehead. "You're soaking wet." She pulled off the sweatshirt that she'd tied around her waist and wrapped it around him. He snuggled into its folds and began ambling back to the blanket. She turned back to Jude and offered her hand. "Come on, Daddy. We still have a bedroom to paint."

Chapter Twenty-Four

Kit was barely snoring when Jude dashed down the hall and made his way back to Harper. Even though he'd only left her for a little while to put Kit to bed, it felt like an eternity. He wanted to be near her again.

Despite his distraction, they'd managed to finish the first coat of paint and a large pizza by Kit's bedtime. Hopefully, Harper would stay, and they could start getting the new guest bed put together. Of course, once they got the bed together, Jude would be tempted to break it in with her. *Stop it!* he scolded himself. If he didn't stop getting lost in his fantasies, they'd never get the room finished in time. His parents hadn't said exactly when they were coming, but they never did. They had a tendency just to show up, usually at the most inopportune time.

By the time Jude reached the guest room, Harper had nearly finished touching up around the crown molding. She stood at the top of the ladder looking absolutely beautiful. A pair of oversized, ripped jeans clung to her generous hips. Each time she reached over her head, her ratty t-shirt rose and exposed a tiny strip of sun-kissed skin. He liked to watch her while she was unaware and uninhibited. Little subconscious things she did were endlessly fascinating. The way she chewed at her lip when she was concentrating. The little tune she hummed when she was stretching for a tiny spot on the wall that was just out of reach.

Damn. I'm doing it again. He couldn't help it. Every single thought rattling around in his brain was of Harper. It probably wasn't healthy to feel so strongly, but he was helpless to resist.

Harper stepped back and surveyed her work. She wiped the sweat from her brow, taking care to keep the paintbrush from slopping across her face. She turned and saw him standing there staring.

She gasped and gripped the ladder when it wobbled under her. "Damnation, boy. You shouldn't sneak up on people like that."

"Sorry," Jude said. Before she could reach the bottom of the ladder, he scooped her up into his arms.

She shrieked, giggling as she crumpled against him. "Careful. We can't have anyone breaking their back."

"Please," he said. "Methinks I'm made of sterner stuff, milady." He stepped over a roller pan and brushes to sink to the couch in the corner. It was covered with a paint-speckled drop cloth and a cloud of dust spewed around them as they fell. "Besides, you're light as a feather."

"Yeah, tell that to the scale."

"Psssht… the scale can kiss your ass."

"My incredibly wide, luscious ass."

"You're gorgeous." He slid his hands down to cup her ass and squeezed playfully. "And so is your luscious ass." He placed a soft kiss at her temple. "Don't ever let anyone tell you different."

Harper snuggled against him, tucking her head beneath his chin. He listened to the soft rush of her breath, and he could feel her heart beating against his own chest. Jude couldn't believe how relaxed he was, lying here with her on the sofa. The last few years, he'd resigned himself to being alone. He'd forgotten how nice the feeling of just being with someone felt. They didn't need to talk. He was perfectly happy just to be.

"You will stay tonight, won't you?" Jude asked finally. He nuzzled into the tangle of curls around her shoulders. It smelled clean, like ocean waves and sunshine. Hidden in the depths was a soft shoulder that peeked out from the slouchy t-shirt. Her skin was smooth and just barely browned from the afternoon sun. As he brushed his lips lightly along the curve, he could taste her sweetness.

"I don't think I have much choice," she whispered, leaning into the caress. She took his hand that rested on her hip and lifted it to her mouth. She kissed each of the fingers and suckled lightly on the tips.

"Good," he said. "Because I don't think I can let you go."

"Then don't."

"I have such a hard time believing that you've never been married."

Harper laughed and leaned over to where his beer bottle was perched precariously on the windowsill behind them. "Obviously, you don't know me too well."

"What do you mean?"

"Well, I have lots of eccentricities that probably aren't conducive to being married." She took a swig of the beer and shuddered. "Blech."

"How so?"

"Well," she said, hiccupping. "I don't like beer, for one thing."

"Hardly a dealbreaker."

"I'm messy. I'm kind of a workaholic. My cat is extremely temperamental."

Jude laughed. "What's so bad about that?"

"Seriously, Matthew—that's my cat—ran off the last guy I dated. Every time he'd come over, Matthew would dive bomb him from the entertainment cabinet. One night, during some… amorous activities…"

Jude put his hands over his ears. "No… I don't want to hear about your previous amorous activities. I don't think I could stand hearing about your other conquests."

"Oh please," she said, rolling her eyes. "I hardly have conquests. Anyway, we're on the sofa and in a rather compromising position. Matthew is on top of the cabinet. I can see him out of the corner of my eye doing the kitty dance."

"The kitty dance?"

"Yeah, you know the one where they shake their butts back and forth right before they pounce? Anyway, I can see him. Before I can warn the guy, Matthew launches himself off the cabinet and lands on his back. So he starts screaming and jumps up from the sofa, causing Matthew to claw his way down the guy's side."

"Oh no…" Jude said, already starting to giggle. "I think I know where this is going."

"Sadly, he didn't. Apparently in Matthew's panic at being swatted away, he was grabbing on to whatever was available. And the guy's uhm… ah…" Harper tried to get the point across with a gesture. "You know… I mean, it was hanging down there and Matthew grabbed at it with his claw. Which then got stuck…"

"Oh no…" Jude unconsciously crossed his legs.

"Oh yes. I'm afraid the poor man was never the same."

Jude couldn't contain his laughter and before long, both of them were giggling uncontrollably. "I bet not."

"He moved away the following month. Never saw him again."

"Ah well," Jude said, wiping his eyes. "It was a sign that you were destined for better things." He wiggled his eyebrows suggestively, and Harper nearly lost it again. "Bigger things."

"Ooh… sounds promising." She moved into his waiting arms and let him embrace her tightly.

Jude relished the feel of her warm softness against him. The scent of her hair and the sound of her breath as it quickened were an intoxicant. This must be what was known as 'love drunk.' He had it bad for Harper, and she was just going to have to resign herself that they were meant to be together.

"So, pretty lady... wanna see my stamp collection?"

"Hmm... is it bigger than a pickle jar?"

"You'll just have to come see." He stood up and took her hands, pulling her up off the sofa. Their bodies collided, and Harper wrapped her arms around him. They kissed, slowly at first and then more urgently. As if the only breath they got was from one another. Before long, they were pulling at each other's clothes.

"Jude... let's go to bed..."

"That's the best idea I've heard all day."

He broke away from Harper, and she slipped past him, dashing up the stairs. "Last one naked is a rotten egg."

Chapter Twenty-Five

The sun streaming through the window woke Harper early. At first, she was disoriented, not sure where she was. Her normal wake up routine involved Matthew swishing his tail under her nose. As her eyes adjusted to the dim light, she remembered that she was tucked into Jude's bed. She rolled over, and there he was, sleeping soundly beside her. His arms were around his pillow, and he clutched it like a lover. She reached out, stroking his cheek gently. His skin was so smooth save for the rough edge of his jaw, already bristled with stubble. Dark, sooty eyelashes that most women would kill for rested lightly on his cheek. "What did I do to deserve you?" she whispered.

Harper started to lean in to kiss him awake when a terrible clatter startled them both. Jude's brown eye opened, and he got to his feet in an instant. He was groggy and as he stumbled around looking for pajama pants, he stubbed his toe on the corner of the footboard. "Damnation…" he growled, rubbing his eye.

"What the hell was that?" Harper yawned and began pulling Jude's bathrobe around her shoulders. Out of the corner of her eye she could see the glowing numbers of the alarm clock screaming 8:37.

"There's no telling," Jude said, shoving the door open and rushing down the stairs. "But I'm sure it has something to do with my child breaking it." Harper followed close behind but stopped in her tracks as they rounded the corner toward the kitchen. Kit sat on one of the stools at the island while an older woman stood over a mixing bowl by the stove.

"Mom?"

"Hello, dear. I hope pancakes are all right for breakfast."

"Can I have chocolate chips in mine, Nini?" Kit asked.

"Darling, you can have whatever you like." She looked up at Jude. "Would you like chocolate chips in your pancakes too?"

"Mom, what are you doing here?"

"I thought we were invited."

"You were. I mean, you always are." Jude wound around the island and wrapped his arms around his mother tightly. "I just didn't know you'd be here today."

There was no doubt that the woman in question was Jude's mother. They looked almost exactly the same with their beakish noses and full lips. When she smiled, the resemblance deepened, her big brown eyes sparkling with the same mischievous gleam. Her gray hair was a wild tangle of gray and blondish curls that were piled on top of her head in a messy bun. Her bohemian peasant blouse and flared jeans left no doubt where Jude got his artistic spirit.

"Well, your father's last gig was cancelled, and I was crazed with need of Kittie kisses." She reached over and ruffled Kit's hair. "Besides, the flight was cheap."

"I'm glad you came, Nini."

"Me too, sweetheart." She winked, picking up the skillet and flipping Kit's pancake with one hand.

Kit giggled and clapped his hands. "How do you do that, Nini?"

"It's all in the wrist."

Harper took a tentative step into the kitchen and cleared her throat. "Jude?"

Jude let out a startled gasp then gave a nervous laugh. "Oh, Harper. I forgot you were standing there." He held out a hand, and she took it, letting him pull her over. "Mom, this is Harper. Harper, this is my mom, Elizabeth Renfro."

"Well," she giggled. "Now I understand why you haven't called." Jude's mother wiped her hands on the kitchen towel next to her and offered a hand to Harper. "Call me Betts. Everyone does." The older woman's eyes were kind but inquisitive as she gave her a once over, obviously taking note of the bathrobe. "Would you like some breakfast?"

"Umm… I should probably…"

Kit ran over and threw his arms around her waist. "Please stay, Miss Winslow. My Nini's making chocolate chip pancakes."

"That sounds delicious, Kit. But I really should be going. Your Nini wants to spend time with you and your dad. I'd be imposing."

"Not at all, dear," Betts said. "I can even make them without the chocolate if you prefer."

Harper glanced toward Jude. She could tell that he was uncomfortable, having been caught with a half-naked woman in his kitchen. She couldn't really blame him. Especially considering that she was almost certain that he'd left a couple of marks on her neck from their activities. "No, I really have to go. Matthew, my cat… he'll literally be climbing the walls if I don't go home to feed him."

Jude sidestepped around the island and caught Harper before she could get over the threshold. His voice was low as he leaned in close to whisper. "Come on, babe. I'd really like you to stay." He accented his words with a gentle kiss just below her earlobe.

"Jude, don't press the girl," Betts said. "He's always been like that, Harper. Never wanting to let people leave. He slept with his father and I until he was nearly twelve."

"Mom…"

"It's why we don't have any other children."

"Mom!"

"But you really should stay. He gets so peevish when he doesn't get his way." Betts winked at Harper. "You'd really be sparing us all from his growly mood."

Harper giggled. "All right. Maybe I can stay for a cup of coffee. But let me go up and put on something decent." She slipped from his grasp, brushing her fingertips along his belly. She didn't want to leave him, but she was also afraid of getting so serious so quickly. She thought of him every minute. When she wasn't with him, she counted the seconds until they would be together. She was absolutely in love with his kid. Then, there was the insatiable desire for him she'd been cultivating. They'd made love twice more in the night, and it wasn't enough. It was only pure exhaustion that forced her to sleep in the wee hours of this morning. Harper had never been a believer in those silly dime store romance novels where the heroine fell in love with the guy after two days, met his family, and was ready to marry him by the end of the week. But then again, none of those sad-eyed heroes was Jude.

Harper inhaled deeply when she threw back the door to the bedroom. Everything smelled like him. The heady scent of balsam and leather was underscored with a whiff of sex — dewy sweat and perfume. She couldn't stop herself from pulling the lapels of his bathrobe against her nose and breathing him in. Her heart beat faster, and she could feel the fluttering sensation in her belly.

"I shouldn't be falling in love so easily," she said to herself. "I barely know him." She gave a reluctant sigh and threw the bathrobe over the end of his bed and began looking for where her clothes landed. As she pulled her jeans, spotted with paint, over her hips she caught sight of herself in the mirror. Her hair was in a tangle around her shoulders and last night's mascara was a little smeared, but her skin was glowing. She ran her hands through her hair, pushing it back from her face. Normally she'd have been gawking at the little imperfections: a blemish on the side of her chin, the beginnings of crows' feet at the temples, a slight double chin, chunky jowls--- all those little things that had always made her feel small and inadequate around her other boyfriends. But this morning, she felt beautiful. She felt like none of those things mattered. Maybe this inner light that she could see radiating out of every pore was her love for him. Like everything she felt was too big to fit, so it had started pouring out of her.

"Hey Harper!" Jude's voice, shouting from the stairs, startled her out of the sappy thoughts. "Can you bring my cell phone down when you come?"

"Sure," she hollered back as she buttoned her blouse. She turned, looking around for his phone. It was one of those enormous monstrosities that looked more like a laptop than a phone. He'd left it sitting on the nightstand, off the charging cable. When she picked it up, it buzzed in her hand. There must be new messages, she thought. Of course there were. Guys like Jude always had messages. When her thumb hit the screen, it immediately illuminated to show the message previews. Harper didn't want to pry, so she started to hit the lock button when a name caught her eye.

MIKE: *I need to see you.*
MIKE: *Are you ignoring me?*
MIKE: *I needed to talk to you about the other night.*
MIKE: *Hey there bad boy. Remember me? You were supposed to call me back.*

She wanted to open the phone so that she could see the whole thread, but that would be a betrayal. Whatever they were talking about, it had nothing to do with her. Her mother had always accused Harper of being too nosy. More often than not, she'd figured out more than she wanted to know.

"Hey there bad boy?" she whispered. That wasn't something one normally said to a casual acquaintance. It was flirtatious. Jude hadn't said a word about talking to Michaela again. Not that he had to tell her everything. Or anything, even. But she couldn't keep the jealous thoughts from rearing their heads. After running into her and Mia at the furniture store the other night, he'd given Harper the impression that she was a person from his past that he didn't care to reconnect with. So why did she have his cell number?

"I'm sure it's nothing," she said, trying to shake her anxiety. "She's an old friend." That he used to sleep with. A lot. And not too long ago.

Harper stood there staring at the texts. They were the cold, fishy reality slapping her in the face. It's not like it wouldn't be par for the course. Alan left her for a boyfriend that he'd been seeing for the last year of their relationship. Reign left her after banging every other woman in the English department at school and a few of the men. Harper was just one of the girls you enjoyed until someone better came along.

"Did you die up here?" Jude called, as he sprinted up the stairs.

When she turned to look at him, she could already feel the tears burning in her eyes. She tried to take a deep breath, but it shuddered in her chest. "No. I'm here."

"I'm so glad," he said, pulling her into a bear hug. "I don't think I could go on." He kissed the top of her head. "Did you find my phone?"

"Yeah. I did." She passed it to him and slipped past to reach for her purse. She pulled it over her shoulder and started searching for her keys. "You know, I think I am going to go."

"What? I thought you were going to stay for coffee."

Harper shrugged. "I was, but I think it would be better if I just left. I mean, you've got your mom and dad here. I have like… a billion papers to grade."

"Harper? Is something wrong?"

She gave a nervous chuckle and shook her head. "No, of course not. I just… uhm… I have a lot to do. In case you forgot, the carnival is less than a week away."

"We have it all under control," he said. "You said yourself that we were ready ahead of schedule."

"Yeah, but I have to finish the treat bags and the decorations for the food tables." She was frantically going around the room, searching for her keys. She had to get out of here. If Jude kept talking, she'd fall for his eyes and his boyish smile all over again. Then, he'd make an even bigger fool of her than he already had.

"Well, after we eat, we can go over to the school and I'll help you…"

"No!" She winced at the harsh tone of her voice.

"Why not? I mean… I thought we were doing this together."

"I just… I don't want… I don't want you to." She tried to push past him to get to the safety of the hall, but he grabbed her arm, stopping her.

"Just wait, Harper." He gripped her shoulders gently, turning her around to face him. She bit the inside of her cheek, desperate to keep from bursting into tears. "What's going on? Does this have something to do with Mrs. Nettles? Or Mia Goddard?"

"No. I just need to go home."

"You're lying. And you never lie, so there must be something wrong."

Harper sighed and shook her head. "Look, I think you and I are just… things are going too far too fast."

"Why? Because my mom caught us together?" He laughed, but there was no humor in his eyes. He was obviously dumbfounded by her sudden cold shoulder. "Trust me, you are not the first girl she's ever been surprised by."

"Oh yeah? How about Mike?"

"What?"

Harper's voice was low, almost inaudible as she stared at the floor. "Mike Arliss. Did you and Mike ever surprise your mom?"

"What does Mike have to do with anything?"

Harper shrugged. "You tell me. She seems pretty desperate to talk to you." She grabbed Jude's hand that held the phone and pulled it up so he could see it. When his thumb brushed the screen, the previews of Mike's messages flashed. And evidently, she'd texted a few more times.

Jude's eyes scanned the screen and he looked up, confused. "I can call her later."

"Oh, don't mind me. Call her now. I was just leaving."

Jude gave her a sideways glance, like he couldn't believe what he was hearing. "You can't possibly think that I'm interested in Mike." He chuckled and shook his head. "I mean, do you?"

His laughter only served to inflame Harper's anger. "Oh I dunno, Jude. She seems way more like your type than me. She's an 'industry person'. She's gorgeous…"

"Mike is a friend, but I'm not interested in her."

"She seemed to think you were."

Jude hesitated, pushing his hands through his hair. "I can't believe that you can possibly doubt how I feel about you. I thought I'd made my feelings pretty damn clear."

"Maybe it's just hard to believe that you would prefer the spinster schoolteacher over the jet-set music producer."

Jude slapped his hand over his face. "Look, don't make me a party to your silly insecurities." His expression had turned serious, and his brown eyes that were usually so full of warmth had gone a cool black. "If you must know why she was texting, she wants me to record a solo record."

Harper had a witty retort planned but the revelation took the wind out of her sails. "What?" she croaked.

"She wants me to fly out to LA with her and record a new album. My big comeback, can you believe it?"

"Uhm…wow…" She started to say more but she couldn't seem to find her voice. While she wanted to be happy for him, she couldn't help the pang of selfishness that was currently working its way from her belly to three back of her throat. It had a bitter taste that made her want to snap angrily at him. Even more than the ugly moment of jealousy over Mike.

"I thought you'd be happy, but I guess not."

"No. I mean, yes, I'm happy for you."

"Certainly looks like it," he grumbled.

"Why didn't you tell me about this before?"

"Before what?"

"Before I slept with you!" Harper's voice sounded shrill and desperate to hear ears. She was choking back a wave of tears threatening to come through. She bit the inside of cheek hard. There was no way she was going to let him humiliate her further by crying. "I thought we had something. Something more than just… just a one-night stand!"

"What makes you think I don't want that too?"

"Well, if you traipse off to California to cut a record with Mike…I mean… Where does that leave us? Do I get to just be the groupie that sits around in this little pig turd town waiting for you to show up to fall on top of her?"

"Harper, don't be ridiculous…"

"Or maybe I get to be wifey-poo that keeps the home fires burnin' while you're on tour, doing whatever you like with whomever you like." With every breath she was getting angrier. "Maybe I can even take care of your kid."

Jude whipped around. His eyes were wild, and she could tell that what she'd said had punctured the bubble of patience. His mouth opened and closed like a gasping fish, but no words would come. Finally, he could only grunt and throw up his hands, walking out of the room without another word.

Chapter Twenty-Six

The day of the Fall Crawl was the chilliest day so far this autumn in Crawford's Landing. The skies were gray, but Harper was hopeful that the clouds would break soon. According to the weatherman, the weekend was supposed to be cool and slightly overcast. She could only pray that the rain would hold off until tomorrow. She couldn't believe how everything seemed to be falling into place. The rental company had been on time delivering the games. The inflatables would be delivered around 11:30. An entire army of parent volunteers had showed up to help set everything up. Everything was going so well.

Except that Jude was noticeably absent.

Harper couldn't exactly blame him. Their argument had been terrible. Not that she felt wrong. It wasn't fair that he hadn't even bothered to talk to her about the new album. Or working with Mike. Maybe she'd been a heinous bitch about the innocent texts, but any idiot could see that the woman would be waiting right there in the wings if Jude found himself single. As irrational as it might be, there was a thought tickling the back of her brain that this whole solo album was a ploy to get Jude back into her bed.

It figured, though. Just as she'd gotten comfortable with this whole thing, one little argument had managed to ruin everything. Story of Harper's life. Still, it wasn't fair to the children to abandon them on the day of the carnival. Everyone had worked so hard. And all because of some stupid argument. Maybe her gut instinct had been right from the start-- don't get involved.

"Harper, you easily have outdone yourself. "

She turned, and Mrs. Nettles was staring in awe as the giant castle was slowly inflating in the center of the playground. "I wouldn't call it easy, but it is coming together. I just hope it turns out okay."

"I'm sure it will. No matter what, you and Mr. Renfro made this happen. You really pulled it off for our kids."

Harper could feel herself blushing. Andrea wasn't exactly overflowing with praise for anyone, so this sudden declaration was surprising. "I hope it helps."

"I think it will. The Communities in Schools committee will be here this afternoon. I can't wait for them to see this."

"Do you really think we'll get the grant?"

"I think we have a fighting chance. I know that Highgate is heavily competing to get it, but I can't imagine their staff and parents pulling together the way you guys have."

Harper had to grit her teeth to keep from offering a few choice words about Highgate and Mia Goddard. "You know, I heard that they were going to have their own carnival today to compete with ours."

Andrea smiled, "Same old Mia. She never could stand a little healthy competition."

"What do you mean?"

"I've known Mia Goddard for a long time. Since she was Mia Faircloth and we were competing for head cheerleader. That was... God, at least thirty years ago. We went to school together here on the island. Then college on the mainland. Both of us wanted to be teachers."

"I didn't know she was from Crawford's Landing. I thought she was from up north someplace."

"Oh yes. She ran off to New York and married the Goddard man. He was some ritzy lawyer, if I remember correctly. He made his big break defending some real estate mogul... Oh what was his name? It was in all the papers.... Randy Arliss."

"Arliss?" That explained a lot, Harper thought. Mike's mom owed Mia a favor.

"That's right, he was accused of murdering his business partner, and Mia's husband got him off. Anyway, after that he was untouchable. He and Mia were apparently the 'it couple' among the New York society crowd."

"Were?"

Andrea nodded. "Mia's husband was killed in a car accident about six years ago, and she moved back down here with a sack full of money. Which she used to open up Highgate. I guess I shouldn't be surprised by all of her petty competitive tactics. She's always had to be better than everyone else, especially me."

So that was what this was all about. Mia was such a twisted and bitter woman that she wanted to see the public school, headed up by her former friend and rival, closed up. Her own silly jealousy being more important than the children of the island. Harper could feel her cheeks burning with anger that one person could be so selfish. "She has no business with children."

Andrea chuckled. "Mia wanted to be a teacher because she thought it would be easy. After all, she liked nothing better than telling other people what to do. Plus, she'd have the added benefit of job security and what she assumed would be copious amounts of time off."

"Boy, was she stupid," Harper grumbled.

"Indeed," Andrea said with a sly wink. Harper couldn't help laughing. She'd never seen Andrea as a real person before. She had always been this goddess of elementary education, held on a golden pedestal of righteous indignation. Now, for the first time, Harper saw her as a woman that she could be friends with. "At any rate, I'll let you know when the committee gets here."

As Andrea walked away, Harper looked down at her watch. Nearly eleven. The inflatables would be here soon, and she was going to need Jude's help to get them placed. He had the map. Her stomach rolled over at the thought of seeing him. The more she thought back over their fight, the more she thought this might all be for the best. The quick conclusions and the jealousy that followed were not exactly conducive to being involved with someone like Jude. Harper realized that she barely knew this person. She'd never known Rockstar Jude. This new album would likely be a huge hit and a major comeback for him. Would he still be the same sweet, poetic man that she fell in love with when success and fame came back to town? She doubted it. Old habits were hard to break.

"Food tent's all set up, chief." Sondra jogged up to her wearing an enormous chef's hat. "We have the tables for the food and Trae just got here with the truck. As soon as Mr. Langsdale gets here with the charcoal, we can light up the grills."

"Charcoal? I thought we were renting gas grills from the Super Saver market."

Sondra shook her head. "They called this morning and said that their gas grills had all been borrowed for today."

"That stuck up..." Harper growled. "Lemme guess. Super Saver lent their two grills to Mia Goddard."

"They didn't say, but the way the manager sounded on the phone, I'm betting so. He did offer some charcoal grills though. And he gave us the charcoal half-price."

"Well that was good of him," Harper said, her tone dripping with sarcasm. "But how are we going to pay for the charcoal?" Harper held her head. The throbbing headache she'd been holding off all morning was threatening to blossom into a full migraine.

Sondra patted her arm. "No worries. Mr. Renfro took care of it already." He pointed to where Jude was standing by the food tent unloading bags of charcoal off the back of a pickup truck.

When did he get here? She must have missed him slipping by while she was talking to Andrea. He hadn't even come to say hello? Which meant that he was avoiding her. "When did he get here?"

Sondra shrugged. "Just a few minutes ago." He smiled and nudged her with his elbow. "I'm surprised he wasn't with you."

"What do you mean?"

"Well, everyone is talking about you two."

"Everyone?" She brushed her hair away from her eyes and tried to look innocent. "There's really nothing to tell."

"The hell there isn't. You two have been inseparable for weeks. The coffee shop, the beach, all over town…"

"We were just doing stuff for the Fall Crawl."

"Oh, come on, Harper. Sell that someplace else. I have known you almost your whole life. The way you look when that man's around—it don't happen very often, honey. When I say everyone's talking about you two, I only mean that everyone is so happy that you've found someone."

"That hard to believe, huh?"

"Not at all. Harper, you've always been the one that takes care of everybody else. When your daddy left, you kept your mom from losing her mind. Then, when she got sick, you took care of her until the bitter end. And it was bitter."

"But those things were my responsibility. She didn't have anyone but me." She paused, looking down at the red and yellow leaves that blew around her ankles.

"And you're in serious danger of being just like her, Harper."

"Maybe I saw how losing my father nearly killed her, and I don't want that to happen to me."

"I loved your Mama, but after your daddy died, she pushed everybody that might be good to her away. It was you and her against the world, and that was okay. Until now she's gone and you're on your own."

"I like being on my own."

"And there ain't a thing wrong with that. But everybody needs somebody to love. You been so busy taking care of everybody else, that you never got around to findin' somebody to take care of you. And you deserve that. You're so happy with Jude. Don't throw that away too lightly."

Harper smiled and embraced her friend tightly. She'd never thought about it before, but Sondra was right. She had been pushing Jude away with both hands. This sudden feeling for him scared her. No, terrified her. Maybe she'd been looking for a reason to run. When she looked across the field, Jude was there with Kit. His smile was radiant, even from this distance. He was wearing tatty jeans and a black, long-sleeved shirt that clung to his torso like a second skin. So beautiful that she could hardly stand to look at him. But even more, watching him kneeling down to Kit, she could see the love he had for his child. His kindness and care. Every second since they'd met, he'd been selfless and kind. How could she have possibly thought that he would hurt her?

How could she have hurt him by losing her faith?

"How'd you get so wise, Sondra?"

"Just born with it, I guess." There was a crash and she looked over her shoulder to where Trae was standing in front of a food table. The brightly colored, plastic autumn tablecloth had been blown to the side by the wind, sending plastic cups and napkins all over the courtyard. Trae was holding a napkin and watching as

Jax ran to catch everything. "Good Lord... that boy's going to be the death of me."

Harper giggled, watching Sondra run to where her son was currently making a fool of himself alongside Jax. Those two were headed toward an adorable relationship, and Harper couldn't wait to watch. She heard a shout of delight that could only be Kit Renfro, and she turned just as he ran off to join the other boys across the field. She'd have to run them off before long so they could set up the ball pit. But before that, she had to get to Jude. She had to talk to him while she still had a chance.

****

Jude rushed over when he saw the food tables blowing into the parking lot. Trae and Jax were laughing as they ran after the cups and napkins that were currently littering the courtyard. Evidently the wind had gotten under the plastic tablecloths before they could get them tied down. It wasn't a surprise, really. It was a chilly day, and the wind had picked up as if to herald the coming of the new season. Trae dove to catch a sleeve of cups and crashed into Jax. The two of them tumbled to the ground, still cackling. Jude smiled, thinking that they looked like such a cute couple. Their attraction was obvious. He just hoped that a small town like Crawford's Landing was as accepting as he thought it was. He'd been disappointed by small towns in the past, and this one was in the south — a region not known for their progressive spirit. Everyone should have a chance at that kind of happiness.

As if he were being taunted, he caught a glimpse of Harper across the quad. She was sprinting to the rental truck that was pulling up in the parking lot. God, she was beautiful. Her golden hair sparkled in the sun as it blew back from her face. She was wearing a pair of jeans, slightly ragged at their flared hem, and a form-fitting plaid, flannel shirt with checks of orange and black. He couldn't stop from thinking about how that shirt would look all crumpled in the corner of his bedroom. Was she wearing the black underwear with the little silver stars? Was she wearing that sexy little toe ring? Would he ever get to hold her naked body against his again?

Jude hadn't seen her in more than a week, and it was killing him. He'd tried calling so many times to tell her he was sorry for their argument, but what could he say? Truth was, he wasn't all that sorry. She'd hurt his feelings to think that after everything that had happened, he could even consider running off with Mike Arliss.

"Daddy?" Kit was tugging on the hem of his shirt while he'd zoned out. "Are you listening to me?"

"Of course, kiddo." He knelt down to his son's level and ruffled his hair. "What's up?"

"Can I go play with Ezra?"

"Where's Ezra?'

Kit pointed to where a group of little boys were playing in the open field on the other side of the vendor tables. "Please?"

"Okay." Kit started to run off, but Jude caught him. "Hey, don't leave that area. I need to be able to see you."

"Okay, Dad."

"And your grandparents will be here in a little while, so keep a watch out for them."

"Is Nini bringing my cake?"

Jude laughed. His mother had been up half the night before making enough cupcakes with candy corn tops to build an addition on the school, and a special pineapple upside down cake just for Kit. "I think so. But just remember, Nini's stuff is for the bake sale."

"As long as I get a piece."

"I know you will."

Kit threw his arms around Jude's neck and squeezed. It surprised him, and he hugged back tightly. The kid wasn't usually clingy unless he was sick or sleepy. Maybe he sensed that his father needed a hug this morning. Whatever the reason, Jude was glad of it. "Now, go play, but be good."

"I will." He broke away from Jude and ran toward the other kids. On his way he spotted Harper. He ran over to her, giving her a hug. Jude couldn't hear them, but after a few seconds of chatting, Kit pointed to where Jude was standing. She held up a hand and Jude returned her wave. Hmm. Chilly. But maybe there was some hope if she was communicating across the field.

"Okay, Jude… you just have to go up to her and say hello." He started toward her, giving himself a pep talk the whole way. "Just pretend like your fight never happened. And if she asks why you haven't called her for a week, just say your phone was out. Be cool." He knew that was a lost cause. When it came to Harper, he hadn't been *cool* this entire time. Maybe he should just blurt out how he felt and be done with it?

Suddenly, he noticed that Harper was coming toward him. She was walking toward him with purpose, and she wasn't exactly smiling, but she didn't seem angry either. Could it be that she was ready to talk? God, he hoped so.

"Hey handsome. I knew I'd catch you here." Jude turned just as Mike jogged up beside him. "Mia told me you guys would be out here super early."

"Uhm… Mike. Hi."

"I'll have you know that I don't roll out of bed this early for just anyone."

Jude could see Harper out of the corner of his eye. She'd stopped dead in the middle of the quad and was watching as Mike embraced him. "Uhm… actually Mike…" He tried to turn away, but she grabbed his hands.

"Anyway," she continued, pulling him closer. "I have been texting you all week and you haven't given me an answer."

"About what?"

"About what? Are you kidding? About coming to LA and cutting the solo record."

"Well, Mike… about that…I'm just not sure that would be the best idea."

"Come on, Jude. I know you're not seriously going to give everything up for this…" She looked around, the disdain clear on her face. "Place."

"I happen to like this place. And so does my kid." Jude glanced over to where Harper was still standing in the middle of the quad, hands on her hips and staring at them. Her hair was blowing back from her face and the sun kissed the high points of her cheeks and the end of her nose. After a second, she shook her head and turned away, heading back to the trucks.

"Oh please. Kids like everywhere. He'd love LA. Always warm, lots of sunshine, Disneyland. And after this record becomes a hit—it'll be a party every day. You can't tell me you don't miss that."

Jude thought it over. Funny, at the time it had seemed like such a great life. More money than he could spend. Friends all around telling him how great he was. Every day a new party. But then Shelby had come along and changed everything. Suddenly all those golden dreams of his had tarnished. Going out on tour had started to seem more like a chore than a party. All he'd wanted to do was be with her and make a life for the two of them, then the three of them. That was where his heart was. Stability and family. Love that was real. And all the money in the world couldn't give him that, but just maybe Harper could.

In that moment, it didn't matter what else happened, he belonged with her. Even if she told him to get lost and he couldn't win her back, the thought of being away from a world where Harper existed seemed like torture.

"So what do you say, Renfro? Wanna go make beautiful music together?"

Jude smiled, knowing what he had to do. "No. Not a chance, Mike. Not a chance in hell."

Chapter Twenty-Seven

H arper was trying not to cry as she stormed back to the vendor trucks. It wouldn't do for her to have a complete nervous breakdown right here in front of everyone. The school was depending on her to pull this off, and there was no time for childish tantrums. At least she'd seen him before walking over there and making a complete fool of herself. That should bring her some sort of comfort, but when she reached the cafeteria doors, she couldn't stop the tears any longer. She shoved the door open, praying that no one else was inside.

"I'm such an idiot…" she scolded herself, slamming her fist into the wall behind. "I told myself not to get involved. This is exactly what I always knew would happen." Her breath was coming in short gasps, and she couldn't stop it. She had to get it together. Harper was not going to let some stupid, romantic drama ruin this day for her kids. She had worked far too hard for this.

She fanned her face, looking up at the ceiling in an attempt to slow the tears. If her nose started running, it would be all over. Her face would get red, her eyes would swell, and her mascara would melt down her face. At some point she'd have to look Jude in the face, and she didn't want him to think for one second that she'd been crying over him.

"Miss Winslow? Are you in here?" Elizabeth Renfro's face peeked into the heavy doors. Great. Just who Harper wanted to see.

She sniffled and wiped her face. "Oh yeah. I just… got hot."

"Oh no. Are you all right? Should I call Jude?"

Harper snorted before she could help herself. "No, I'm all right. Just a little too much sun and too little water."

"I completely understand, dear." She was holding two large bakery boxes, and Harper could barely see the woman over them.

"Do you need some help with those?"

"Actually yes. I wasn't sure where I was supposed to put them."

"I'll show you where to take them." Harper grabbed the box on top. "Here, let me help you. Follow me." Harper led Mrs. Renfro out of the cafeteria doors and back into the quad that had now been set up with food tables, vendor booths, and a giant castle inflatable. They crossed the field to where the bake sale had been set up. She handed the boxes over to Trae.

"Make sure you get these on the table, will ya?"

Trae looked down into the boxes with their clear tops. "I don't know, Harper. I might take these on back here for myself."

"As long as you pay for them," Harper joked.

"Thank you, dear. Those were a bit unruly."

Harper nodded. "We really appreciate your helping us out. I was afraid we weren't going to have enough for the bake sale."

"Jude mentioned that. I hope Kit and I made enough cupcakes."

"Are there ever really enough cupcakes?"

Mrs. Renfro laughed. "Not really, I suppose. I think Jude ate at least three of them last night before I could get the frosting on the tops." She shook her head. "He's just the same as he was when he was a little boy. I remember one time, I'd made a cake for my bridge circle and left it sitting on the counter, all frosted and beautiful, while I went to finish my face."

"I think I can already sense where this is going."

"At some point in the ten minutes I was upstairs, Jude had come in and helped himself to some cake. Of course, knowing he'd be in trouble, he scooped a piece out of the center, ate it, and frosted over the hole. When I cut into it, the darn thing was completely hollow."

"Oh no!"

"Oh yes. I still don't know how he managed to keep the whole thing from caving in."

Harper could just picture him, a small boy not unlike Kit, with huge brown eyes and a mop of black hair, creeping into the kitchen with devious intent. Just before their fight, Harper had started to think about what it might be like for the two of them to have a child together. Would it be another rambunctious boy that would torture Kit and follow him everywhere? Or maybe a girl with chubby cheeks and a crooked smile like hers? She'd indulged in little fantasies about trips to the beach, family Christmases—all those little threads that made up the tapestry of life. And now, she'd never get to enjoy that. At least not with Jude. Maybe she'd been stupid to think there was ever a chance.

"But, despite all that. Jude was a good boy. Is a good boy." She turned Harper toward her and stared up into her eyes. Bets was a tiny woman, but Harper could see shades of Jude everywhere. "I make it a point to never get involved in my child's love life, but I need to have my say."

"All right..."

"I don't know what happened between you and Jude. I don't want to know. But ever since that day we met, he's been lost. The worst I've seen him since poor Shelby died. I know it's a lot to ask, and it's none of my business... but talk to him. Just let him talk.

He's just like his father. He lets things stew, but just... let him talk. Let him explain. Give him a chance to make things right."

"Mrs. Renfro—"

She patted Harper's hand. "It's none of my business. But what can I do? Jude's my child and whatever he wants, I want to get for him. And he wants you, Miss Winslow. I can see it as clear as I'm seeing you now. Just give him a chance."

Before Harper could reply, she spotted Nicole running toward them out of the corner of her eye. "Harper!"

"I'm sorry, Mrs. Renfro. I... I have to go."

Bets smiled and patted her cheek. "Just promise me you'll think about it."

"I'll try..."

"Harper," Nicole said, breathing hard as she reached them. "Come on quick. The grant committee is here. We need you now."

"Already? We aren't even ready to open yet."

Nicole put her hands on her knees, breathing heavily as if she'd run ten miles to get there. "I know. They're early. Probably... going to Highgate too..."

Harper rolled her eyes. She pressed her nails into the heels of her palms to keep her cool. It wouldn't surprise her if Mia had orchestrated their early arrival. After all her scheming, it would be just like the old battleax. She could feel herself getting tense and then suddenly, an epiphany. Her anger and animosity toward Mia wasn't hurting Mia at all. All it was doing was making Harper a bitter old woman, paranoid and competitive. Like Mia. The thought was so clear that it was like running headlong into a brick wall. Harper had to let go. These walls she'd been subconsciously building for most of her life had to come down. It was keeping her from getting the things she wanted. Not just the grant for the school, but Jude. She wanted Jude and Kit more than anything she'd ever wanted before. And damnit, she wasn't going to let him go this easily. She would fight for him.

Harper took a deep breath and threw an arm around Nicole's shoulders. "Come on, Nic. Let's go get that money."

Chapter Twenty-Eight

"You were brilliant!" Jax exclaimed, hugging Harper tight as they strolled away from where Andrea and Nicole were still shaking hands with the Communities in Schools board. While never one to toot her own horn, Harper thought she'd done a damn fine job convincing five middle-aged white dudes to give their school a half-million dollars.

She, Andrea, Jax, and Nicole had shown them around the school, newly adorned with student work that celebrated autumn. They pointed out all the after-school programs that served their at-risk student population. Harper had explained that their school was a center of a community where people mostly worked in the tourist industry during the summer and didn't have much money to spare in the off-season. But what they lacked in funds they made up for in enthusiasm for educating their kids.

When the party arrived outside, the gates to the carnival had just opened and the kids of Crawford's Landing had done the rest of the convincing. The whole community had come out to support them, and Harper had never felt so proud in her entire life.

"Thanks, Jax. But I think the kids are mostly to thank. Once they saw how happy and involved everyone was, how could they tell us no?"

"Only if they're heartless bastards."

"Never say never," Harper said, then giggled. "But I don't think we have anything to worry about."

"I just wish Mia Goddard was here so I could see her face when they give us that giant check."

"It's a small town, and word travels fast. I don't think you have a thing to worry about." She hugged Jax again and he swung her around, both of them laughing in triumph.

"Hey, how'd it go?" As Jax set her back on her feet, Harper turned to see Jude jogging up to them. "I saw the guys in suits. How'd it go?"

Harper could feel the flush her cheeks deepen. She didn't want to have an awkward conversation in front of Jax. "Uhm... well..."

"It went great," Jax finished. "The Communities board loved the school. And Harper."

"Well, who could blame them?" Jude said, offering a wink.

"I think it had more to do with the kids than it did with me," Harper said. "But it's looking pretty good for the grant."

"That's great!" Jude exclaimed, exchanging a fist bump with Jax. "Well, congratulations, Harper. You did this."

She shook her head, her eyes downcast. She didn't think she could look up at him right now. "Oh, come on. You helped. If it hadn't been for you, we wouldn't have all this stuff." She motioned to the games, rides, and inflatables that had been assembled around the quad. "We could never have afforded it if you hadn't been so persuasive."

"But it was you," Jude said, stepping closer. "Crawford's Landing wanted to support you, Harper. People like you and they know you care about their kids. I was just backup."

Harper wanted to say more, but when she looked up at him, all of her words became twisted and died in her throat. Finally, she just said, "Thanks."

There was a moment of silence between them. For a second, Harper thought he might try to embrace her. Or maybe lean in for a sweet kiss, but instead he just smiled. "Anyway, congratulations." He gave a friendly pat on the shoulder before walking away back toward the food tents.

Jax watched him walk away, then back at Harper. "What the hell was that?"

"What do you mean?"

"A congratulatory pat on the shoulder? I thought you told me that Andrea was fine with the two of you being... you know... more than friends."

"It just didn't... work out."

"Didn't work out?" Jax was starting to become animated. He was about to go off on one of his moral tirades. "What is that supposed to mean?"

Harper shrugged. "We're just in different places right now. Maybe... maybe we should just be friends."

"Friends? Girl, people don't look at their friends like that. You need to go after him before he gets snatched up by one of those desperate housewives over there." Jax motioned to a flock of women who were standing on the edge of the quad. As Jude passed them by, their sunglasses dropped in unison and they were leaning hard on each other.

"Wait, what about you?"

"What about me?"

"Before you start judging me for missed opportunities, what's going on with you and Trae Robinson?"

Jax's eyes grew wide and his mouth opened and closed like a fish out of water. "What do you mean?"

Harper giggled. "You know exactly what I mean. And the two of you are adorable."

"Well…he is a rather attractive fellow."

"Indeed. And obviously smitten with you."

Before Jax could reply to Harper's obvious gushing, a bunch of kids shouted and began running toward the fence. A fire truck screamed around the corner and down the street past them. Kids tended to love watching fire trucks, but once the truck had passed them by, they usually went back to what they were doing. This time, though, the kids weren't moving. Most had abandoned the games and were making their way out of the bouncy castle to run toward the fence. Some were even climbing up and looking over as their parents ran into the commotion.

"What in the world?" Harper said absently as she sprinted across the quad. "What's going on?"

Kit found her quickly and grabbed her hand. "The school down the street. It's on fire."

"What? Highgate?" More kids and parents were coming in behind them, pushing toward the fence to get a better look. Harper strained to see over the crowd but couldn't see much. "Is that Highgate?"

"Kit!" Over the din of noise, Harper could hear Jude calling Kit. She looked around and saw him on the fence. He'd climbed up to get above the crowd, looking for his child. "Kit where are you?"

"I've got him!" Harper shouted. She grabbed Kit's hand and started to make her way through the crowd to where he was. "Jude! I've got him!"

"Oww… Miss Winslow…" She turned back and Kit stumbled to his knees. She reached down and scooped him up. "I think I skinned my knee."

"Okay, kiddo. We're getting to your dad."

"The Highgate school is on fire!"

"They were having their carnival today too."

Harper tried to block out their voices and concentrate on the problem at hand. Once she delivered Kit safely to his father, she could think about the fire. "Sorry... excuse me... pardon me..." She picked her way through the gathering mob until she finally got to where Jude was jumping down from his perch.

Kit covered his ears as another fire truck squealed by, its lights flashing. "Too loud..." he whined.

"Thank God," Jude said, taking Kit from Harper. "I saw the kids swarming, and I guess I panicked."

"He's okay," she said, brushing off the back of Kit's shirt. "Can you see what's going on?"

"A little. It looks like the courtyard in front of Highgate is on fire." The two of them ran to the side, trying to get away from the onlookers. Jude set Kit on his feet and looked him over.

"I fell down, Daddy."

"Oh no. Are you okay?"

Kit nodded and rubbed his eyes that were moist with tears he was trying so hard not to shed. "I'll be okay."

"Harper! Jude!" Sondra was running toward them. "What do we do?"

"Get those people back in the quad," Jude said. "If they start climbing the fence, someone could get hurt."

"One step ahead of you," Sondra said, nodding to where Trae, Jax, and several of the other teachers were herding the kids and parents back toward the games. "But all those kids at Highgate. Do you think they have help?"

Jude nudged Kit toward Sondra. "Kit, you stay here with Sondra and Miss Winslow. I'm going to run down and see if they need help." He looked to Harper. "My parents are here someplace. If you could see that Kit gets to them."

"I'm going with you," Harper said.

"No," Jude said. "It might be dangerous."

"Exactly why you shouldn't go alone."

Sondra took Kit's hand. "Come on, little one. Let's go sell some cupcakes and find your Nini." Kit nodded and the two of them walked off toward the food tents. Luckily, the teachers had been successful in distracting everyone from the fire, and the crowd had started to disperse.

Jude motioned for Harper to come on, and they took off across the quad and through the gates. More emergency vehicles were racing down the street toward Highgate as they ran down the sidewalk toward the blaze. The closer they got, the more they could smell the heavy smoke. Soon they could see it, and by the time they reached the school, it was so thick that it was hard to see and breathe.

The courtyard where the carnival had been set up was in chaos. Kids were crying, parents were shouting and jerking up their children. Firefighters were trying to shove people toward the street and imploring them to stay calm. The petting zoo animals were braying and squawking while their handler tried desperately to keep them from breaking their gate to run away. The flames were behind the food tables and Harper could see that several of the canopies were on fire. Luckily, it didn't appear that the fire had spread to the building yet, but it was only a matter of time.

Jude caught one of the Highgate teachers as they herded children toward the sidewalk. "Hey, what happened?"

"One of the grills blazed up and caught the canopy on fire. It must have gotten to the propane tank and boom."

"Oh my God," Harper said. "Was anyone hurt?"

"Luckily no, but the guy working the grill probably lost his eyebrows."

Harper stared past the teacher as he talked to Jude. Mia was standing in the middle of the courtyard, looking around at the disaster. For the first time since they had met, Mia didn't have her nose in the air, staring down on everyone else. She looked almost lost. Her perfectly coiffed bob was tangled, and her glasses were crooked. The smart blazer she wore over her Highgate Academy t-shirt was torn at the hem and pocket. Suddenly, Harper felt sorry for the woman.

"Mia?" Harper said, walking over to her. "Are you okay?"

Mia seemed startled that anyone was speaking to her. Then, even more so when she realized it was Harper. "Oh! Harper... I uhm... well, yes. I guess I'm okay."

"Was anyone hurt?"

Mia shook her head. "No, thank God. None of the children were anywhere near when the propane tank exploded."

"And adults?"

"Everyone's fine. I think." She shook her head. "I can't believe it. I thought... I thought I'd planned everything so perfectly." She took her glasses off and then did something that left Harper completely shook. Mia Goddard began sobbing uncontrollably.

"Oh, Mia..." Harper reached for the woman before she could help herself. "There now, everything is okay. No one was hurt."

"But they could have been," she wailed. "And now look at this mess. All the children will be so disappointed. We'd barely gotten started."

Harper looked around. She was right. The place was a mess. The fires had been squelched by the firemen, but the food tents, most of the games, and the petting zoo were a complete disaster. Kids and their parents were milling around on the sidewalk watching the collapse, some of them crying and pointing toward the destruction of their fun-filled afternoon.

"I mean, they came for a carnival and now look..."

In the blink of an eye, all of the contempt Harper had been holding against Mia and Highgate evaporated. She had an idea how to fix this mess in an instant. "They came for a carnival, and a carnival they shall have. Let's bring them all down to Sojourner Truth. We have a lovely carnival with rides and games and cotton candy. We… we'd love to have you."

Mia wiped her eyes and stared at Harper. "You mean, you'd let us come to your festival?"

Harper smiled. "Of course. Why wouldn't we?"

"After I did everything I could to sabotage your event, and you'd welcome me and my staff to your carnival?"

"Of course. After all, this isn't about us. It's about the kids, right? That is, unless you think you're too good to slum it with the public school kids."

Mia stared for a moment as if still trying to work out Harper's motives, but then she sighed and nodded. "No, we'd love to join you."

Mia and Harper worked together to gather all of the teachers and parent volunteers. In a matter of minutes they'd formed lines of kids and their families, marching down the street to Sojourner Truth Elementary. Even some of the vendors followed with their wares. Jude and some other teachers organized adults to carry tables and lead some of the ponies down to the Fall Crawl while the firefighters finished putting out the smoldering tents.

When they got to Sojourner's courtyard, more teachers and volunteers were on hand to help them rearrange and set up. Within the hour it was no longer the Sojourner Truth Elementary Fall Crawl, it was the Crawford's Landing Fall Crawl.

Chapter Twenty-Nine

The Fall Crawl drew to a close as the sun dipped down below the horizon. All in all, it had been a rousing success. They hadn't been able to add up all the proceeds just yet, but by Jude's rough estimate, they'd made several thousands of dollars in profit. Certainly enough money to keep the school's after-school programs going. Jude had even agreed to start a club for students that wanted to learn to play guitar. A few phone calls and he'd managed to get several guitars so that the kids wouldn't even have to rent them. And on top of all that, the Communities in Schools grant had been awarded to Sojourner Truth Elementary. Everything seemed to be falling into place.

Andrea had insisted on ending the event with a speech and presentation of the Communities in Schools grant award. He figured everyone would be gone by now, but all of the parents and kids didn't seem to want the night to end. They stood around the stage waiting for the closing ceremony with eager anticipation. But all Jude wanted to do was go home to a hot shower and his bed. The day had been good, but now that it was almost over, that lingering sadness over Harper was starting to weigh on his shoulders.

Jude stared across the makeshift stage set up in the center of the courtyard. He could see Harper standing there, listening intently and looking everywhere but at him. She was smiling and laughing with the other teachers but hadn't even so much as glanced his way. After the incident with the fire, he'd wanted to corner her and tell her once and for all how he felt, but everything had happened so fast. Maybe whatever hope they'd had had gone up in smoke like Mia's canopy.

"Hey, Dad." Kit stood at his feet looking like an unmade bed. The kid had played hard all day, and it was obvious that he was running on fumes. But it was a good tired.

"Hey there, Kit," he said, hoisting the boy up on his hip. "Having a good time?"

"Yeah. Miss Robinson and Miss Thompson was showing us how to make s'mores in the bonfire."

"Oh wow! I love s'mores."

"Me too. I like my marshmallows burned."

Jude laughed and nodded. "You get that from your mom. She wanted hers completely black on the outside."

Kit laid his head on his dad's shoulder. Poor kid. He was going to be asleep sitting straight up pretty soon. Jude figured he'd better say his goodbyes and get home. His parents had offered to take him when they left a couple of hours previous, but Kit had been having such a good time. Jude hated to break up the party.

"Dad, can I ask you somethin'?"

"Sure."

"Do you like Miss Winslow?"

Jude's heart thumped against his sternum at the mention of her name. "Uhm… well of course I do, Kit."

"I miss when she used to come over to our house."

"I… I guess I do too."

Kit sat up and looked at his father seriously. It was such a stern expression and reminded him so much of Shelby that Jude almost had to sit down. "If you like her, then you should tell her you like her."

"You think so?"

Kit nodded. "Don't be scared. She likes you too. I know she does."

"How do you know that?"

Kit shrugged. "I don't know. It's just the way she looks whenever you're around. Her eyes sparkle. And she smiles a lot."

"She smiles at everybody."

"Not like she does at you. Even when she's mad, she still likes you. You should tell her you like her too."

Jude gnawed at his lower lip. "I dunno, Kit. I think maybe it might be too late. I just don't know what to say to stop her from being mad at me."

Kit shrugged. "Sing her a song."

"What?" Jude chuckled.

"Sing her a song. It's what you do best. Nini said you used to sing songs to Mom when she was mad. I bet it would work on Miss Winslow too."

"That's all well and good, Kit, but how am I going to sing her a song?"

"Do it right now." Kit wiggled in his father's arms until Jude let him slide down to the ground.

"I can't..." As soon as both feet hit the ground, Kit ran off into the courtyard. "Kit!" he called. "Christopher Renfro! Get back here!" he shouted, but the boy didn't turn back. "Damnit..." Jude grumbled. He started to follow, but a heavy hand clamped down on his shoulder.

"Hey, Miss Nettles wants you to say something." Trae started tugging Jude toward the makeshift stage where Andrea Nettles was standing, tapping the microphone.

"I need to go catch my kid."

"Don't worry, man. Jax'll look after him."

He didn't have time to question Trae further before he was shoved on to the stage.

"Ladies and gentlemen, thank you so much for all of your support for this year's Fall Crawl," Andrea said. "I hope that this event will become an annual gathering of our community. We taught our students a lot today about teamwork and the value of community partnerships. But more than that, and probably most importantly, we taught them about being kind and forgiving of others." Andrea glanced toward the other side of the stage to where Harper was standing between Nicole and Mia Goddard.

"Of course, this year's event would not have been a success without the help of our students, parents, and community business leaders who donated their time and expertise. As you can see, things like this are never the work of just one person, but a group effort, and our school cannot thank you enough." The crowd applauded and whistled their approval. "Now, we have a big announcement and since this has all been her baby, I'm going to hand the mic over to everyone's favorite kindergarten teacher, Harper Winslow to tell you about it."

A loud whooping and clapping erupted as Harper crossed the stage. God, just the sight of her made his mouth water. She looked exhausted, but Jude didn't think he'd ever seen anyone look so beautiful.

"Thank you so much, everyone. I just don't know what to say. You've all been so wonderful through this whole thing. Miss Nettles said the Fall Crawl was my baby, but... I can't take credit for all that. A carnival was my idea, but it was all of you who made it a reality. I hope we've done what we set out to do, which was secure funding for our school. Crawford's Landing is an island community. We're kind of cut off from the world around us. I used to think that was a bad thing. That it made us small and insignificant. But I've learned these last few months that us islanders are pretty lucky. We take care of our own. We know that there's nothing more important than family — both the kind you're born with and the kind you make. All you guys are family. My island family." Harper paused, letting the town applaud for her and each other. This was what Jude had been trying to tell Mike earlier. This was something that no amount of LA glamor or money or fame could buy.

"There you are!" Jax and Kit appeared at the side of the stage. Jax was carrying Jude's guitar case and Kit was grinning like the cat that ate the canary.

"I told you he hadn't started talkin' yet," Kit said.

"What are you two doing?" Jude hissed.

"Kit said you needed this," Jax said, setting down the large guitar case. "That you had a new song to sing for everyone."

"What?" he knelt down to Kit's level. "What are you doing?" he whispered. "I'm not ready to sing, kid."

"You're always ready, Daddy," Kit said, matter-of-factly as he opened the case and handed the enormous acoustic guitar over to his father. "Sing that song for Miss Winslow."

"It isn't finished."

"It's finished enough," Kit said. "She'll like it."

"Of course, Miss Thompson and I couldn't have done any of this without the help of one-third of our planning committee, Jude Renfro." Jude looked up, completely terrified, as Harper called him up to the stage to speak. She wasn't smiling, but she didn't look like she was waiting to throw him off the stage either. Possibly a good sign. Jude looked to Kit who jerked his head toward the stage.

Jude rose slowly and threw the neck strap around his shoulder as he sauntered over to the microphone. The crowd was silent as he took the stage, all their eyes burning holes into his stomach. His boots seemed to boom loudly over the boards, and the creaking of the nails was deafening.

He cleared his throat. Singing in public was no problem, but speaking was a different matter. This had all the earmarks of disaster. "Ahem... uhm... thank you to all of you who came today. I think I speak for all of the committee when I say that we've had a wonderful time with all of you." He glanced over, and Harper was standing on the edge of the stage, watching every move that he made. Their eyes met for just a second and everyone else faded into the background. All of a sudden, he knew exactly what to say.

"I've never been particularly good at speaking my mind. I think I became a musician so I wouldn't have to talk. Music is a language that I understand, and when I can't think of the right words to say, I always go back to music to say it for me. So, here goes." He locked eyes with Harper one more time. "Miss Winslow, I hope this says it all."

Jude began to strum the chords of the song he'd been working on for the last few months. At first, he hadn't realized that he was writing about her, but the first time they kissed, it all became clear. The soft melody on the strings wasn't overly complicated. It had a simple hook and a steady heartbeat on the bass string. It wasn't sad, but a clean, soaring tune that immediately put him in mind of Harper's blue eyes and all-in smiles.

"Just let me hold you for a while. Hearts beat together, breath for breath in perfect time. You and I are fallin' into rhythm. One more kiss and you'll be mine."

When the song ended, Jude opened his eyes to the silence of the crowd. They all seemed to be locked in place and for a moment he was sure he'd made a terrible mistake. He turned around and there was Harper. Any anger she'd still been harboring was long gone now, and her eyes were wet. On either side of her Jax and Nicole looked like they were holding her up and as the applause in the audience began, they pushed her toward him on the stage. It was all she needed. She sprinted across the stage and threw herself into his arms. His guitar fell with a dissonant screech as she pressed her body against his, kissing his mouth with unabashed enthusiasm. He wound his arms around her, holding her close and getting lost in the scent of her hair.

"I'm so sorry," Harper said against his lips. "I never should have doubted you."

"It's okay. It wasn't all you. I doubted myself a little there. But I swear. I'll never doubt again."

"You won't have to." She kissed him again and this time there were no reservations or doubt. "Because I'm telling you now, Jude Renfro, and I don't care who else can hear. I'll love you forever."

Just then, Kit ran to them on the stage and threw his arms around their waists. "Finally!" he exclaimed.

The two of them laughed, kissing again as the crowd's cheers drowned out their words. There was no one else on Earth right now, just the two of them in the center of their own little universe.

Perfectly in rhythm.

The End

Meeting Her Match

A Crawford's Landing Love Story (#2)

Sneak Peek

Chapter One

Sondra Robinson was half past give a damn with this crap. She'd been on hold with these people for at least an hour and *still* no luck. In front of her was the wreckage of a brand new cappuccino machine. It looked like some great copper beast that had been slain and ripped to pieces all over her hardwood floors. No surprise, really. The stupid thing had been the bane of her existence since her son, Trae, pulled it out of the box a week ago. *Top of the line*, the salesman had bragged. *"No ma'am. No other coffee shop in Crawford's Landing has anything like this. The Grindmaster 4000 is a whole coffee system."* Funny, she'd been doing better with that ancient commercial pot that she'd bought secondhand when she opened Common Grounds four years previous. But Trae had insisted that they move ahead with the times. The trusty old EX-presso was too slow and completely inadequate to meet the demand of their customers.

Slow indeed, Sondra thought. At least it worked.

"Thank you for your patience. Your call is very important to us. Please hold the line for the next available service representative."

That cheerful, computerized voice made Sondra want to smash the phone into a million tiny pieces. "Oh sure," she said to the smooth jazz coming out of the receiver. "It ain't like I got anything to do today except wait."

Waiting wasn't exactly a new thing for Sondra. It seems she'd been waiting her whole life. Sondra was an army brat who had spent her childhood waiting on her father to retire so that their family could finally settle in one place. Then she'd waited all through high school for it to be over so she could get started on her own life. Sondra had always been a dreamer with big aspirations to be the first girl in her family to go to college and go on to conquer the business world. Then she'd met her husband, gotten married, and had Trae. While their life together had been more wonderful than anyone could hope for, Sondra had found herself waiting again. Once Trae was grown, she'd told herself, she could finally open the business she'd always dreamed of—a coffee shop and bakery. Then her husband got sick and suddenly all her dreams didn't seem so important anymore. Now that he was gone, it was finally her time and she didn't appreciate having to wait any longer.

The bell over the front door rang behind her as someone came in. Sondra rolled her eyes. Usually, the hours between ten and twelve were pretty quiet. That's why she'd chosen to call the coffee company now instead of waiting until Trae came back with their grocery order. "Just a minute," she called over her shoulder, trying not to sound irritated. If she hung up, she would likely have to start this process all over again and spend another hour on hold. She'd come too far to give up now.

"Ahem... Miss... excuse me..."

"I'll be right with you."

"*Thank you for your patience. Your call is very important to us. Please hold the line for the next available service representative.*"

"Look, I know that this is the only place in town to get a cup of coffee, but..."

Sondra whipped around, pulling the phone down on the counter and preparing herself to blow this guy's eyebrows off with her wrath. "Sir, I know that you probably aren't used to waiting, but…" She stopped short as her eyes focused. An impossibly tall white guy stood in the light of the doorway with the early morning winter sun glowing around him like a halo. He was wearing an expensive tailored suit and his blue eyes glowed with growing annoyance. "But if you could just give me another second."

"I'm already late," he said, a tinge of an Irish brogue coloring his words. "Since you don't seem interested in my business, I'll just have to go elsewhere."

"You don't have to be so rude," Sondra called as he turned his back.

He paused. "Oh yeah? You're just the latest in a long line of people standing in my way this morning. I know they say things move slower down here in Grover's Corners, but some of us have lives." With that he turned and stormed out of the shop, nearly bowling over Trae and knocking out the doorbell.

"What the hell was that all about?" Trae asked, setting the boxes from the market down on the counter.

"Over-privileged white dude," Sondra said, turning back to the phone. She put the receiver back to her ear, expecting to hear the perky drone of the computerized operator advising Sondra that her call was important. Unfortunately, the line was dead. "Damn it!" She slammed the phone back on the cradle.

"Whoa, Mom. Take it easy." Trae went around the counter and caught the receiver as it banged against the wall. "What's going on?"

"That monstrosity you made me buy is broken," she began, pointing to the pieces all over the floor. "I've been on hold with the company for over an hour to try and get it fixed only to lose my place in line because of that… person. I haven't finished prepping for lunch. I have brownie batter going bad in the refrigerator, and I have to make those cake layers for Kit Renfro's birthday cake today or it isn't going to get done in time…"

Trae grabbed his mother by the shoulders and looked in her eyes. "Mama, you got to calm down."

Sondra pushed away and looked up at him with her arms crossed defiantly. "Son, has that ever worked?"

"What?"

"Telling a woman to calm down?"

He thought for a second. "Look, what happened to the coffee machine?"

"I was just trying to grind some beans before the lunch rush. I dumped them in, there was this awful noise and smoke started coming out the back. I turned it off, opened the top, and beans started spraying everywhere. I got that stopped and cleaned up the beans, but I thought maybe something was stuck in there. So I took it apart and here we are."

Trae threw an arm around his mother's shoulder and hugged her gently. "Okay, why don't you let me take care of this? I'll call the coffee place back and take care of customers."

"How? The coffee pot's broken."

"I'll hook up the old one for now." He led her through the double doors into the kitchen. "You just come on back here and finish up prepping for lunch. I'll take care of everything."

"Trae, I'm really all right."

"Of course you are. But as usual, you're doing too much."

"How does somebody do too much for their own business?" Common Grounds was Sondra's baby just as much as Trae was. She'd dreamed of having this place since the day she moved to Crawford's Landing and there was nothing she wasn't willing to do to make it successful. When Trae transferred to a college close by, he'd come to work for her full time at the shop. He was so full of ideas to make the place better and so far, he'd been right. But with that success came more work.

"I know. I just wish you'd let me hire a couple more people to help out. Especially with the Sweethearts' Dance coming up next month."

Sondra rolled her eyes and pushed past him to the fridge where today's fresh chicken salad was waiting. "Why would I want to do that?"

"Oh, I dunno, Mama. Maybe so you could have a life?"

Sondra snickered as she tossed the container on the counter. "I have a life, Trae. In case you missed it, Common Grounds is my life."

"No, I didn't miss it. I'm saying that's your problem."

"What's that supposed to mean?"

"You spend every waking minute in this place, Mama."

"Not every one…"

"Just about. And when you aren't here, you're taking care of everyone else in this town. Bake sales and church raffles and… school carnivals."

"Being a part of the community is important, Trae. You should know that. After all, the Sweethearts' Dance was your idea. Just like the open mic nights and the live bands…"

Trae went to his mom and grabbed both of her hands. "I do, Mama. And I learned everything I know about hard work from you. You built this place from nothing. Literally. Remember when you bought this building from old man Gaston?"

"I do. It was falling down."

Trae nodded. "You practically rebuilt the place with your own hands. We were selling coffee and pastry on the sidewalk at a picnic table because people couldn't go inside. Remember?"

"Very well."

"You made it into this great spot for everyone to enjoy. Don't you think it's time you relax a little and enjoy it?"

"Trae, I've never depended on anyone to do my work for me…"

"It wouldn't be like that, Mama. Just a couple of people to help you in the kitchen for a few hours a day. Do some of the cleanup. Prep the chicken salad." He gestured to where she'd sloshed mayonnaise out of the big mixing bowl and all over the counter.

"Oh lord…" she said, immediately going to wipe it up.

"Asking for help isn't a crime, you know. And I'm worried about you, Mama."

Sondra shook her head. "What? Why would you be worried about me?"

"You're running yourself ragged lately—"

"Because of all your brilliant ideas."

"—and I don't want you to fall over dead. You need to do something just for you. Relax. Have some fun. I dunno… go on a vacation. Get a massage. Go on a date."

Sondra sighed and pulled away from Trae. She pulled out the loaf of bread she'd made fresh this morning and began slicing it vigorously. "Not this again…"

"Come on, Ma. It isn't like you haven't had your share of offers."

It was true. Crawford's Landing had nothing if not an entire subculture of geezers out there waiting to take her to an early bird special. At least once a week one of the old guys who regularly came in to wile away their mornings with a cup of her decaf tried to convince her to go out with him. The problem was, the average age of these guys was about eighty. And Sondra wasn't a spring chicken, but she was hardly old. She was only forty-five, but everyone assumed that since Trae was in his early twenties that Sondra was in her fifties, at the very least.

"Trae, we have been over this a thousand times. There ain't a man in this town that I'd be interested in goin' out with. They're either too young or way too old, and I just ain't got time for that right now." She threw the soiled towel in the sink and turned to her son. "You and this place are my greatest loves. I don't need anything else."

"Life isn't always about what you need, Mama. It wouldn't kill you to have a little fun."

As he walked away, Sondra's belly flopped. He had that look in his eye. The same one he'd had since he was a toddler. Trae Robinson was up to something.

About the Author

Alexandra Christian is an author of paranormal and contemporary romance with an occasional foray into horror. Her love of Stephen King and sweet tea has flavored her fiction with a Southern Gothic sensibility that reeks of Spanish moss and deep-fried eccentricity. Her guiding principle as a romance novelist has always been to write romantic adventures for people who think they hate romances. After all, love itself is life's greatest adventure.

Lexx is a native South Carolinian who lives with an epileptic wiener dog and her husband, author Tally Johnson, in a small town just south of Charlotte, NC. In addition to her writing, she also has unhealthy obsessions with supervillains, Sherlock Holmes and Star Wars. Her long-term aspirations are to one day be a best-selling authoress and part-time pinup girl.

Questions, comments and complaints are most welcome at her website: http://lexxxchristian.wixsite.com/alexandrachristian

Connect with Alexandra

Website
http://lexxxchristian.wixsite.com/alexandrachristian

Blog
http://lexxxchristian.wordpress.com

Facebook
https://www.facebook.com/TheSouthernBellefromHell/

Facebook Group
https://www.facebook.com/groups/TheHellsBelles/

Newsletter
http://eepurl.com/b5c_Un

Instagram
https://www.instagram.com/lexxchristian/

Also by Alexandra Christian

For updates, visit Alexandra's website:
http://lexxxchristian.wixsite.com/alexandrachristian

Beast of Burden
Huntress (also available on Audible)
Strange Bedfellows (also available on Audible)
Sanguine Kiss
Chasing the Dragon: A Sherlock Holmes Romantic Mystery

Phoenix Rising Series
Naked
Neo-Geisha
In Absinthia
Out of Ashes

Shadow Council Archives
The Ghost and Dr. Watson
Dr. Watson and the Ladies' Club Coven (coming soon)

Crawford's Landing Series
Falling Into Rhythm
Meeting Her Match (coming soon)

Anthologies:
Witches, Warriors, and Wise Women (Concrete Dreams #1)
Lawless Lands
An Improbable Truth: The Paranormal Adventures of Sherlock Holmes (as editor)
Curious Incidents: More Improbable Adventures (as author and editor)

www.ingramcontent.com/pod-product-compliance
Lightning Source LLC
Chambersburg PA
CBHW020440270626
47155CB00022B/788